Ancient Enforcer

Ancients Rising Series

KATIE REUS

Copyright © Katie Reus 2021

All rights reserved. Except as permitted under the U.S. Copyright Act of 1976, no part of this publication may be reproduced, distributed, or transmitted in any form or by any means, or stored in a database or retrieval system, without the prior written permission of the author. Thank you for buying an authorized version of this book and complying with copyright laws. You're supporting writers and encouraging creativity.

Cover Art by Sweet 'N Spicy Designs
Editor: Julia Ganis
Author Website: https://katiereus.com

Publisher's Note: This is a work of fiction. Names, characters, places, and incidents are either the products of the author's imagination or used fictitiously, and any resemblance to actual persons, living or dead, or business establishments, organizations or locales is completely coincidental.

Ancient Enforcer/Katie Reus.—1st ed.

ISBN-13: 9781635561593

eISBN: 9781635561586

*For Piper and Jack, the inspiration behind the dragonlings.
(And the silliest pups a writer could ask for.)*

PRAISE FOR THE NOVELS OF KATIE REUS

"Exciting in more ways than one, well-paced and smoothly written, I'd recommend *A Covert Affair* to any romantic suspense reader."
—Harlequin Junkie

"Sexy military romantic suspense." —USA Today

"I could not put this book down.... Let me be clear that I am not saying that this was a good book *for* a paranormal genre; it was an excellent romance read, *period.*" —All About Romance

"Reus strikes just the right balance of steamy sexual tension and nail-biting action.... This romantic thriller reliably hits every note that fans of the genre will expect." —*Publishers Weekly*

"Prepare yourself for the start of a great new series! . . . I'm excited about reading more about this great group of characters."
—Fresh Fiction

"Wow! This powerful, passionate hero sizzles with sheer deliciousness. I loved every sexy twist of this fun & exhilarating tale. Katie Reus delivers!"
—Carolyn Crane, RITA award winning author

"A sexy, well-crafted paranormal romance that succeeds with smart characters and creative world building."—Kirkus Reviews

"*Mating Instinct*'s romance is taut and passionate . . . Katie Reus's newest installment in her Moon Shifter series will leave readers breathless!"
—Stephanie Tyler, *New York Times* bestselling author

"I just can't get enough of these sexy, growly, dragons and the women who are strong enough to put up with them." —Edgy Reviews

"Katie Reus pulls the reader into a story line of second chances, betrayal, and the truth about forgotten lives and hidden pasts."
—The Reading Café

"Nonstop action, a solid plot, good pacing, and riveting suspense."
—RT Book Reviews

"Enough sexual tension to set the pages on fire."
—*New York Times* bestselling author, Alexandra Ivy

"…a wild hot ride for readers. The story grabs you and doesn't let go."
—*New York Times* bestselling author, Cynthia Eden

"Has all the right ingredients: a hot couple, evil villains, and a killer action-filled plot. . . . [The] Moon Shifter series is what I call Grade-A entertainment!" —Joyfully Reviewed

"*Avenger's Heat* hits the ground running…This is a story of strength, of partnership and healing, and it does it brilliantly."
—Vampire Book Club

"*Mating Instinct* was a great read with complex characters, serious political issues and a world I am looking forward to coming back to."
—All Things Urban Fantasy

PROLOGUE

Two months before The Fall

Mikael stared out the window of the home the Alpha of New Orleans had just brought him to. After waking from a millennia-long sleep, he and his brothers had just been passing through so they'd checked in with the Alpha. Originally they hadn't planned to stay long, but they all liked the territory.

He and his brothers had already been "vetted," as King put it, but the Alpha still required that they have what was the equivalent of a babysitter. A *human female*, of all people. It made no sense. If King had said a dragon female would be keeping an eye on him, he would have understood—dragon females were the fiercest of warriors.

But this human was apparently going to be their new boss at a construction site as well. King had offered him a job there and had hinted that if this worked out, he would like Mikael and his brothers to be on the pack's security detail.

Mikael wasn't sure how he felt about that. He wasn't sure about anything since waking from a long Hibernation. He and his brothers were still adjusting to this new world where humans were in charge of things—and the world appeared quite dysfunctional. Things were very different than when he'd gone to sleep millennia ago. Supernaturals weren't out to all humans, only to a small group.

Most humans had long since forgotten about his kind's existence. The city of New Orleans was different, however—many people knew of supernaturals and accepted them. There was a deep magic here that sang to his dragon half. It was the same with his brothers so they had decided to stay.

To test the waters.

So here they were, waiting to meet this "babysitter" or *guardian* as King had called her. He'd assured Mikael and his brothers that they would like her—he said everyone did.

King stepped into the living room suddenly with a litheness that was usually reserved for feline shifters, and motioned that the three of them should follow.

Mikael and his brothers did, making the short trek out to the back patio that had a bunch of overhead lights strung up in a crisscross pattern, potted plants, and big umbrellas shielding a good portion of the patio from the bright sunlight.

But all he could focus on was a pretty human standing in between two human males, her stance protective even though the males were bigger and taller than her. It was clear there was a familial relationship, given the shade of their skin and the shapes of their eyes and mouths.

He flicked a brief glance at the two males, but his gaze strayed right back to her. Her chocolate-brown hair was wild and curly. It was pulled back into a ponytail, and under the sunlight, wild streaks of red shot through some of the strands. Her skin was sun-kissed and glowing and… He realized King was staring at him.

He blinked and cleared his throat.

"Mikael, this is Avery. She's been gracious enough to allow you and your brothers to live here," King said.

"We appreciate it very much," he said, stepping forward and closing the distance between them. He held his hand out in the way he had seen humans do, but only because he wanted to touch her, to feel how soft her skin was.

Her cheeks flushed a delicious shade of pink against her bronze skin. Her hands were soft but had little calluses that he liked. He probably held her hand a little bit too long, because one of his brothers cleared his throat.

Not wanting to come off like a weirdo, he turned to her brothers and shook both their hands as well. "These are my two brothers, Casimir— you can call him Cas—and Ivyn. We promise to be good roommates for as long as you will have us." *How about forever?* his dragon half purred.

He ordered his other half to be quiet.

Her smile never wavered as she looked at all of them and he understood why King had said he would like her. She was like sunshine incarnate. There was a glow that rolled off her. Hell, even her scent was intoxicating—like sunshine and sweet, fresh peaches.

"King explained that you three have just woken up and are still adjusting to the world, right?"

His brothers murmured affirmations behind him even as he nodded. He still hadn't stepped away from her, hadn't put any distance between them. That was not happening any time soon. He liked being close to her too much. This whole sensation was strange. He had not spent much time with humans, but this one... He inhaled again.

"Well, I've worked with various supernaturals over the years. There are a ton of bears in construction," she said on a laugh. "So anything you need, I'm sure we can help out. The only thing I ask is that if you're going to bring someone back to the house, give us advance warning. I don't want to walk in to find strangers here. Also, no wild parties, please."

"We will bring no one back here," he said immediately. "And have no parties."

She seemed startled by his vehemence, but her smile remained in place as she nodded. "Okay, then. That's perfect. So I should also warn you that even though we'll be living together, I won't be cooking for you guys just because I'm a woman."

"We would never expect that," Ivyn said from behind him. "In fact, I love cooking, so if you have any requests, just let me know. I've been experimenting with a lot of recipes lately."

Mikael watched as her eyes widened slightly and pure joy rolled off her. He was going to have to punch his brother in the face for that later. He was suddenly overcome by the most insane need to be the only one to make her smile and laugh.

He vaguely remembered talking to King after that, saying goodbye and promising to basically be on his best behavior, but all he could really do was soak in the warmth and presence of Avery.

Avery... He let her name roll around in his head. Perfection.

He would never leave New Orleans now, not as long as she was here. That was something he knew on an intrinsic level. It should have scared him, being tethered to some place—to *someone*.

It did not.

"What the hell was that?" Ivyn asked him hours later once it was just the three of them upstairs in Mikael's new bedroom. They didn't have much so it hadn't taken long to get them settled.

He'd chosen the bedroom closest to Avery's.

"What are you talking about?" He shut the closet door and turned to face his brothers, who were staring at him expectantly.

"The way you went all moonfaced over our new babysitter," Cas said, quoting him when he'd grumbled about having a babysitter.

Moonfaced? Where did his brother come up with this? It must be a human phrase he had learned. "Her name is Avery," he growled, his dragon flaring to the forefront. "She's being kind enough to let us live here. You will be respectful."

Ivyn elbowed Cas. "Told you. He's totally smitten."

Cas laughed lightly and fist-bumped Ivyn—something they had recently picked up. "You were correct. I concede."

He blinked, realizing they had been messing with him. "You guys are assholes."

"That may be true," Ivyn said. "But we weren't the ones practically drooling all over our new roommate."

"You two better keep your distance from her. I would hate to have to gut you and feed you your entrails." The words came out as a growl, which only made his brothers laugh uproariously. *Yep. Assholes.*

CHAPTER ONE

After The Fall

Mikael stepped through the front door of the three-story brick building downtown and looked around. He'd received a phone call about twenty minutes ago from King, saying that he was needed here. Since it was after work hours and Avery was home with Mikael's brothers—meaning that she was protected—he'd slipped out.

"Thank you for coming," King said as he stepped out of a half-open door where two other wolves were sitting inside talking quietly.

He shut the door behind him. In jeans, boots, and a long-sleeved black T-shirt, the male with brown skin and his wolf in his eyes reverberated with power. Especially for one so young—King was only a hundred or two hundred years old per Mikael's information. But energy sang around him, a soft, lilting melody right underneath the surface.

Mikael thought the place they were standing in was called a lobby. There was a cluster of chairs off to the right, exposed brick along two of the walls, and a big desk to the left that appeared to be a hundred or so years old. The only reason he even knew that was because his Avery—who was not really his at all—liked to tell him about different types of designs, and he paid attention to everything about her.

"What is this place? And why am I here?" He didn't like being separated from Avery for long. His dragon rippled impatiently underneath his skin, wanting to get back to her.

Always.

"This way." King's expression was dry as he jerked a thumb over his shoulder.

Mikael had been a general long ago, was used to giving orders and undertaking covert missions, though he'd always had an Alpha, so he knew how to take orders as well. His dragon hadn't quite decided if he was fully committed to following a wolf, but he found he liked this young

Alpha, regardless. They strode down the quiet hallway decorated with random artwork on the walls, and Mikael could smell plenty of humans behind some of the doors. But not many supernaturals.

That was interesting. Then he scented two very familiar humans, Avery's two younger brothers.

King jerked open the door and Mikael's eyes widened.

Anthony and Riel were stretched out on a hard-looking bench against a wall, both dozing, their soft snores filling the air. Mikael narrowed his gaze on Axel, the annoying lion who liked to flirt with Avery. The lazy male was a little farther down the same bench, reading a paperback book, one leg crossed over his knee, looking perfectly at ease as he glanced up at Mikael.

Axel gave him an obnoxious grin. "You're here to bail me out, dragon? I've gotta say, I'm touched… Also, I'm not even sorry about last night."

Mikael took in the lion's rumpled appearance, his torn shirt, the jeans ripped at one of the pockets. It looked as if there was…some type of frosting in the lion's thick hair. Mikael didn't respond, but looked at King instead.

It was clear that the wolf was fighting a bit of amusement.

"I'm afraid to ask what happened," Mikael muttered.

King lifted a shoulder. "I don't actually know. There was a fight, that much I'm clear on. My people are still trying to figure out what started it."

Around that time, Anthony and Riel both stirred, sitting up. Anthony, the youngest, looked at Mikael with wide eyes. "Did you tell Avery we're here?"

Mikael was an ancient dragon warrior, millennia older than the two human brothers, but the young men were more afraid of their older sister, who was not even thirty. Mikael understood, however, because while he wasn't afraid of her, he never wanted to disappoint her. "It's just me, younglings," he murmured. They might not be supernatural, not dragons, but he still viewed them as his to protect. "What happened?"

The two human males flicked a glance at King, who still stood next to Mikael, all humor and amusement gone as he stared them down like the Alpha he was.

"May I have a couple minutes alone with them?" Mikael asked. It was pretty clear this place was a makeshift holding center. Not a jail exactly, but given the bruised and bloodied knuckles of both brothers, and Axel's condition, it was clear they'd all been in a fight. He also scented blood in the air. Faint though it was, it still lingered.

King nodded and stepped out. Mikael knew the male would hear every single word he said even from outside the room. At least it would give the young humans the illusion of privacy, however.

"You two got into a fight?" That didn't sound like the two young men he knew. "Did the lion start it?" Mikael crossed his arms over his chest. He knew he was intimidating to them and that they looked up to him. He would use that to his advantage.

"Hey! I didn't do shit," Axel grumbled. "I was just there to have a good time."

Anthony looked at the floor, studying his scuffed-up sneakers. He was about twenty-three, but looked even younger in that moment.

Riel's jaw jutted out. "I got into a fight, I started it. And I'm not sorry either."

Anthony's head snapped up. "It's my fault! My ex-boyfriend was there and he said something nasty about my mom."

Their mother had died from cancer ravaging her body.

"So I punched him right in his stupid smirking face," Riel continued. "He was trying to hurt Anthony and had the nerve to talk shit about our mother. Screw him!"

Mikael simply nodded. "Punching him sounds like it was likely the right decision." Speaking ill of one's mother was simply not done.

Both men looked surprised but settled back on the bench.

He flicked his gaze to Axel. "Why are you here?"

The lion just grinned and shrugged.

Mikael gritted his teeth, deciding that he was going to ignore the lion today. He turned back to the brothers. "Are you ready to go home?"

They both jumped to their feet, then winced and slightly swayed, and he had a feeling alcohol had played a huge part in last night's activities. That was when he saw there was frosting smushed into the brothers' hair as well.

"You're not going to bail me out too?" Axel asked, still looking like the smug asshole he was.

Mikael snorted softly. "Ask one of your crew to get you out."

Axel stretched out on the bench, putting his hands behind his head as he did. "I think I'll just take a nap."

"Why am I not surprised? Come on." He motioned for the boys, who weren't boys at all but somehow seemed like actual children some days.

As they stepped out into the hall together, the brothers' eyes widened to see King standing there, leaning against one of the walls.

The wolf pushed up, the motion languid, almost feline despite his lupine status. "The human you got into a fight with last night," the Alpha murmured. "He was speaking disparagingly about your mother?"

"Yes," Riel answered, his shoulders straightening. "My mom died of cancer and he was trying to upset Anthony. He said... I can't even repeat the words. But they were hateful and ugly. No one talks shit about my family like that."

King's wolf flashed in his eyes for the briefest of moments before he nodded. "You're free to go. Don't get into any more fights. You have them?" he said to Mikael.

Meaning, would Mikael take full responsibility for them now? Of course he would. "Do you need me to escort the lion home too?" He couldn't believe he was even asking, but...Avery liked that jackass.

The wolf was back in King's eyes. "Aurora is coming to get that troublemaker."

Ah. Okay, then. Mikael nodded once at the wolf and headed out. He knew King was busy figuring out how to set up a currency system, an education system, and if they ended up having a prison of sorts, a system for that as well. Though in the shifter world, things were run differently than in the human one, so he had a feeling that things would look far, far different than what humans were used to once King had full control of New Orleans. Not that any of that was Mikael's concern right now.

As the three of them stepped out into the waning sunlight, he gripped the back of both Riel and Anthony's necks and squeezed with just enough pressure to make his point. "You're too old to be getting into fights." Or maybe they weren't. Hell. His own brothers were almost as old as him. Old and jaded, they'd retreated from the world and gone into Hibernation millennia ago once they'd grown tired of humans and shifters and treachery in general. They'd lost most of their family, and sleeping had been the respite they'd needed. But his dragon had decided it was time to wake up. He hadn't understood why.

Until he'd met *her*.

Both males winced slightly but Riel was the one who spoke up. He was often the spokesperson of the two. "Maybe you don't tell Avery about this?"

"I will not say anything to her right now, but I also won't lie to her." The boys were supposed to have been helping out on a construction site on the other side of town this week, assisting another crew. It was clear that King had held them for a while, probably since last night if Mikael had to guess, likely giving them time to cool off and think about their actions. "We are all rebuilding the world right now. Do you think fighting unnecessarily is helpful?"

He could scent the shame rolling off both of them. Good.

"No," Anthony muttered. "But I'm still not sorry for punching that douche canoe."

"Me neither," said Riel.

Mikael let out a low laugh. "Well if anyone has the audacity to talk about another being's deceased mother, they deserve to get more than their nose broken. I will show you how to take down another human quickly and efficiently without permanently maiming them." Hopefully.

They both gave him a surprised look.

Feeling protective of them, he wrapped an arm around both their shoulders and squeezed once before he let them go.

"Don't worry about that loser," Riel muttered as they continued down the sidewalk. "He's your ex for a reason, Anthony. He showed his true colors and he's a piece of shit. He's not your ride or die."

The two boys started murmuring to each other but their words made Mikael frown. "What is ride or die?" He did not understand a lot of human idioms. And this one was definitely new to him. Not that he'd been awake for very long anyway, but he'd discovered that many idioms were senseless. Much like the actions of many humans.

"You know," Riel said. "Your one and only."

That still did not make sense. "Explain more."

"Basically it means," Anthony started, "that your significant other is someone who you'll always support. You'll always be loyal to *them*... Ah, you have their back no matter what. I think originally it was some biker phrase, something to do with riding or dying, but now it's that one person who you'll ride into battle with or, you know, die trying."

He frowned as he digested their words. Avery was definitely his "ride or die." Though he never wanted her going into any sort of battle. She was too soft and wonderful.

She was his everything, even if she only saw him as a friend.

CHAPTER TWO

Bent over the architectural plans laid out on her desk, Avery scribbled another note. She was in the middle of building a small condominium complex, in the punch-out phase of another one, and in a couple months, she would be heading up another project per King's orders.

This was on a different scale than when she'd been flipping houses and handling small apartment complexes, but she had the knowledge and experience and had been living in New Orleans her entire life so she knew a lot of people—which was a big plus right now. Humans were scared (yes, she was human, although *she* wasn't scared), and working with people they trusted gave humans a sense of normalcy.

As she looked at the plumbing specs, she made a mental note to call her friend and fellow contractor Zia with a question.

She nearly jumped when someone knocked on the front door. Mikael had slipped out earlier—very sneakily, but not sneaky enough— and she had no idea where he'd gone. Her brothers still hadn't come home and she wasn't sure where Mikael's two brothers were. They'd disappeared right after Mikael had. Quiet dragons.

But she wasn't their mother so she wasn't going to worry about it. Still, she was a little surprised that Mikael had left without saying anything to her. He was usually her shadow. A dark, broody, quiet, sometimes grumpy one. And…she had other feelings about him leaving without telling her. Feelings she wasn't going to acknowledge.

Because that was how she rolled—burying her feelings in the healthiest way possible.

Striding to the front door, she tugged it open and froze. Her father stood on the stoop.

Nausea swelled up inside her as she stared at him. She hadn't seen him in nearly six years. Wearing jeans and a pullover sweater that looked rumpled, he was more disheveled than she'd ever seen. His dark hair that had been peppered with gray in a very fashionable way years ago was now turning almost white in areas. He also had a few days' worth of facial hair and looked...old. Haggard. This was *not* the same man who used to get weekly manicures and massages, who'd played tennis four days a week, and swam laps in his pool the other three.

"Shep." She grinded her teeth together at just seeing his face. She refused to call him Father or Dad. It was simply Shep now. Or asshole. He'd lost all rights as her father after what he'd done to their mother. They didn't even share a last name anymore—she and her brothers had rejected every single part of him. Now she was Avery Cortez.

"Avery, how are you?" He tried to force a smile, but it came off strained, fake.

"What do you want?" she asked, because he was very clearly here for *something*. He didn't care about her or Riel and Anthony. He cared about himself and that was it. Experience had taught her that.

He glanced past her. "Are the boys here?"

"No, and they're not boys. They're men." Okay, that was kind of a stretch. At twenty-three and twenty-four, yes, technically they were men, but Anthony and Riel were so immature. A little impulsive at times, quick to fall in and out of love—but that was to be expected. She wasn't that much older than them, but some days she felt light years older.

In response, he walked past her and into her house.

She blinked, her nausea turning to a fiery ball of rage in the middle of her core as she shut the door behind her. "Come on in," she muttered as she turned to face him. Might as well get this over with. She knew he wouldn't leave and she really didn't want to have this conversation outside where her neighbors might overhear—because she had a feeling she would start yelling.

"You look like you're doing well." He looked around the house, a gleam in his eyes.

Eyes that were unfortunately the same pale green as her own. *Ugh.* She hated that she looked more like him than her beautiful mother. Hated that she'd gotten anything at all from him.

She knew what he was seeing: the huge two-story Creole home, the wide foyer, the big chandelier hanging above them, which she'd restored herself. Real wood floors, local art on the walls and in the sitting room—which had furniture her mom had left her in her will. All classic, solid pieces that meant something to her. During the day, the whole house was filled with natural light, but now, with the sun going down and Shep in her personal space, the foyer seemed tiny and...foreign. It jarred her, having him here in her home, talking to her. He didn't belong and he was marring this wonderful place with his mere presence.

"The family home was destroyed...when everything happened," he said.

"Everything" meaning The Fall, when a bunch of power-hungry dragons had outed themselves and other supernaturals to the world and nearly destroyed it in fire. Well not *nearly*— they'd actually destroyed more than half of it. New Orleans had gotten caught in the fray as well, but thanks to a whole lot of badass supernaturals, the city and surrounding areas had been mostly saved. But not all the structures, and the city was definitely still rebuilding. Hell, it hadn't even recovered from the last hurricane, let alone a bunch of evil dragons.

The world was a new place, with no currency system right now. It was...interesting, to say the least. She was embracing this new chapter, however. What she wasn't embracing was her bastard of a father. Hate was a very strong word but she *hated* him with the passion of a thousand fiery suns, as cliché as that sounded.

She wasn't going to let her rage take over, however, so she forced herself to take a deep breath. "I'm working, Shep. What do you want?"

"Look... I've lost everything," he started.

Boo freaking hoo, Avery thought as she stared at this man, this monster in human skin. She didn't respond, kept her expression stony, completely unmoved.

He cleared his throat and looked around again. "This is a really nice house."

Yes, it was. She continued staring. She could wait him out because she had nothing to say to him. She wasn't that little girl who needed his approval any longer. She didn't care what he thought. He'd killed all of her love for him in one awful moment.

"I'm living in a two-bedroom condo." The way he said it, it was as if that was the worst thing in the world.

"And?" she asked against her better judgment, scorn dripping from the word.

"And, it's awful. I'm surrounded by simply *awful* people."

Translation: he probably had perfectly friendly neighbors but he was just a dick. Anyone her father thought was awful was probably lovely. "If you're being harassed or abused in any way, then you need to report it to the Alpha of the territory." She kept her words even and monotone.

"I know that!" he snapped. "What's the matter with you?"

She stared at him, her mouth falling slightly open. Was he really this lacking in self-awareness? What was the matter *with her*? "You need to leave. I seriously don't know why you're here. And really, I don't care. Because if you think I would let you live here, you're out of your mind."

He took a step toward her, putting his palms up in a placating gesture. "No, I just…I know you're friends with that wolf." The way he said wolf was almost…derogatory.

She lifted an eyebrow. "Do you mean *King*?"

"Yes, yes. I know you're doing a lot of work for the city. You can ask him for a favor, get me better accommodations. I'm living like…" He cleared his throat. "I need something better." There was a desperation in his voice.

She couldn't help herself, a burst of laughter exploded from her. "Are you serious right now? You think I would waste a favor on *you*? You're more delusional than I ever could have imagined. I'm not going to ask King for anything. And for the record, I could," she added, because she was feeling petty. She didn't like this side of herself, this angry ball of rage, but years of suppressed anger were rolling to the surface with no warning. "I'm afraid what you're figuring out right now is what it's like to be part of the working class, actually having to *contribute* to society. I'm sure that's a huge revelation to you, but deal with it."

He stared at her, and for a moment raw fire flickered in his pale eyes. But just as quickly he smothered it and it was replaced by an emotion she couldn't quite define. Calculation, likely. "She left me," he whispered in a way that was supposed to sound sad and pathetic.

Okay it *did* sound like both those things. Because he was pathetic.

"Who?" She knew exactly who—his wife. But she wanted him to say it.

"Lindsey."

"She left you? Bet that feels like crap, huh?" Avery didn't like this anger that was pouring out like a geyser. This was…not her. But at the same time, she couldn't stop herself. Couldn't stop the venom if she'd wanted to. It felt good to let it free.

"You don't have to gloat over it," he snapped.

"I'm not gloating. I would have to feel something for you to do that. And now it's time for you to go." She stepped toward the front door, exhausted just from this interaction. And she needed a shower, needed to erase the last few minutes from her mind.

He stumbled toward her, his eyes wide and manic as he suddenly grabbed her wrist. He might look fragile, but his grip was strong, making her cry out in surprise and a little pain. "You have to get me better living accommodations! I'm working in a food center!" he snapped, his voice trembling and out of control.

Before she could respond, the door swung open and Mikael and her two brothers strode in.

Avery met Mikael's eyes. She thought she'd seen him angry before, but she realized that she hadn't. She'd only seen him annoyed. Now…his dragon stared back at her, then he turned to her father, who was still holding her wrist.

She wasn't afraid for herself, but her father should be very, *very* afraid. Mikael's dragon peered out, his eyes a smoky gray of swirling color. He was…not happy. He'd gone still in a way that was eerie, watching her father as if he was a bug.

"Take your hand off her *now*." The words were spoken so quietly, Mikael's voice a deadly sharp blade.

Her father dropped her wrist immediately and held his hands up. "I am just talking to my *daughter*."

"You're not our father." Anthony stepped forward, the anger in his normally affable expression out of character as he glared at Shep. "You're just a sperm donor and a pathetic excuse for a human. Get the hell out of here!" He and Riel stormed into the foyer, planting their bodies in front of Avery protectively.

It was incredibly sweet even though it was unnecessary.

Mikael, however, wasn't nearly as patient. His gaze pinned to hers, he grabbed her father by the back of the neck. "I'll take the trash out for you." Then he dragged her father out the front door in seconds, slamming it shut behind him.

"Avery, are you okay?" Anthony asked as Riel asked another question she couldn't make out because of the blood rushing in her ears.

It was too much. Everything was just…too much.

Swallowing hard, she nodded. Today she did *not* have it in her to be okay, to pretend like she had it all together, to be the strong one. Nope. "I just need a minute," she rasped out before turning and hurrying down the hallway. Instead of stopping in the kitchen, she opened the back door and kept going. She wasn't sure what she was doing or where she was going, she just knew she needed space, to get away right now before she broke down in tears.

That monster didn't deserve her tears, but she was afraid all her repressed emotions were going to bubble up in one awful cry-fest where she ended up looking like a puffer fish. If that happened, she definitely didn't want Mikael to see it.

She shoved the back gate open and stepped out onto the little brick herringbone path that led to a nearby sidewalk. The sun had set now and she could hear some of her neighbors laughing and talking outside. She wrapped her cardigan tighter around herself and picked up her pace.

She nearly jolted when she realized Mikael had slipped up next to her, as quiet as a wraith.

"Where are we going?" he asked in that quiet way of his. He wore simple jeans and a gray T-shirt that stretched across broad shoulders, pulling at his muscular biceps. Everything about the dark-haired male with the strong jaw and sharp cheekbones was honed to perfection, as if he was a weapon himself. Which, she supposed, he was.

She didn't want to admit it, but she was glad he was with her, this quiet dragon with smoky gray eyes who made her feel way too many things. Things she wanted no part of. She'd seen what a lifetime of giving yourself to someone, dedicating yourself to their needs, got you.

A shattered heart.

And she'd only known him a few months—ever since King had asked her to take him and his brothers in. They were dragons living in a city where supernaturals had been outed to humans, and King had thought they needed someone to keep an eye on them. The very thought of her human self "keeping an eye" on Mikael, Cas, and Ivyn was ridiculous. Or it had been, because they listened to her, looked out for her, were...all sort of wonderfully weird.

"I don't know where we're going," she answered.

"Should I bring him back so you can yell at him? Perhaps punch him?"

She snorted as they took a left at the next four-way. Her feet had a mind of their own—and she knew where she was going now. "He's not worth the energy."

"He made you cry." There was a low rumble in his tone, an undercurrent of...something dark.

"I'm not crying," she said petulantly, even as she swept away tears from her cheeks. Damn it, she hated that she was crying. "Fine, I am crying, but these tears aren't for him. They're for my mother. For a lot of things." Like the fact that the world had changed forever a couple months ago. Change being such a pathetic description for the complete seismic shift of the entire planet.

"Here," he said as they reached one of her jobsites.

This wasn't one of the condo complexes she was working on for King, it was a house she'd bought before everything happened, and she, her brothers, Mikael's brothers and Mikael had all been working on this home when they could. It wasn't a priority, just a project she enjoyed that gave her something to do when she didn't want to think about anything else.

Like right now. Though she wasn't going to do any work tonight. She was too keyed up. She strode up to the front porch with him and sat on the top step.

He sat with her, taking up more space than her with his broad shoulders and presence in general. He was quiet, not pushing her about her sperm donor, and she appreciated that. But she also figured he deserved to know. She wasn't even sure why, but she wanted to tell Mikael.

"My father left my mother when she was dying of cancer," she blurted out. She'd only ever told him that her parents were divorced and that her mother had died. She'd never given him any details because it was too painful to talk about. And she never, ever thought about her father anymore. She couldn't imagine that he would come back after his reception tonight, so at least there was that.

Her quiet dragon shifted slightly, looking down at her with piercing eyes, the animal back again, peering out at her. His head tilted to the side slightly as if he was confused. "He left his mate when she needed him?"

She nodded once. "He left her for...another woman. A girl I was in college with. My roommate, a woman I thought I was friends with." She let out a bitter laugh, but cut it off abruptly.

Avery looked away from him, staring out at the overgrown grass of the small yard.

"It was surreal, so unbelievable. He'd never been the best father. Don't get me wrong, he showed up to some things, but my mom was there for everything. She was like this big bright light of goodness. He *never* deserved her and I honestly have no idea what she saw in him. And everyone loved her. I'm not exaggerating either. Even my father's stuffy asshole country club-type friends *adored* her. She was just the kind of person you simply wanted to be around so you could bask in her sunshine. When she got sick..."

Avery cleared her throat.

"The doctors found her cancer too late. There was no help for it, just a way to ease her suffering basically. My brothers were seventeen and eighteen, and I was just finishing up college. My roommate came home with me one weekend... That's how my father met her."

She swallowed hard, knowing that if she shed another tear, she wouldn't be able to finish.

"My father comes from a lot of money. Not that he ever did anything to earn it." She made a scoffing sound. "He likes to pretend that he works hard, that he started from nothing." She let out another laugh because the thought was so ridiculous. "In reality he had a few vanity projects that he worked on, but he lived off his inheritance. Don't get me wrong, I had my school paid for, so did my brothers, and I'm grateful and well aware of my own privilege. We were given so much. But that was from a trust from my grandparents. Am I making sense?" she asked because she realized she was just rambling and that he might not get some references, like the country club thing.

Mikael, steady and strong, nodded. "I understand the majority of what you are saying."

"You sure you want to hear all this?" She had diarrhea of the mouth and God, there was no way he could want to hear her pity party story.

"I want to hear every single thing you have to say." The deep rumble of his voice was all-consuming.

A strange flutter started in her belly but she squashed it. He was nothing but her self-appointed protector. He wasn't interested in her romantically, and she didn't want him to be. That would just complicate things. "So anyway, I guess the short story is my mother was dying, my father cheated on her, and instead of waiting a couple more months for her to die in peace with absolutely no knowledge of his betrayal and infidelity, he decided to *leave* her. He married a twenty-two-year-old, someone the same age as his daughter, while his wife of twenty-five years was dying. He...he actually lost a *lot* of friends. Something that surprised me, given the vipers in their social circle. But I guess he underestimated even his circle's adoration for my mom. That was the only justice, I guess, even though I don't think that's the right word. Because there was no justice, just pain. But he did lose some contacts, and in effect, he lost money, which I know bothered him.

"Anthony turned eighteen right around the time our mom died, so my brothers both moved in with me and we haven't spoken to Shep since. He had the audacity to invite us to his wedding. He tried to reach out a couple times, in that first year, but not to apologize. He tried to explain that he fell in love, that it wasn't his fault, that I would understand when I fell in love, blah blah blah. His...*wife* tried to reach out to me too. Only a couple times, but I cut her off just as quickly." Even remembering some of the bullshit stuff Shep had said made her want to smack his stupid face right off.

"If you wish, I will hunt him down and kill him right now." Mikael's words were softly spoken in that sharp-edged way of his that sent a shiver down her spine. She was pretty sure he wasn't joking at all.

She was going to choose to pretend that he was, however. She nudged him with her elbow. "Don't be ridiculous."

"Not ridiculous. It will be easy. He is old and pathetic. I will make it quick. Unless you want him to suffer." Again, with the dark, rumbly voice. "Then he will suffer greatly."

"Mikael! I…" She sighed, unable to deal with *this* right now. Instead she laid her head on his hard shoulder and stared out at the yard. "We need to trim this lawn. My lawn guy is a slacker."

He snorted softly since he was the one who normally took care of the yard here. "I'll make sure I talk to him."

For a moment she savored the quiet, this little time she was going to simply take, when… She sat up suddenly as she remembered something. "Did my brothers have bruises and bloody knuckles?"

Mikael nodded. "They did."

She blinked at his honesty. "Do you know why?"

"I do."

"Are you going to tell me what happened?"

"They asked me not to, but I won't lie to you."

"Was there…color or something in Anthony's hair?" It had looked purple, and while she'd been stunned by her father's arrival, her brain must have subconsciously picked up on all that. Now she wanted to know what had happened.

"I believe it was cupcake frosting. And no, I don't know why it was in his hair. I think the lion was involved." Mikael's face scrunched up a very particular way every time he talked about "the lion."

She studied his expression. If Mikael wasn't worried, then she wasn't going to worry either. Sighing, she laid her head back on his shoulder. She liked being close to him. She felt safe. Protected. Grounded. "I'm going to pretend I have no idea about frosting or bruises right now."

"With younger brothers, that is often a wise choice. Speaking of…do you know where my brothers are?" There was a tension in his question.

"No. They're grown men, Mikael, and I don't need them watching out for me while you're gone." Mikael could be sooooo overprotective of her and her brothers, which was sweet, but he got kind of grumpy and mulish sometimes if his brothers left her alone for two minutes. She was twenty-eight and she didn't need a guardian, let alone three of them.

He just grunted, which yep, meant things were back to normal between them.

Right now she was glad for it, because she craved normal. Or their new version of it.

CHAPTER THREE

King stepped around the prone body and crouched down by the male's head. It belonged to one of three dead humans.

They all had puncture marks in their necks and wrists. All had been savaged when the vampire had drained their blood. Savaged meaning that the killer had drunk from them as if they'd had no control. And yes, vampires had to have training once they'd been turned, being taught how to drain enough blood to satisfy without killing the victim. It was Vampire 101. Killing food sources was stupid in the long term when you could use them for decades upon decades.

"I've seen this kind of feeding before," he murmured to his lieutenants, Ace and Delphine.

"Yeah, me too," Delphine murmured, her amber eyes flashing once as she looked down at the bodies. She pulled her long, dark brown braids back into a tie before she crouched down and inspected the wounds on the female human.

"They're all clothed," he said, mainly because he wanted to make sure they were all on the same page. "I don't think this was a sexual assault type of thing."

Someone could have re-dressed them, of course, but…these killings were sloppy. That of young vampires not in control of their bloodlust. Because he was certain there was more than one killer. The scents hung heavy in the air.

"The vampires lost control, drained them instead of taking only a little. And…" He inhaled again. His olfactory senses were acute, especially for his age of roughly two hundred years. "They were killed at separate times. Then dumped here." The dumping part was obvious. This area of underbrush was muddy and there was only one set of footprints other than theirs still visible around the dump site. None of the bodies had on socks or shoes—yet their feet weren't dirty. Definitely dumped. "Not a turning gone wrong either."

"There's a moratorium on creating vampires anyway," Ace said, stepping back and scanning the area.

Of course he already knew that—he had set the damn moratorium with good reason.

One of their sentries patrolling the outer limits of the city had discovered the bodies and reported in immediately. King's pack had since secured the area, but finding something like this threatened to disturb the balance of the city. One that was still recovering from…a lot of shit.

So far New Orleans had dodged any serious issues with getting the city resettled. People needed a sense of normalcy, and right now he was making sure everyone's needs were being met. Everyone had enough food, they had running water and electricity, and had limited communication thanks to some of his brilliant packmates. Education was on hold for the moment, but he was working with various educators as well. Any healthcare needs were being met either in the human hospitals or the ones run by supernatural healers. The important stuff was handled, and something like this… Humans being murdered?

It could definitely disrupt things. No, he did not like this at all.

"I want a meeting with all the vampire leaders in the city. Tonight." He looked at Ace. "Make the calls. We'll bring the bodies, see if anyone recognizes them."

His lieutenant nodded once and stalked off, pulling his cell phone out.

"Do you smell that?" King murmured to Delphine, stepping away from the bodies.

She frowned and glanced around the wooded area. The bodies had been left beneath a tree, with a few leaves tossed over them as if the person who'd brought them here had haphazardly tried to cover the bodies, then changed their mind. It was barely a half-assed attempt.

The bodies had been abandoned quickly, discarded like trash. It also told him all he needed to know about their killers.

"You think one of the killers is still here?" she murmured low enough that only he could hear.

"No." The bodies were cold and it would be stupid to hang around.

He stepped between two trees and heard a rustling sound, then looked up, tensing for an attack.

He stepped back in surprise to see a baby dragon the size of a baby elephant staring down at him with wide purple eyes, its gray wings pulled tight against its back.

"Well, hello there," he said in what he hoped was a calm voice.

The dragon blinked at him, then dove down onto the blanket of leaves in front of King, using his wings to glide. He made a loud chirping sound, tilted his head slightly and continued to stare at King with blatant curiosity.

"I have no idea what you just said," he murmured.

"King," Ace called out from across the clearing.

He turned and felt the dragonling sidle up next to him, its wings brushing against his leg and hip.

He'd only interacted with one dragonling before, and she was a little bigger than this guy. He wasn't even sure how he knew the dragonling was male, but he definitely was. And he was now rubbing his face against King's hip with insistency.

Reaching out, he rubbed the baby's head. "What is it?" he said to Ace.

Ace paused, looking at the dragonling, then shook his head and focused. "You're going to need to see this."

He hurried across the clearing, the dragon loping alongside him instead of flying. King shot it a surprised look but the dragonling kept up as they reached a cluster of... *Oh hell.* "Those are dragon eggs." Well, the hatched shells. As in...plural.

The little dragonling moved forward and touched one of the cracked-open eggs with his wing, then pointed at himself. Then it chirped happily, as if to say, "That's mine!"

King scrubbed a hand over his face. There were three more open shells in addition to the one the little guy had pointed at. So it looked as if Willow, the dragonling one of his friends had adopted, wasn't the only one in the city.

This was an interesting development. He...wasn't sure what to make of it. There was a lot he didn't understand about real dragons—which were very different from dragon shifters.

"Everyone can meet you in an hour," Ace said. "Unless I should tell them to push the time back?" He glanced at the shells, his eyebrows raised.

"No. The meeting is still on. But I'm going to take this guy to…" He racked his brain, thinking of all the dragons in the city. He could ask Reaper and Greer to take this dragonling in, but they were both so busy running one of the supernatural hospitals. "Mikael and his brothers. Avery will look after this little guy." Hell, she looked after all the males in that house, dragon and human alike, whether they realized it or not. And he remembered her saying that she wanted a dragonling of her own. He liked the human female who was doing so much for the city and knew this baby would be safe with her.

"What should I do about these shells?" Ace asked.

"Transport them home. To the main compound," he clarified. "I don't know if dragons need them or what, but I don't want to just abandon them here." He couldn't imagine why they'd need their shells, but he figured it was better to be safe than sorry.

"I'll scout the surrounding area, looking for the other babies," Delphine said as if reading his mind.

He nodded, then headed for the open-top Jeep he'd arrived in. The dragonling came with him and jumped in the back open seat like a puppy eager for a ride, as if he'd done it a hundred times before.

King turned around and looked at him in surprise. "Seriously? You're riding in here?" He'd assumed the dragonling would fly, if he decided to come with him at all. He'd been hoping the dragon would so it would make the transport to Avery and the dragons easier.

The baby chirped in response, perched on the seat, its tail wiggling.

Laughing to himself, King started the engine and then took off down the dusty old road.

Two minutes later, the baby jumped from the back seat and started flying next to King, chirping animatedly as if he was having an entire conversation with himself. King just made grunts of acknowledgment, which seemed to please the dragonling.

"What the fuck is my life?" he murmured to himself even as a smile tugged at his lips. Even as he had the thought, he knew he would tell Aurora about this development as soon as possible.

Because she was the one person he wanted to tell everything to.

CHAPTER FOUR

Mikael watched from the back porch as Avery tossed another cherry at the dragonling.

The baby, roughly the size of a small horse, practically preened when he caught it in his mouth and then did a sort of bow, as if he was very proud of himself.

If Mikael was the kind of male who used the word adorable, he might say that the dragonling was just that. He was making Avery smile anyway. The pain rolling off her from only hours ago because of her asshole father had dissipated to be replaced by pure joy.

"What am I supposed to do with him?" He looked back at King, who was watching the interaction between the two with a hint of amusement. If he didn't know that the Alpha was smitten with another female, he might have been annoyed that the male was watching Avery.

Mikael's female.

His dragon swiped at him. *Not your female yet.*

Yeah, and it would never happen. He knew exactly where he stood with her. It was a thing called the friend zone. At least that was what one of her brothers had told him. He didn't mind being her friend, and did not quite understand the phrase, and wasn't sure why her brother had said it as if it was a bad thing. In fact, he liked it. But he wanted more than friendship. He wanted everything.

"I thought since you're a dragon you would be more equipped to watch after the little guy before I can find a permanent housing situation for him. Unless it ends up working out and he stays here," King said.

"What kind of housing situation are you looking at for him?" Because Mikael knew that if they took this dragonling in, Avery would never give him up.

"I'm going to reach out to Dallas and see if any of her neighbors want to house him. Dallas loves Willow and that little dragon helps out around the farm, so maybe she'll want him."

Mikael snorted softly. He'd seen Willow's antics and he wasn't so sure the dragonling actually helped out with anything…but she was sweet. And she also made Avery smile. "I know nothing about dragonlings."

Avery turned, clearly eavesdropping even though she was in the middle of the yard, and chucked a cherry at Mikael. "We'll learn!"

Lightning fast, he reached up, snagged it from midair and popped it into his mouth. Flavor exploded on his tongue and he wondered… Well, he wondered what he always did. If Avery would be as sweet if he ever got to taste her. Especially between her legs. She had a rich, fruity scent that made him crazy on a daily basis. He always craved peaches because of her.

Her eyes widened slightly and she grinned. "That was impressive."

He would catch a thousand cherries for her to grin at him like that again. It was a sucker punch straight to his heart. One he thought had died a long time ago when most of his family had been murdered.

"If he wants to stay, I want to keep him," she said as she strode across the yard, the little dragonling loping next to her instead of flying. "But he seems to have bonded with you, King. He keeps watching you, looking for approval every time he catches a cherry."

Mikael looked between the Alpha wolf and the dragonling, who was looking up at King adoringly. *Oh.* "Avery is right."

Frowning, King looked at the dragonling, who stuck his tongue out at him in what Mikael had heard was called a raspberry.

Avery let out a burst of laughter, the sound a balm to his soul.

"I'm trying to keep the city from falling apart. I don't have time for a pet." King spoke more to the dragonling than them.

"You can stay if you want, sweet boy," Avery cooed, scratching behind his ear.

Now the little dragon looked up at her, that adoration directed her way.

The most primal part of Mikael wanted to snarl at the little thing, then felt like an "utter dick," to quote Riel. He could *not* be jealous of a dragonling getting Avery's affection.

"So you'll do it?" King was already heading for the gate that led to the front yard.

"Of course—" Avery broke off as the little dragon trailed after him, chirping animatedly.

King turned around and held his hands up. "No, you stay here." He pointed at Avery and Mikael as if the beast could understand.

Maybe he did, because the dragonling looked at them, then at King, then he jumped right over King, flapping his wings quickly as he sailed over the gate onto the other side of the yard. That dragonling had made his decision.

"Pretty sure he's claimed you," Avery called out. "And now you need to name him."

King looked...baffled, but didn't argue.

As the two left, Avery let out a happy sigh. "Can you imagine how cute it would be to have a little dragon for a pet? King said they found more than one empty shell, right?"

Mikael nodded and headed up the steps of the back patio.

Avery joined him, sitting on one of the lounge chairs that overlooked the backyard with its pretty lights and hanging plants she'd potted herself. There were touches of her everywhere here, from the bright colors and carefully tended roses and geraniums.

In that moment he wished he had the right to pull her into his lap, to nuzzle his nose along her neck and inhale deeply. To rake his teeth against her sensitive skin as he slid his hand down the front of her pants and— He cut the thought off and rolled his neck. *No.* "He was quite adorable."

"That's high praise coming from you." She gave him another one of those soft grins and stretched her legs out.

You could easily give her a baby dragon, his inner beast reminded him. *Just get her pregnant.*

He bit back another groan. His dragon was such an asshole. "You thirsty?" He needed space for a few minutes, just to breathe in air that wasn't laced with her sunshine and perfection.

"Yes, thanks." Avery gave him a tired smile and leaned her head back. "Hot tea, please. I don't care what flavor."

She had many so he picked the raspberry-scented one he knew she usually chose. Not long after, Mikael stepped outside to find Avery dozing on the lounge chair.

He wasn't surprised since it had been a long day for her. As he'd done a few times before, he scooped her up into his arms—even though it was torture to hold her so close—and carried her inside. She stirred slightly, but burrowed into him as she mumbled something under her breath he couldn't make out.

On the stairs he passed Ivyn, his youngest brother, but he ignored the pointed look Ivyn gave him and continued to the second floor. Even if Mikael hadn't known where her room was—which he definitely did—he would be able to follow her scent easily.

Perfection on a summer day.

She mumbled something under her breath, curling into him with complete trust. Her eyelids fluttered but she didn't open them, just murmured something again, her nose scrunching up in what was definitely an adorable way. Because Avery was adorable—he would always use that word for her. Along with kind, beautiful, *his*.

Her bed was neatly made, no surprise. With one hand he tugged the comforter down and eased her against her pillow. She automatically turned onto her side and he pulled the covers up to her shoulders. Gently he pulled the tie from her curly, chocolate brown hair so that it fell all around her head and shoulders. She'd once told him that if she slept with the ties in, they gave her a headache.

What he wouldn't give to run his hands through it, to cup the back of her head as he took her mouth with his. For a long moment he watched her, and reached his hand out to brush her hair out of her face.

But he drew his hand back. Touching her was a special brand of torture—and he had actually been tortured. But this was different, worse. Because she wasn't his. And he didn't have the right to touch her anyway.

Instead of leaving her tie on the nightstand, he tucked it into his pocket. Then he snagged a little dragonfly hair clip and added that as well. When he stepped out into the hallway, he found Ivyn standing there leaning against the doorway two bedrooms down.

"What?" The want and need he'd buried for Avery bubbled up inside him in the form of anger at his brother. His nosy fucking brother.

Ivyn simply lifted a shoulder. "What are you doing with her?"

"What does it look like?" And he didn't answer to his younger brother.

"Like you're trying to hurt yourself." Now there was…a touch of pity in his brother's normally hard gaze.

Annoyed, wanting to punch something now, Mikael turned away and stalked to his own room. His brother was right about hurting himself—maybe he deserved it.

If he'd been home when his family had been attacked, slayed…they might all be alive now.

CHAPTER FIVE

With her hard hat and boots on, Avery ducked into the third floor of the condo complex where they were having an issue with some of the plumbing.

There was a shortage of supplies—even though witches could duplicate *some* things that they needed. So could some half-demons, she'd been told, which was fascinating.

But her construction crews couldn't depend on them for everything. Some things had to be manufactured to specification.

"Look, boss," a big bear shifter said, one meaty hand on his hip as he pointed at the open, unfinished bathroom. "I can finish in here. And we have enough for the rest of this floor, but next week we're going to be moving on to the fourth floor. We don't have enough and I don't know how we're going to get what we need." She knew Santiago, had known him before The Fall, as it was. He'd been in construction for probably longer than she'd been alive and he was damn good at what he did. She was glad King had put him on her crew.

"Let me worry about that. Just finish up everything you can, plumbing-wise, this week. If for some reason we stall on this job, we've got plenty to do at other jobs."

He grinned, half saluting her. "Okay. I know you'll come through. You always do."

She certainly hoped so. She'd already let King know what her crew needed and he was going to reach out to Finn Stavros, the Alpha of the Southern Mississippi and Alabama area. There were a few warehouses in bigger cities like Biloxi and Mobile filled to the brim with stuff that had been untouched during the dragon attacks.

Finn and his pack had provided food and the ability to grow food to other areas with no strings attached, and she had a feeling that the Alpha of Biloxi, as he was commonly called, would give them what they needed with no strings attached either.

It truly was a new world. People were simply helping out because it was the right thing to do. There were a lot of crappy things about this new world but also a lot of really good new ones. Like the fact that if she got hurt, she could go see the supernatural healer and get healed without having to worry about going bankrupt or going into debt. Insurance wasn't a thing right now, simply getting medical care when necessary *was*. So yeah, she could get on board with that.

"What's that look?" Anthony asked, coming up to her.

"Hold on." She answered the call on her radio and headed toward the stairs.

Anthony fell in step with her. He'd transferred back to her crew for the rest of the week, but hadn't told her why. She knew that both of her brothers had gotten into some sort of trouble the other night, but neither of them had opened up to her and she didn't want to push.

When their mom had died, she'd taken on more of a maternal role with them. She'd actually taken it on when their mom had gotten sick, helping them fill out college applications, being there for Anthony when he "came out" as bisexual, though no one had been surprised. In general, she'd just tried to make sure they were okay. "So what's up?" she asked.

"Nothing. You just look stressed. How can I help?"

"Everything's good. I promise. I'm just trying to get some small things in order." She gave him a sunny smile, ignoring the worry burning low in her belly. If they couldn't get what they needed for the next few floors, it would slow down everything. Which meant the people on the wait list for housing would have to wait even longer and she hated that. People were already in a sort of holding pattern, displaced and afraid, and she wanted to make sure they had a warm, safe place to lay their head at night.

"You sure? We didn't really talk about what happened last night."

Meaning when their douchebag of a sperm donor had shown up. She definitely didn't want to talk about that, and never at work. "There's nothing to talk about," she said as they headed down the stairs. "He was just showing up looking for a favor. It's not like he cares what happens to us."

"I wish I'd punched him," Anthony grumbled, flexing his fingers.

"Hey, where's this coming from?" Anthony had always been more of a lover than a fighter.

He shrugged, grinning. "He has a punchable face."

She giggled slightly as they reached the bottom floor. "I'm not going to argue with you there, but he doesn't deserve any space in our brains. I'm going to do my best to forget he ever stopped by." She didn't like thinking about him; he brought up too many painful memories. And he certainly didn't deserve her time or tears.

"What the hell?" Anthony murmured as a shout went up from the parking lot.

She hurried across the gravel, sliding her sunglasses on to block out the bright sun, Anthony hot on her heels. A small circle of shifters had gathered and once she pushed her way through the group, she found Logan, a big bear shifter she recognized from her friend Zia's crew working on the complex next door, and Mitch, a human male on her crew, facing off with each other.

Zia was on the sidelines, wearing her own hard hat—a purple one—as she looked up at Logan, the bear shifter who drove her crazy. "We need to—"

Avery took the whole scene in and hurried over to Zia's side. "What's going on?"

"This asshole stole my Makita." Logan looked directly at the human male who was trying to stand his ground, but Avery could see the fear in his dark eyes.

If Avery didn't know Logan, she would probably be afraid too. He was likely six foot five inches, maybe taller. But he was normally so jovial and kind to everyone. "Why do you think he stole it?" She'd seen Logan's brushless rebar tying tool—and was jealous of the expensive piece of equipment. Avery shifted slightly so that she stood directly in front of the human. She knew without a doubt that Logan would never hurt her, but she wasn't so sure about Mitch. He was new to her crew, had been put on last week. She didn't know him.

Zia shifted with her, using her body as a block.

Logan frowned but some of the tension in Avery's shoulders eased as he looked down at the two of them. "I saw him take it. He thought he was being sneaky, but I came back from my break early. He's a shitty thief."

Annoyed, Avery turned around and faced Mitch. "Give it back."

"You're just going to take *his* word?" Anger flared in the human's dark eyes as he took a menacing step toward her.

But she'd worked with men for most of the last decade and she was *not* worried about this guy. He was all bluster. So she took a step toward him, hands on her hips. "Yes, I am. I've known him for years. Give it back now and get the hell off this job. One of King's people can place you somewhere else, but you don't work for me anymore." She had a feeling King would be very, very pissed about the stealing.

"You stupid bit—"

Faster than she thought possible, Logan somehow moved her and Zia out of the way and smashed his fist into the human's face.

Avery winced at the crunching sound. That had to hurt.

"Holy shit," Zia murmured.

Heart beating fast, Avery stared at the groaning, crumpled human on the gravel lot. Holy shit was right. Blood covered his face and the front of his shirt.

"That's enough, Logan," Zia said quietly, placing her fingers gently on his forearm.

The bear shifter stilled, though his body was still vibrating with anger as he stared at the human.

"That's right, listen to your bitch," the human said as he spit out blood, shoving to his feet.

Okay, it was actually impressive that Mitch could even stand up at this point. And he wasn't shouting in pain, though she knew he had to be in a lot of it.

Logan started to take another step toward the guy but Avery slid in front of him and held up a hand even as Zia clutched onto his forearm. "He's not worth it. He's done for. He won't be working in any area around here again." Because she would make sure of it.

Logan leaned around her to glare at Mitch. "If you call Zia or Avery any name again, you'll have to worry about more than my fist in your face. And I do listen to everything my female says. I'm not sure why you think that's a bad thing, to listen to the most beautiful woman in the world. You're a thief *and* a fool."

Zia groaned and mumbled something under her breath.

"All right, show's over!" Avery snapped out. Just then Mikael appeared as if out of nowhere. She'd sent him on a run to grab supplies—because she trusted him and had needed a little space from his hovering. But he was back and his dragon was in his eyes now, all smoky gray rage. She didn't even have to tell him what to do, he simply grabbed the human by the back of the neck and started dragging him off the jobsite.

Everyone started dispersing, thankfully, getting back to work.

"Logan," Zia murmured, nudging him in the stomach—though Avery doubted he could even feel it.

"Princess, just tell me what to do and I will do it."

Zia scrubbed a hand over her face. "Please go back to the jobsite and finish the drywall. And *stop* calling me princess."

"I can do anything but that, my Princess." Then he basically *bowed* and strode off—strutting as if he was a peacock, which was ridiculous for such a big bear shifter.

Once the bear was gone, Avery turned to her friend and giggled. "Now he calls you princess?"

Zia shook her head, her short, dark curls bouncing around her face. "He announced to everyone that he is my hammer and does as I order. Something is seriously wrong with that bear. I have no idea why he keeps saying these things. I'm human and it's not like we're mated. But he says," she whispered, glancing around once, "that he would follow my commands even over the Alpha. I don't think that's a good thing." She kept her voice low so only the two of them could hear.

"Shifter hierarchies are really weird." But she was also pretty sure that Logan was obsessed with or in love with Zia. He looked at her as if she'd hung the moon and she'd heard him refer to himself as her hammer more than once. The bear really was kind of ridiculous.

If adorable.

Avery wondered what it would be like to have someone be completely devoted to her, but then...shelved the thought. It would never happen.

Fairy tales were just that. Fairy tales.

CHAPTER SIX

Three weeks after The Fall

Listening to her iPod, Avery stared up at the stars, unable to shake the...blah feeling ruminating inside her. Today had been long and uneventful, but in the quiet when she'd gotten home an impending sense of doom had settled around her shoulders like a familiar ache.

Just...sitting there, pushing in on her.

Suddenly Mikael's face was in front of her as he looked down at her on the chaise longue. He had a blanket rolled up under his arms.

She nearly jumped, but pulled her earbuds out. "Hey, you scared me."

"My apologies," he said in that formal way of his. He had the faintest hint of an accent that could maybe be linked to modern Russia. Or...what would have been considered Russia before three weeks ago.

She wasn't actually sure how he'd learned English but he and his brothers seemed to know it and a few other languages. From what she'd gleaned they were old—ancient, really. As in, they'd gone into Hibernation so long ago she couldn't even wrap her mind around it. They didn't know much about modern history—as in the last thousand years—at all.

"What is wrong?" he continued.

She didn't move from her position as he sat on the chaise next to her. It was one of those oversized ones that could fit two people. "Nothing. Just tired."

"I can scent your lie and your sadness." He nudged her hip with his big hand—a hand she'd had fantasies about.

Well, not his right one in particular, but both giant callused hands. And his mouth. And...other things. He and his brothers hadn't been living with her and her brothers long, but her crush had developed pretty damn quickly. It was impossible not to like him. He was just so...adorable. To be fair, all of them were, but Mikael was different. Sweet. Always doing little things for her without telling her.

Like, she'd noticed that he sometimes folded her laundry when she left it in the dryer too long. Or he made sure she had a fresh cup of coffee every morning doctored exactly the way she liked it before they all headed to work. And all his kindness didn't take away from the fact that the male was a walking, talking weapon. She absolutely understood that he was dangerous.

Just not to her.

She scooted over and he stretched out next to her, all long, thick, muscular legs and a spicy, woodsy scent she wanted to bathe in. He tossed the blanket over them, because he was always thoughtful like that.

"I'm just...feeling overwhelmed, I guess. Working on this new housing for King has been keeping me busy, but it's hard to shut my brain off. Hard to process how many people around the world died so suddenly. Some days I'll force myself to not think about it, but others...it's just a lot sometimes."

"That makes sense. We all need time to process things. And the loss to the world was abrupt and violent. If you are not used to violence, it will be harder to adjust."

"Did you...see a lot of violence? Before you went to sleep?" She knew he must have, but asked anyway.

"I did." He leaned his head toward hers so that his was sort of right over hers as he curled his body against her ever so subtly, giving her some of his wonderful warmth.

She breathed deeply, taking him in, glad he was here right now. Her brothers and Mikael's brothers were out for the night. She hadn't felt like going anywhere or seeing anyone. "Want to expand on that?" There was so much she didn't know about him and she was curious.

He was silent for so long she didn't think he was going to respond. That was okay. The fact that he was here was good enough for her. "I saw a lot of war. Death. Caused it too. I don't wish to talk about it though."

"I understand." Maybe not the war stuff, but she understood not wanting to talk.

"I'm sorry for your pain," he said quietly.

She tugged the soft navy blue blanket she'd had for years up higher and curled into him. "You're warm," she murmured. And he made her feel waaaaay too many things.

"I am a dragon."

She laughed lightly, her breath curling out in little wisps of white smoke. "So you're always hot?"

"Yes."

She nearly sighed. Yes, yes he was. The hottest male she knew. The fact that he didn't seem to realize it made him that much more attractive.

"What were you listening to on your music machine?"

She snorted. "It's an iPod. Or you can call it an mp3 player." Though music machine made her giggle and she vowed to call it that from now on. "And I was listening to The Cranberries. They're sort of my go-to for anything when I'm...in a mood. Any mood at all." Happy or sad, didn't matter.

"Can I hear them?"

"Yeah." She handed him one of the earbuds. "Dolores O'Riordan was the singer. Her voice is...simply beautiful." Hauntingly.

"Was the lead singer?" he asked as he slipped it into his ear.

"She died a couple years ago. The world lost an incredible artist that day. I like to think she's living in a multiverse though, still singing her heart out."

He paused for a moment. "What is a multiverse?"

"I don't even know if it's real. It's just a theory about how there are other universes that exist parallel to ours and different versions of ourselves are out there living their lives just like we are. I figure if dragons and other supernatural beings exist and our whole world has been changed so dramatically, multiverses exist too."

"Then I hope she is in one too."

Avery smiled slightly and pressed play, looking up at him now instead of the blanket of stars scattered across the sky. She wanted to watch his expression, hoped he enjoyed O'Riordan's voice as much as she did.

Mikael wasn't wildly expressive—at least he wasn't normally—but she could see the shift in him, the way his smoky gray eyes lit up as he listened to her lilting, distinctive voice. Eventually she laid her head on his chest as they both listened to the full album.

When his arm curved tighter around her, she savored the sensation of feeling safe and protected. Savored him. This male who she shouldn't want because she knew there were no happy endings.

But that knowledge did nothing to douse her growing feelings for this ancient dragon who had awakened something inside her she didn't even know existed.

CHAPTER SEVEN

"I think my brothers are avoiding me," Avery said as she and Mikael stepped into the foyer. It had been a long day and she was beyond exhausted. And she couldn't find one of her favorite hair clips, a sparkly dark blue claw she liked to pull her hair back in after her shower. None of the males in the house had taken it, so she hadn't bothered asking them. And it had nothing to do with her brothers at all except she was feeling annoyed right now.

"Why do you say that?" He locked the door behind them.

"I don't know, they're being weird."

"So are *my* brothers. Maybe it is a younger sibling thing."

She laughed lightly because both sets of their brothers had disappeared after work tonight, acting all cagey. If they wanted to go hook up with people...who cared? She just hoped they weren't getting into trouble. "Hey, want to go out tonight? I'm tired but I could have a couple drinks and unwind." For some reason she didn't want to be alone with her thoughts, didn't want to think too much on...anything.

"Of course."

"Okay, I want to shower first." She was covered in a fine layer of dust.

He simply nodded and she hurried up the stairs.

She was so thankful that the city had running water and electricity. She might like getting all sweaty and putting in a hard, physical day's work, but she absolutely loved running water, thank you very much.

She actually put on a little makeup that she hadn't used in months—it wasn't like she could go to the store and buy any more right now—and slipped on a dress that made her feel sexy, feminine. Not like the boss of over fifty men—mostly—who viewed her as one of the guys. Which was good, but still, she needed to feel feminine tonight. Needed to feel alive, sexy.

More than she'd realized until that moment as she put her mascara wand back into the tube. Because right now too many emotions swirled inside her, as riotous as a hurricane. She knew it had everything to do with her father showing up and the stupid feelings she ignored whenever she was around Mikael. Which was often now. Going out with him alone was probably stupid but she was feeling reckless enough not to care. And he was the sole reason she'd dressed up—put on makeup. Yeah, apparently she was vain enough to want to look nice for him. *Ugh.* What was wrong with her?

As she reached the bottom of the stairs, Mikael appeared out of nowhere, as always, a freaking ghost. God, he looked so damn sexy in jeans and a gray T-shirt that molded to every delicious muscle. She bit back a groan. How was he so effortlessly sexy? His hair was still damp and she guaranteed he'd put absolutely no thought into what he was wearing. He'd just taken a shower and tossed on clothes and now looked like a walking, talking wet dream.

His eyes widened slightly when he saw her, that smoky gray sweeping over her from head to foot and then back up again.

"What?" She fought the heat spreading across her cheeks. "It's not that cold out." The weather was in the weird in-between stage where it got chilly-ish at night but into the eighties in the day. And screw it, she didn't care if it was chilly out, she was showing some leg tonight, hence the blue summer dress with light gray polka dots. It pulled in at her waist, had little flutter sleeves, and while it had give in the material, it hugged the rest of her as well. She loved the way it made her feel.

He made a sort of coughing sound, his eyes pinned to hers. "You look...stunning."

"Oh," she murmured. She cleared her throat again as butterflies danced inside her. "Thank you." The dress was definitely better than her jeans and flannel work shirts. "I don't really have a chance to dress up anymore, obviously, so I figured why not tonight." She was such a liar! She'd dressed up for him and now that he'd noticed...what did she even want to happen?

He made a sort of rumbling sound as he opened the door. He stepped outside in front of her, something she'd discovered shifters simply did out of habit. Especially those of the warrior class; they entered rooms before anyone they saw as more fragile than themselves. And Mikael was so overprotective of her and her brothers. He always went into any room first to ascertain danger. Not that she was expecting any on her front porch. But she appreciated the thought. He had this way of making her feel so damn safe and protected all the time.

Inhaling, she savored the fresh air as they stepped outside, could smell just a hint of rain on the air and was glad for it. Even if it might slow down their job a couple days, they needed the rain. "Riel texted me that he's going to be late tonight. I think he's hanging out with Axel, something I'm not so sure about."

Mikael's gaze skimmed over her again before he scanned the neighborhood in that intense way of his. When he looked at her like that, his expression so damn unreadable, she had no idea what to make of it. "The lion is no good, I told you."

She nudged him with her hip as they headed down the sidewalk. They hadn't discussed where they were going, but there was a local bar close enough to walk to. They rarely drove anywhere anymore; living and working within a small radius made the most sense for everyone. At least in New Orleans. She hadn't heard much about what was going on in the rest of the world except for a few cities. The news and internet were spotty here—everywhere, she'd heard—and they didn't get things as quickly as they had before. She knew that King was in touch with Alphas all over the world, and really, she was trying not to worry about any of that since their territory was functioning.

"I don't understand why you and Axel don't get along. He's so sweet, if a little mischievous."

Mikael mumbled something under his breath, his face doing that cute scrunchy thing he did if anyone even brought up "the lion."

Which she could admit she liked. Because she liked everything about the sexy male. Tall, dark and brooding. That was Mikael. His eyes were what had first drawn her in. The smoky gray was mesmerizing—and so were his broad shoulders and ripped body. She'd seen him without a shirt on a couple times since they lived together and holy hell, the gods had been created after *him*, no doubt.

"Have you heard from your…ah, sperm donor?" he asked cautiously as they reached a four-way stop.

Under other circumstances she might have giggled at him using the term sperm donor. It sounded strange coming from him, especially when he often spoke semiformally. "No. He doesn't have my cell phone number anyway. I don't actually know how he found out where I live, though I imagine it's not that hard."

"If you need me to do anything about him, just let me know."

"Well you're not going to kill him, if that's what you're saying." They'd never really discussed what he'd said last night about killing her father, and there was so much about Mikael and his brothers she didn't know.

She obviously trusted them since she was living with them, but still, he was from a completely different era. Like thousands of years ago. Not to mention a different culture entirely. Hell, species. He'd literally offered to kill her father like it was no big deal.

She knew he'd fought in a bunch of wars too. The concept was so foreign to her. It was hard to wrap her mind around him and his brothers battling with swords—or dragon fire, probably. She'd tried asking him about his previous life once but he'd shut down quickly so she hadn't pushed. She understood the need for privacy, the need to keep some things to yourself. Even if she did wish he would open up to her some.

"I will do anything you ask of me," Mikael said quietly as they reached the neighborhood dive bar. He placed his hand on the small of her back, something she liked.

"You're a really good friend, Mikael," she murmured as he opened the door and a cacophony of noise greeted them. Too bad he was just a friend.

Inside was busy, as normal. The red walls had always seemed garish to her, but they were growing on her a little. Three guitars were on the back wall, signed by some famous Irish musicians. There was a bit of exposed brick on three of the four walls, and little round-top tables that fit four people max and took up the majority of the bar. Little twinkle lights lit up the undercarriage of the bar top and behind it, intertwined with all the bottles. One thing that hadn't changed since The Fall—still no smoking inside. Something she was grateful for. Still, it smelled like beer, too many people, and perfumes. She'd been coming here since college and something about this place was comforting to her.

They'd taken three steps when Avery's gaze landed on *her*.

Oh my God. All the breath sucked from Avery's lungs. She hadn't seen Lindsey in six years.

Mikael shifted his body in front of hers in a subtle, quick motion. "What's wrong?"

She clutched his forearm, digging her nails in. "Her. *She* is here. The woman my father…" She couldn't finish. She tried to tear her gaze away from Lindsey Baird, the woman who she'd once lived with, once thought was her friend, until she'd stabbed Avery in the back in the worst kind of betrayal possible. The one who had apparently left her father, if he was to be believed.

"The one you told me about yesterday?" he asked quietly, his gaze trailing across the bar.

She took a step back, wanting to leave right now.

Just then Lindsey turned and looked at her, her lips a shiny ruby red, her blonde hair soft and perfect, falling around her shoulders and breasts like she was a freaking model. She looked paler than Avery remembered but it looked good on her, like she was a porcelain doll or something.

"Let's grab a drink," she gritted out to Mikael, looking away from Lindsey. Because she wasn't going to let that woman drive her out of a place she liked. Now that she'd actually seen Avery, she couldn't leave on principle.

As they moved to the bar, she barely blinked and Lindsey was right next to her and Mikael, smiling widely at her. *What the hell?* How had she moved so fast?

Oh no. A sinking sensation filled her gut as she realized…Lindsey looked different. She'd always been beautiful, no way to deny that. She was like a modern Marilyn Monroe. But oh God, she had to be a vampire. It was the only thing that Avery could guess, and she knew a decent amount about supernaturals at this point. She'd known about them before The Fall. You didn't grow up in New Orleans and not know that the things that went bump in the night existed. And Lindsey looked even more beautiful than she remembered.

"Avery," she drawled, stroking her long fingers against the delicate necklace around her neck. It had a single emerald pendant.

It had been Avery's mother's—her father had told her it belonged to him, had refused to give it to Avery. And since it hadn't been specified in her mother's will, she hadn't been able to fight him. Lindsey might as well have slid a stiletto through her ribs. Seeing the necklace around Lindsey's neck... It was just one more betrayal, one more stab in the back.

"I have nothing to say to you." She'd started to turn away from her when Lindsey looked Mikael up and down, actually licking her bottom lip.

"What have we here?" She reached out a hand as if to actually stroke Mikael's chest but he slapped her hand away.

Lindsey's grin grew even wider. "Is this your idea of foreplay?"

"Oh my God," Avery muttered and looked at Mikael. This was pathetic. "You know what I like. Order for me while I run to the restroom?"

He simply nodded, but his gaze was pinned firmly on Lindsey.

It was a strange look, one she wasn't sure how to decipher. All Avery knew was that her stomach muscles pulled taut as she walked away, a brittle tension settling in her shoulders. She didn't like feeling like a coward, that she was running away, but she needed some breathing room to process the fact that Lindsey was here in the flesh. And seemed to be a vampire—which was terrifying on another level. She didn't think Lindsey would hurt her or anything, but she'd also never thought the woman would screw her father. So.

In the bathroom she turned on the faucet and splashed cold water on her cheeks, the chill grounding her a bit. Seeing that woman was a jolt to her senses. She'd moved in a way that was far too fluid, too quick to be just a human.

Once Avery felt more in control of herself, she stepped out into the little hallway, only to be inundated by the noises of the bar once again. A man stumbled past her, heading for the bathroom door. As she headed down the hallway, it sounded even louder than before. It probably was. This was around the time people were getting off work, and especially after The Fall, people needed to unwind more than ever.

As she stepped out of the hallway and into the bar, she immediately sought out Mikael.

But as soon as she spotted him, she froze.

He was still at the bar, with Lindsey. He was leaning down talking to her, had his hand wrapped around her neck, his thumb along her jaw as if embracing her, like a lover would do.

Avery stared in horror at the picture the two of them made. She knew she didn't have that kind of relationship with him, but still, he knew *exactly* how much that woman had hurt her.

He spoke in Lindsey's ear, as if he was whispering to her. He wasn't pulling back. No, he was…still embracing her, talking to her. Everything looked so damn intimate.

Feeling as if she'd been punched in the stomach, Avery ducked back into the hallway.

Nope. She couldn't do this. She could not walk up there and act like everything was normal. She was… Well, she wasn't going home. That was for sure. And she wasn't staying here. Thankfully this place had a back door and she was going to use it.

Because she wasn't going to stand around and watch that shitshow, that was for sure. If Mikael wanted Lindsey, he could have her.

This was exactly why Avery didn't believe in fairy-tale bullshit.

Because that was exactly what fairy tales were.

CHAPTER EIGHT

Mikael waited until Avery was out of sight before he approached the female who was most definitely a vampire. The one who made Avery smell like pain. The scent coming off Avery before had been the same as when her father had come to see her.

Avery hadn't allowed him to end her father, but this vampire was about to get her head ripped off.

He leaned in close, wrapped his hand around her throat and squeezed. He didn't care that he was in public, didn't care about anything but taking away Avery's agony.

The vampire gave him a smile she probably thought was seductive. "So you do have good taste after all," she purred.

He tightened his grip as he leaned close to her ear. "You are going to want to be quiet now. You're simply going to listen to everything I say, you stupid little vampire." His words were subvocal, so only she could hear him.

A trickle of fear intermingled with her lust. *Good.* His dragon half was ready to burst out, take out this threat with fire and destruction, and destroy the whole damn bar, but he kept his control.

Barely.

"It would be nothing for me to rip out your jugular right now. Or drag you into the parking lot and burn you alive. You will turn to ash under my fire, as if you never existed at all."

He let his dragon flare in his gaze now, his beast wanting to do just that, to stop this vampire who had caused Avery even an ounce of pain.

"I am thousands of years old. I know ways to torture that you cannot even imagine." A solid truth she heard in his words if her jerk of fear was any indication.

She was breathing hard now, not from lust either. She hadn't tried to yank away, very likely her fight-or-flight instinct telling her to be very, very still or the predator with his hand on her throat would end her life.

"I could drag you into the mountains, shackle you in a cave and torture you for decades for what you've done to Avery. Make sure you receive the barest hint of blood so you won't die. Just exist in pain. Give me one reason why I should not."

The stench of her fear was acute now, overpowering him and his beast. He did not like weak bullies.

"This necklace," she whispered. "Take it, give it to her."

He stilled in surprise. "Why do I care about a necklace?"

"It was her mother's," the vampire rasped out, from fear or because he was squeezing her throat so tight she could barely talk, he wasn't certain.

With his free hand he opened the clasp and grasped the necklace lightning quick before it fell. "You will leave New Orleans—"

"What?"

"You will leave this city and never come back. You have two days to pack your things and find a new place to live." He wasn't the Alpha, didn't have that authority. But he didn't care. This female was leaving.

"That's not—"

"I told you to be quiet. If you are smart, Avery better never see your face again. Or I will do everything I said I would. And worse. Do you have anything else of hers?"

There was a long pause, then she tried to nod but could barely move her head at this point. Thankfully no one was paying any attention to them. He'd already waved the bartender off and everyone else was all huddled up in their own conversations, not worrying about the two of them.

He glanced over his shoulder, looking for Avery. He wanted this done before she returned. "What is it?"

"Just some jewelry."

"You will bring them back to me. And if I have to hunt you down, you won't like what happens." His dragon was still in his eyes, watching her.

The acrid stench of her fear intensified but she nodded. "Give me half an hour," she whispered. "I'll meet you in the parking lot."

"Good." He released her and she practically sprinted from the bar, stumbling in her skinny heels.

His beast wanted to hunt her down, fillet her alive, do all the things that Avery would look at him in disgust for. He was not a good male, not the right type of male for her, but it didn't matter to his dragon. He would do anything to keep her safe, to make sure she was happy. And if that stupid vampire didn't listen to him, well…he might eat her as a snack. His dragon rumbled an agreement in his head. *With barbecue sauce.*

He'd recently discovered barbecue sauce and his dragon half was now obsessed with it.

He glanced around the bar again, looking for Avery. She'd been gone for too long. The place had gotten crowded in the last few minutes, with people caught up in their own conversations, and trying to wave down the lone bartender.

He slipped off his barstool and made his way through the crowd. It was easy enough. Most people moved to the side so it didn't take long to make it to the little hallway where the bathrooms were. Avery should have come out by now. Maybe she was still upset.

He knocked once on the door. When there was no response, he opened the door. The lights were off and it was empty.

His dragon clawed at him, the foreign emotion of worry spiking inside him. He had never worried about anyone before Avery. He immediately called her, but she did not respond.

To his surprise he received a text from her.

I've gone to a friend's house. Have fun with her. Then she included a red-faced, angry-looking…emoji, he thought the symbols were called.

Have fun with who? He frowned even as he realized what she meant. She must have seen him with the vampire and thought… Hell, she must have assumed the worst. He'd been whispering in the female's ear, but only so no one would overhear his threats to kill and torture her.

Damn it.

He texted back. *Where are you?*

Avery didn't respond.

He wasn't going to wait or try to text her so he called her again, wanting to clear this up immediately. But it went straight to voicemail. He growled low in his throat as he stepped out into the parking lot.

He understood enough about these cell phones that he knew she'd turned her phone off. He inwardly cursed to himself. He had a feeling he knew where she'd gone at least, especially since she was on foot.

He wanted to rush after her, but he would wait to get the rest of her jewelry. Once he brought this treasure to her and explained everything, Avery would understand.

Twenty minutes later, which seemed to stretch on for an eternity, the vampire was back in the parking lot, a purple bag in her hand. She shoved it at him, her entire body trembling, the fear rolling off her pathetic.

She was a vampire, not completely weak. Yet she had no backbone.

"Everything is in here?" He didn't bother looking inside. He would have no idea if all of Avery's jewelry was inside or not.

"Yes. Everything." She took a step back, her movements jerky.

"Good. Remember what I said? Tick tock. Two days," he growled, his dragon watching her like the prey she was. Riel had taught him the phrase "tick tock" and it seemed to have the effect he wanted.

More likely, she was just terrified he'd burn her to death.

* * *

Mikael made his way up the long walkway to where he suspected Avery had gone—the mansion where the stupid lion lived. He'd tracked her scent and it was strong here.

The females who lived there were all right. He didn't like most people, but they had always been kind to Avery. Before he'd made it to the front door, one of the redheaded tiger shifter twins dropped down seemingly out of nowhere in front of him, tall, lean and... She looked annoyed. *At him.*

She crossed her arms over her chest, her expression pulled into a scowl. "What are you doing here?"

Okay so she was annoyed at him for certain. And he knew that Avery was here, partially because of the tiger's reception but also because her scent was growing stronger. If he had to guess, this tiger was Brielle. Her twin, Harlow, always looked as if she was deciding whether she should kill you or not. Which he appreciated. He liked to know where he stood with other shifters.

"I'm looking for Avery."

"She's not here." Brielle's tone was flat.

"You are not a good liar."

The tiger shifter looked at her nails, as if bored. Then he watched as two of her claws started to grow. "You can come see her out back. If you upset her, you'll get to see more of these." She waved her claws at him and then her tiger flashed in her eyes once before she gave him her back. Which was definitely an insult.

He didn't care what this tiger thought of him. He didn't care what anyone thought of him. He only cared about Avery.

He fell in step with the tiger, following the sunshine scent of the sweetest female he'd ever known around to the back of the mansion.

He'd been here a couple times before and it looked much the same. There were chickens running around, little round lights hanging over a patio set, and a greenhouse in one corner of the yard, as well as another garden they'd started growing. But all his attention was on Avery, who was curled up on a lounge chair next to Lola.

Lola's hair was still that bizarre rainbow color.

"You left." Apparently he was saying obvious things as he stalked up to Avery. He knew his dragon was in his gaze too.

"Why are you here?" she sniffed and he thought he detected tears glittering in her eyes.

No. He could not handle tears. Not from her. "I had to take care of something."

Now a sharp sense of rage rolled off her as she glared up at him. "Take care of...something?" she said through gritted teeth.

The rest of the females—Axel thankfully was not there—stirred in their seats, giving him death glares.

"I was not fucking that female," he spat out, because clearly she must've been thinking something along those lines. He crouched down in front of her so they were more at eye level. He wanted her to see the truth, to know he could never betray her like that. How...could she even think that of him?

"I saw you. And I know we're friends and you can do whatever you want, but I told you about my past. I told you what she did to me. I just… I *saw* you." Her voice cracked on the last word and something inside him cracked as well.

Show her the jewelry, dumbass, his dragon snarled at him. *Now!*

Moving quickly, he laid the small, soft bag on the table in front of her. Though he hated to tear his gaze from hers, he unrolled it so that all the pieces were visible. They sparkled under the lights above them.

She gasped in shock and jumped from her seat, the blanket around her shoulders falling behind her. She stared at him, then at the jewelry, her pale green eyes going wide. "This is my mother's. Which…you obviously know. How…how did you get this?"

He leaned down, knowing he was pushing into her personal space and not caring. Because he needed to make something clear. "The only reason I was touching that vampire was because I was threatening to torture her. She's lucky she's still walking." He decided not to tell her that he had contemplated ripping out her jugular. "She returned your mother's jewelry to you as an offering—so I wouldn't kill her. And she will be leaving the city within the next two days. You'll never have to see her again."

He couldn't believe Avery thought he would be with someone else. He couldn't even *look* at another female. Clearly she didn't understand what she meant to him. He wasn't even sure he'd understood how much she meant to him until that moment. But he still couldn't fathom touching another woman. Never. Now he'd told her what kind of male he was, that he would kill another being. She was watching him still, her eyes wide, her scent unreadable.

She…was probably disgusted by him. But he'd had to tell her the truth.

Taking him off guard, she suddenly threw herself at him, wrapping her arms around his neck and holding him tight in a hug.

He didn't pause, and wrapped his arms around her as well, inhaling deeply. *Sunshine.*

She leaned back, grabbed his face and planted a kiss right on his mouth.

Before his brain had time to register that Avery's mouth had actually been on his, she'd already pulled back and crouched down in front of the jewelry. "I can't believe you did this," she whispered as the other females crouched down with her, looking at the sparkling jewels. "I never thought I would see any of this again. Some of these actually belonged to my great-grandmother, were passed down to all the females in my family."

Brielle handed him a beer, the tiger shifter able to move with more stealth than any shifter he'd ever known. "So you're not an asshole. Apologies for threatening you," she said as she tipped the top of her own bottle to his.

Mikael nodded at her because he wasn't sure what to say and took a sip of the beer as he watched Avery pick up one of the necklaces—not the one the vampire had been wearing—and put it on around her neck. It was a simple gold chain, but the way she touched it... *Hell.*

He knew the others were talking, could hear the hum of their voices as he watched Avery's brilliant smile light up the entire backyard. But he couldn't make out any words.

The only thing he could actually focus on was the fact that she'd kissed him. She also...didn't seem to care that he'd threatened to torture that vampire either.

He filed that away, not quite sure what to do with the knowledge yet. But just maybe he had a chance with her.

And now that he'd had a tiny taste, it would never be enough. Would never satisfy him.

CHAPTER NINE

Four weeks after The Fall

Mikael ducked as Cas swung his arm at his head.
He jabbed quickly into his brother's ribs, a sharp punch he pulled back just as lightning fast.

Cas swiped out at him, trying to knock him off his feet—which was the purpose of this exercise.

He stumbled, righted himself and ducked to avoid another rapid-fire incoming punch.

"You should just concede," Cas said, a grin on his face as he jumped back out of reach. Normally his brother was so serious. Both of them were. Had been that way for a long time, but today things felt different.

After a long day at work, they'd all needed an outlet. Mikael had already sparred with Ivyn and then Cas had challenged him.

"To my baby brother? Never." He ducked low and rammed his head straight into Cas's middle, taking him completely off guard. Ignoring the rain of punches to his back and then ribs, he twisted and flipped Cas in the air.

Instead of landing on his back, his brother righted himself midair and landed with the grace of a panther.

He heard a gasp of surprise from the patio and turned, scenting her even as he heard her short gasp.

Avery was standing there, the female of his fantasies. Her eyes were wide, her mouth slightly open, and all he could think about was biting that bottom lip between his own teeth before he fully claimed her mouth. Her body.

And that was when his brother slammed into him, tackling him to the ground.

"That's what you get for being distracted," Cas said as he jumped to his feet, holding out a hand.

Grumbling, Mikael grabbed his brother's hand and jumped up with ease.

"I get the winner!" Ivyn jumped down from the patio railing where he'd been sitting.

When he looked up, Avery had disappeared and he fought disappointment—until she strode back outside with something in her hand.

"Are you okay?" The petite human who smelled like peaches and sunshine and shared music with him seemed so concerned about him. He was not certain why, but he could admit that he liked it. It meant she cared.

"We were just sparring." His gaze flicked down to what he now realized was a bag of ice in her hand.

She pointed at him to sit, then joined him on the bench. Her fingers gently skated over his skin as she held the bag to his forehead. "You guys are so rough," she murmured.

He wanted to tell her that he didn't even feel this injury she was so concerned about, that he would be healed within ten minutes, but he really, really liked the sensation of her soft fingertips moving over his skin.

"Yes, my brothers like to fight dirty," he murmured, fighting a smile because he did too.

"We learned it from you!" Cas's voice carried out from the yard.

Mikael didn't even bother looking at his brothers. All his attention was on the dark-haired beauty with the big green eyes who was watching him carefully.

Her eyes dilated slightly and a curious scent played in the air for a moment before she cleared her throat and glanced away. "So is this normal for you guys?"

"What?"

"The fighting? My brothers don't fight like that so I don't have a reference if it's...normal."

"It's more sparring than anything and yes, we spar to keep in shape and test our reflexes. It's wise for any warrior to consistently practice as we do." Because an out of practice warrior was a dead one.

She nodded once, letting the ice drop, but she gently skated her fingers over his forehead again as she inspected whatever wound was there.

All he could feel was her gentle fingers and he instinctively leaned his head into her touch. He wanted so much more than this, wanted to feel her hands all over him, ripping at his clothes, wrapping her fingers around his cock... Hell, he had to shut this down or it was about to get really uncomfortable.

When she dropped her hand away he was glad she didn't get up or leave, even if he was disappointed not to feel her touching him anymore.

"What are you doing tonight?" he asked. Sometimes she went out and met friends, but usually she stayed in. She'd even taken him and his brothers out, trying to help them get a feel for the city. He only went out if she did, not liking to be separated from her.

"I was actually coming out here to see if you guys wanted to watch a movie. My brothers are out for the night."

"I would love to," he said. She had introduced him to movies as well. He *found that he liked them. Most of them anyway.* "Cas and Ivyn are going out too, so it will just be us." *Cas and Ivyn had no plans that he was aware of, but his brothers would hear him, even over their fighting, and if they decided to stay, he would kick their asses for real this time. The chance to spend alone time with Avery? This did not happen often and he would take it with both hands.*

"I hope you're ready for a superhero movie."

He grinned at her, inhaling her sweet scent. "I will get the popcorn ready." *She had introduced him to that as well.*

"It's a date, then." *She gently touched her fingertips to his forehead again and frowned. Then she looked away from him in his brothers' direction.* "Cas, you need to be more careful!"

He heard his brother sputter out a response and turned just in time to see Ivyn body-slam him.

Mikael grinned and stood. "Now I get the winner."

"I'm starting the movie in an hour," *she said as she stood. Then she sighed.* "Try not to kill each other before then."

CHAPTER TEN

Lindsey took a drag from her cigarette, glad they didn't hurt her lungs anymore. She just liked the taste, had quit years ago only because she hadn't wanted them to age her. Her body and looking young were her best commodities. Now smoking didn't matter so she did it whenever she wanted.

Darren, the newly turned vampire in bed with her, went to take her cigarette, but she flicked his hand away. "My pack is over there." Freaking greedy.

He simply rolled his eyes and grabbed one.

He'd been annoying when he was a human, and he was annoying now, but he had a big dick. And he knew how to use it. His only redeeming quality.

"When does he get back?" Darren asked.

No need to explain who he referred to. He, as in the vampire who had made them. *Magnus.*

"I don't know." And she was a little worried. Tonight hadn't remotely gone the way she'd planned. "It wasn't my fault. The guy was so...powerful." Mikael no-last-name-that-she-knew-of had exuded a terrifying sort of power. Her maker had ordered her to talk to him—seduce him—but she had no idea why. She just knew that she'd been instructed to approach him and get a feel for what he liked—hopefully her. But things had gone completely sideways. He'd barely looked at her, except when he'd been threatening to torture her and set her on fire.

She wasn't used to that reaction from men. Normally they threw themselves at her feet.

She blew out another puff of smoke as she stared at the ceiling. She wasn't staying in the city proper, but in a farmhouse in a fairly rural area on the outskirts. A few different farms surrounded the area, but she didn't know their neighbors, and had been instructed to stay away from them.

"What wasn't your fault?" Magnus stepped into the room in dark pants and a long-sleeved dark shirt. He had a slight lilting accent, and she guessed he was from somewhere in Europe. *Maybe.*

He didn't tell them much about his past, or even how old he was. But she could sense that he was powerful. And when he'd asked her if she wanted to be turned into a vampire, it had been a no-brainer. He'd asked her right before The Fall, approaching her when she'd been out on a "girls' night"... At least that was what her now ex-husband had thought. She'd taken one night a week to go out and do what—and who—she wanted.

She'd been smart about it, however. She hadn't wanted to get caught. No, she'd liked her life—liked being able to afford to live. People who said money didn't matter had never had to worry about things like dental care, or health care—or being able to afford to turn the heat up on cold nights. Or having enough for food. Then when The Fall happened, she'd lost everything, the life of luxury that her ex had given her. She wasn't going to be stuck with that old bastard for the rest of her life, and her maker had come at the perfect time. So she'd told him yes and hadn't looked back since.

Unfortunately she couldn't manipulate Magnus, but he'd given her immortality and she would be forever grateful. She was also trying to learn from him. The little she was coming to understand about supernaturals was that even though they had immortality, it didn't mean they couldn't be killed. And supernaturals could be savage. She would have to be smart if she wanted to survive this new world.

Clearing her throat, she sat up and set her cigarette to the side. She didn't bother to cover herself. They'd already slept together a few times, though he didn't seem interested in fucking anymore, which annoyed her. She was used to men doing what she wanted. She licked her lips, nervous. "I went to see that male, Mikael, like you told me to. It seems..." She cleared her throat again, hating the nerves humming through her. But when Magnus stared at her with those dark, fathomless eyes, she felt as if she was looking into a vast wasteland. As if she could fall into those eyes and never escape. The feeling was...terrifying. "He's friends with someone from my past."

"I am aware of this."

She blinked. *Oh.* But of course Magnus had known. Maybe...that was why he'd asked Lindsey to approach Mikael? Oh God, of course that was why he'd asked Lindsey. It hadn't been a coincidence. God, she was so stupid. And she'd screwed up. *Damn it.* "He's very protective of her. He didn't have a reaction to me at all." The blow to her ego still stung. As a vampire, she was even more stunning than she had been as a human.

"He threatened to kill her," Darren said, blowing out a ring of smoke. He hadn't moved from his position except to cover up his dick with a pillow.

She gritted her teeth.

"He threatened you." It wasn't a question so much as a statement, so she remained quiet as Magnus watched her, the weight of his stare heavy and intimidating, pressing her into the mattress.

When he looked at her, she felt like prey. Powerless.

"I gave him my jewelry," she blurted, even though she hadn't planned on telling him. She found that sometimes around Magnus she said things she didn't plan to, they just spilled out. The compulsion was disturbing.

"Why?"

She glanced down at the expensive sheets, picked at the material with her fingernail. "Technically the jewelry belonged to my ex-husband's first wife. She was going to leave it to her daughter, but my ex gave it to me instead. Mikael…ordered me to hand it all over." The jewelry had been her insurance—before The Fall anyway. Now jewelry didn't mean shit, couldn't buy her anything.

"You already handed everything over to him?"

She nodded.

He stepped farther into the room, a wave of rage rolling off him, making the pictures on the wall tremble ever so slightly. "It seems I had more faith in you than I should have, you stupid female. You should have *waited* and spoken to me first."

She swallowed back her fear, though he would have to scent it. "Waited for what?"

His jaw tightened again. "You really are stupid trash."

Anger popped inside her as she jumped to her feet against her better judgment. "I'm not stupid! You just told me to meet him and try to seduce him. You didn't give me any other instructions. He threatened to torture me unless I gave him the jewelry. So I did. If you had other instructions, I would have followed them." She wasn't going to tell him about Mikael's other threat, that he'd told her to leave New Orleans. She...couldn't. She didn't have anywhere to go. She wasn't even sure where she *could* go as a vampire at this point. There were all sorts of territory rules she wasn't sure of. She knew there were vampire covens in New Orleans, but Magnus wasn't aligned with any of them—he was not in this territory legally.

Magnus's head tilted to the side slightly and she worried she'd gone too far because he was watching her with that predatory gaze again.

For a moment she thought he would lash out, strike her. He'd hit her once when she'd been a smart-ass months ago. It had taken her by surprise more than actually hurt her, but she thought she understood him better now. He wasn't a human or some simple male she could manipulate with her body. At least she could respect that.

"Go find me some humans to turn."

She stared at him, wondering if this was a trap somehow. They had a whole coven living here at the farm, though most of his creations were out tonight, hunting. They hadn't been controlling their appetites either, which was stupid, in her opinion. You didn't kill your food source. That was how you got food shortages. Stupid.

She'd been too upset to feed so had crashed back at the farmhouse with Darren. Too bad his dick hadn't helped her mood much.

"I'm not angry," Magnus continued, still watching her in that eerie way of his. "You're right, I should have given you more instructions. I still need Mikael and you are going to help me. He's protective of the female? You're sure?"

Lindsey snorted. "Oh yeah. He seems obsessed with her." Granted she'd only seen them together for a few moments, but the way that male had watched Avery—instead of being interested in Lindsey—was disconcerting. She wasn't used to feeling jealous, but Avery was one of the first females she'd ever been truly jealous of. That bitch had been given everything and people gravitated to her. It was revolting. And now a male had chosen Avery over Lindsey?

The male nodded as if satisfied. "Good. Now hurry before the sun rises." Then he looked at Darren, who was still smoking. "You too," he snapped out. "Two humans each."

She hurried from the room, grabbing her discarded dress as she raced out. She wasn't going to mess this up. Her maker was far too relaxed about her screwup right now—she didn't trust it. Didn't think he would let her off so easily unless she did exactly what he asked. Two humans should be easy enough. Who didn't want immortality?

CHAPTER ELEVEN

"It's time to go home." Mikael's quiet voice startled Avery.

She turned away from the worktable in her job trailer. She shouldn't be surprised by how quiet he was by now, but it still amazed her that he could sneak up on her so easily—and without even trying.

"I just have a few more things to go over. You should go home without me." The last few days had been kind of weird between them.

Okay there was no "kind of" about it. Things had been plain weird.

She'd gotten so angry at him when she thought he'd been… When she thought he'd made a move on Lindsey, a red sort of haze had descended. She'd been angry, but also so damn hurt, the pain of it slicing right through every barrier she thought she'd put up.

Then to find out that he'd threatened to torture Lindsey instead? And gotten Avery's mother's jewelry back for her? The jewelry was just stuff—the materialistic part didn't matter—but the fact that it had actually belonged to her mother did. The fact that Mikael had gotten it back for her mattered as well.

And then she'd kissed him. Right on the mouth.

It wasn't like tongue had been involved or anything but… She'd felt a jolt all the way through her system. One she'd been pretending did *not* exist for three long days. He'd barely seemed affected anyway, and he hadn't brought it up.

She'd thrown herself into work every day, which was normal, but she'd also been avoiding him after work. Holing up in her room after dinner instead of hanging out with everyone. She'd been feigning headaches, then saying she had work to catch up on. Sad, pathetic lies because she was a coward.

And Mikael had been watching her for three damn days. Every time she turned around there he was. Even if he was working, she *knew* he was aware of her. He was always in her line of sight.

It was jarring. She didn't know what to say to him either. The anger she'd felt… She didn't know how to handle the aftermath, the fact that she'd been so mad at all. If she didn't care about him, obviously she wouldn't have been so angry. So now he knew she cared—and she'd kissed him. *Gah*. She needed to get out of her head.

"I'm not leaving without you," he said. "So you will leave now. You have been working too hard." The set of his jaw was tense, his gray eyes in full-on dragon mode.

Which just served to get her hackles up. "Are you trying to annoy me today?"

He gave her a half grin that made something flutter in her chest. A whole burst of butterflies, really. "No."

"Then stop being so bossy and go home."

He leaned against the open doorway, casually masculine. Everything about him was so sexy and it wasn't fair. She'd seen women look at him, men too, but he just didn't seem aware when people did double takes of him. Maybe he *didn't* care. She didn't know what went on in that sexy dragon brain of his. Ugh. "*You* are always bossy," he murmured, his gaze tracking her as she moved to the other side of her desk.

"It's because I'm the boss."

"At work, *yes*."

There was something in his tone that she was not touching with a ten-foot pole. It was wicked, dark and made all sorts of feelings curl in her belly. And it was not good. So, so, so not good. There couldn't be anything romantic or physical between them. They lived in the same house. He was like…a billion years old, and a dragon shifter. She was human. She knew things didn't work out the way they should, that happily-ever-afters were a lie. And…there were other reasons. She was having a hard time remembering them, however, when he watched her with those smoky gray eyes.

She turned away from him and tried to focus on the paperwork in front of her. Maybe Mikael would simply fade into the background. Avery nearly snorted at the thought. Fat chance of that.

As she scanned the list of plumbing fixtures she'd just received, she breathed out a sigh of relief. At least King had come through like she'd known he would. He'd gotten her every single piece she needed. And they were working on making this place completely solar, which would be a big feat. One she was excited to tackle. But she needed to stop trying to get any more work in now and just go home. She wouldn't be able to work with Mikael hovering.

"King's here," Mikael said abruptly.

Surprised, she looked up to find him in the same position by the open doorway, but looking outside instead of at her. "Seriously?"

He simply nodded and stepped forward, waiting for her. Of course he stepped out first, but she hurried after him into the parking lot to find King and a couple of his people there.

"Hey," she said as she reached the other male. "Where's..." She trailed off as she spotted the dragonling flying in figure eights over one of the other work trailers. "Ah." She grinned, unable to stop herself. "He's following you everywhere, isn't he?" Her friend Dallas had a pet baby dragon, and sweet Willow followed Dallas everywhere too.

"He's impossible. He whined so much last night I had to sleep outside with him in my wolf form," King muttered, but a smile reached his eyes, taking all the heat out of his statement.

"He's adorable is what he is."

"Manipulative is more like it. He's got everyone in the pack spoiling him now." King glanced over and upward, shook his head as the dragon burped out a small burst of flames that thankfully just sputtered into nothing.

It was kind of funny to see King like this. The big male was always a little intimidating, the predator inside him clear half the time, but he had a sort of warmth that drew people to him. And he'd done a lot for the city because he cared about it. Like, truly cared about it in a way she'd found that human politicians never had.

Not all of course, but in her very short life she wasn't impressed with the people in power who were supposed to make things better for their cities. Instead they mostly seemed to be more concerned with their own power. King...he wore his power like a mantle and he wanted the people of New Orleans to be safe, happy, secure. Which was why she liked working under an Alpha like him. Thinking the word Alpha was still kind of surreal but she was getting used to it.

"Is everything okay?" Mikael asked, his body tense.

King gave a brief nod. "Everything is fine. I hear you guys are ahead of schedule and I just wanted to check things out."

"Okay," she said. He didn't actually need her permission or anything, he ran the whole city—er, territory. "A couple of the bears are on security tonight."

He nodded but still stood there, as if this wasn't the reason he'd come at all. Then he cleared his throat and flicked a glance between the two of them. "Avery, I'd like to speak to you alone."

Next to her Mikael bristled. He didn't actually move, but his body went preternaturally still and his dragon flickered into his eyes as he watched the Alpha.

Uh oh, this might not be good. She might not understand shifter hierarchies completely but that looked a little bit like a challenge.

"Will you grab the paperwork I was reviewing?" she asked Mikael, digging her fingernails into his forearm. "I want to go over some things tonight."

He looked down at her, his dragon peering back at her…curious as he watched her. For a long moment she thought he would say no, but then he simply nodded once and turned away from them.

King's jaw tightened and his expression didn't exactly convey anger, but…he was annoyed.

"So what's up?" Avery knew Mikael wouldn't leave them alone for long. And he could likely overhear anything from this range given his supernatural hearing, so King asking to speak to her alone felt almost like a cursory request.

"Your father came to see me," King said bluntly.

She almost took a step back, his words surprised her so much. "What?"

He watched her carefully, his ice-blue eyes searching for…something. "He's requesting better accommodations. He said he was there on your behalf because you didn't want to bother me."

She took a steadying breath, trying to get her wild heartbeat back under control. "My father is a liar. I apologize that he came to see you. I have no idea what his accommodations are and I certainly did *not* request that he get something different."

"He's in a very nice condominium complex on Canal Street." King's tone was neutral. "My pack has been making sure humans in the older age bracket are in areas within short walking distance of everything. They have a pool, an exercise facility, and we are also accommodating any sort of disabilities."

Mikael was there suddenly, paperwork in hand as he stood next to her, his arm brushing against her shoulder.

She wasn't sure why, but it grounded her somehow.

"Her father is a garbage human," Mikael said abruptly, his words stiff, but the anger rolling off him was like a live wire.

King actually looked surprised as he blinked at the other male. Before the Alpha could respond, Mikael continued.

"He abandoned his mate after twenty-five years of marriage when she got cancer. He left her for another female." He said the words so bluntly, and she felt every single one of them like a hammer.

King's wolf flared in his gaze for a moment, and it was as if she could actually see his animal beneath the surface before his expression went carefully neutral.

He gave her a brief nod. "I'll have a conversation with your father. He won't bother you or me again. Also, you're doing incredible work here. If you need anything, you know you only have to ask." Then he walked away, the two males who had arrived with him and his new dragonling leaving as well.

"You shouldn't have told him that," Avery muttered as she looked at Mikael.

"He abandoned his mate when she was sick. That is one of the greatest crimes in the shifter world. He should be *living* in a pile of garbage." Anger popped off him with each syllable.

"Maybe so, but...I told you that in confidence. I don't normally tell anyone that." She'd made herself vulnerable, opened up to him. It embarrassed her to have the ugliness in her family exposed to the Alpha she admired so much.

He winced, took a step toward her. "I apologize for telling King." Then his mouth curved up ever so slightly and he didn't look sorry at all as he said, "Your father isn't going to like his accommodations after this."

"I..." She had no idea what to say to that. She hoped King didn't mess with his living situation. Her father was awful but...for some reason, a bit of guilt bubbled up. She quickly squashed it, however. She'd done nothing wrong, just told King the truth. And she couldn't believe Shep had gone to the Alpha and tried to pretend he was there on her behalf.

Actually, she could believe it. Because she'd never really known that man at all. She rubbed a hand over her face. "I need to go out tonight."

"Then I will accompany you," Mikael said immediately and she realized she'd said the words out loud.

"I don't need a babysitter."

Mikael's gaze flicked to her mouth, heat flaring wild and chaotic.

She stilled, looking away from him because that was *definitely* heat. And she didn't know what the heck to do with that. Everything had gone crazy three days ago. She needed to keep her distance from him. He had complication and heartbreak written all over his hard face.

Why had she kissed him? It had been so quick, so innocent, but the raw hunger she'd experienced afterward had not been so innocent. She realized she'd started walking toward the exit of the parking lot when he fell in step with her.

"I know you don't need a babysitter. Do you not like my company?" His tone was mild, but there was a hint of...vulnerability in the question.

She nudged him with her hip. "Don't be ridiculous. I love hanging out with you." It was the truth, and he made her feel safe. "I just don't want you to feel like you have to supervise me or whatever." God, she was just talking out of her ass right now and she needed to rein it in.

"I watch you boss around a bunch of males every single day. I know you don't need supervision." He snorted and she found she liked the sound of his amusement. "Maybe I'm looking out for everyone else."

She nudged him with her hip again. "Silly dragon." Yes, going out tonight was the right idea. Staying cooped up at home where she could obsess over so many things? Not so good.

CHAPTER TWELVE

Five weeks after The Fall

Avery leaned forward as she got into the balasana yoga pose—aka child's pose. She'd been out on her back deck for twenty minutes and could already feel the tension and stress of the day easing from her bones.

At a soft shuffling sound, she glanced behind her. Her cheeks immediately flushed hot to see Mikael standing there. "Hey, what are you doing?" She kind of felt weird in this position with her butt up in the air.

"Trying to figure out what you're doing," he said, his expression unreadable.

Sometimes she thought she understood this sexy, ancient dragon who was living in her house, but it was all an illusion. He only let her see what he wanted, she was certain. So far, he and his brothers had settled in perfectly to their house. They were shockingly quiet, much quieter than any former roommates she'd had, and definitely quieter and neater than her brothers who she sometimes still cleaned up after.

"Yoga. I'm sure it's been around as long as you have."

He paused once, as if searching his memory bank for a definition of the word. Then he nodded. "I know it by a different word, but yes."

She fell out of her pose and turned to look at him, crossing her legs and sitting on her mat as she faced him. "A friend of mine recommended it over a year ago. I'd always thought it sounded really silly but after a long day at work it really helps my mind sort of untangle, I guess."

He glanced over at the piece of paper she had next to her mat.

"I don't know all of the poses yet, I'm still practicing some of them. This is my cheat sheet."

He walked toward her, and she resisted the urge to drink in every inch of his body. She didn't want to be the weirdo who ogled her roommate and stared too much. It was really hard when he walked around without a shirt on. Thankfully he had one on now—and he smelled so good, as if he'd just taken a shower. Given his damp hair, he probably had. That brought up other thoughts. Naked ones. So she shut that down.

"This looks interesting," he said as he crouched down next to her.

His masculine scent invaded all of her senses and she tried not to sniff overtly, because again, she didn't want to be a weirdo roommate. "Oh yeah? You think you can do this one?" She pointed to the bakasana pose, one she hadn't mastered yet.

She watched as he got down on the patio deck next to her and twisted his body into a pretzel, his forearms and neck muscles flexing so that his veins were visible as he lifted his body up with just his arm muscles.

She stared. "Have you ever done this before?" He hadn't even looked at the step-by-step instructions. He'd just...done it.

"No." He moved with a liquid grace that was astonishing as he relaxed and sat next to her, stretching one leg out and lounging all casual and sexy as if he hadn't just shown off an incredible amount of balance and strength.

"That's so not fair," she said as both his brothers strode out onto the deck.

"Dinner's going to be ready soon," Ivyn said. "Also, what's not fair?"

"Mikael was showing off his yoga moves."

"Showing off?" Cas said, his gaze falling on the sheet. "I bet I can do better than him." Making a scoffing sound, he nudged Mikael out of the way and proceeded to attempt to twist himself into a pretzel as well—he wasn't as successful as Mikael.

Ivyn, not to be outdone, decided to make his own poses and stripped off his T-shirt before going into a handstand. Then he pushed up on just his fingertips so that he was suspending his entire body that way, and started walking on his fingers.

She looked at him in fascination and a little horror because holy hell, that had to hurt. Avery glanced over at Mikael to find that his expression had darkened. He stripped off his own shirt and she didn't bother trying to avoid staring now.

If he was going to put everything on display, she was going to enjoy this little peek of godlike perfection.

"What the hell is going on?" Anthony asked a few minutes later when he and Riel walked out to find all three dragons doing handstands and walking across the deck and all the way back, seeing who could last longer.

They'd long since given up on doing yoga and were basically doing random acrobatics now. And it was hot.

"I have no idea but I guarantee if we took a video of this, and if currency was still a real thing, we could make like a million dollars after putting this up on YouTube." Which also didn't exist anymore.

While her brothers laughed, she couldn't take her gaze off Mikael.

They were acting so ridiculous and silly and... She loved it. Not to mention his display of upper body strength was beyond impressive.

They hadn't been here very long, but very quickly the three dragons had become sort of like family to her, which was a scary thing in itself. Of course, she only had sisterly feelings toward Cas and Ivyn. Her feelings for Mikael, however, were a different story.

Suddenly, Mikael, still holding his body up on just his hands, lashed out with one of his legs and knocked Cas down.

Then he kicked out at Ivyn's hip, knocking him over as well.

Springing upward, Mikael landed on his feet like a cat.

"Take a bow!" Anthony said, still laughing.

Mikael, his gaze pinned on hers, did just that. But then Ivyn tackled him, grumbling about cheaters right before Cas jumped on both of them.

She winced as they started rolling around with each other in a way her younger brothers had never done. She'd quickly learned that these brothers fought like savages sometimes. Maybe it was a dragon thing.

"I say we go inside and see what's for dinner. Maybe get dessert first," Riel said, backing away from the three males.

Anthony and Avery hurried inside with him, and even though her yoga session had been cut short she realized she hadn't laughed like that in a long time.

She also realized she was falling head over heels for an ancient dragon who couldn't be interested in her the way she was interested in him. He was in a different league—stratosphere—than she was. So there was no sense dreaming.

CHAPTER THIRTEEN

Only half listening, Mikael glanced over at Arthur as he said something. "What?"

Arthur and Prima both gave him dry looks. They were dressed similarly, both in dark pants and T-shirts. Apparently Arthur had forgone his kilt tonight. Unlike most of the people in this club, who seemed to be having a contest for who could show the most skin, his old friends did not even appear to want to be here. He could understand. There were too many people, too many sounds. Crowds didn't necessarily bother him—not that he enjoyed them—but he did not like so many people close to Avery. At all.

"Sex has made your brain stupid," Prima said, absently toying with an intricately carved blade.

He grunted. Maybe lack of sex, but *not* sex. Unfortunately. His gaze strayed back to Avery, who was dancing with some of her girlfriends—the females who lived with the lion. He liked all of them, and he liked that they were all shifters and were capable of taking care of themselves. Not that Avery could not, it was simply that she was human. That made her more fragile in some things.

Mortal.

It was…disconcerting. There was always this sense of powerlessness humming under his skin where she was concerned, knowing that she could be snatched from him at a moment's notice. If she was his, he would be able to claim her, protect her more.

"So what were you saying about dead humans?" he asked quietly. See, he had been listening. Sort of.

"King's pack has found humans drained of blood. It's very clearly the work of vampires. But not any vampires local to the city. So far the killings have been in more rural areas around the city. Nothing in the city proper or even in the direct outer radius. A few look like campers. Others he hasn't been able to identify using the technology they have access to, so they might be from another territory," Arthur said.

"Campers?"

Arthur grunted. "Humans who like to get out in nature and temporarily live in tents."

Mikael had lived in tents at one point. Well, when he'd been in human form while fighting wars. He did not care for it. He preferred a cave big enough for his dragon half to rest peacefully.

"So far there is not an outcry about these deaths, but it is coming," Prima said.

"Why do you two even care?" He looked at both of them. They were both warrior dragons, both of different clans, currently living in New Orleans. He wasn't sure why either. Well, he knew the reason Arthur was here was because of Prima. But he hadn't figured out why Prima was here, not when her twin was elsewhere and her entire clan was in an area called Montana.

"Why wouldn't we help?" she asked.

"You haven't given allegiance to King."

"No," Arthur said simply. "But I trust him. He's doing something important. And right now he needs help building up this territory into what it should be. Into something he and his pack can rule and truly care for. Humans have screwed up this world for too long. I would like to be a part of something good. I think King is on the right path."

Okay, that was good enough for Mikael. He kept Avery in his peripheral vision as he spoke. "So why are you telling me about these vampires?" And dead humans.

"You're a good tracker."

He snorted. "Good?"

Arthur gave him a dry look. "You're an excellent tracker. Don't you...get bored? Doing construction?"

"No." He didn't even have to think about it. "The city needs rebuilding." It was important to build a solid foundation. In more ways than one.

"You used to lead men. You carried out covert missions. You were an enforcer for your clan. You laid waste to—"

"I know who I used to be." And now most of his family was dead. He was living in a foreign world where Avery and his brothers were the only things that made sense. "I know exactly what I'm supposed to be doing with my life."

Out of the corner of his eye he saw Prima punch Arthur in the arm and she muttered at him to shut the fuck up.

He smiled to himself. She never had been subtle.

Mikael looked back at them. "I'm tired of death and fighting. I saw enough of it to last far too many lifetimes." He'd more than just seen it. He'd caused deaths. So many. And…he was in a new phase of his life. One that involved a fragile, sweet human he wanted to make his.

When he saw the stupid lion start dancing with her he slid off his chair. "I will help track vampires if necessary. You know how to contact me."

Mikael stalked toward the dance floor, his dragon clawing right under the surface as Axel spun Avery in front of him and pulled her back up against his chest. He looked at Mikael with a wide grin.

Maybe he could cause just one more death.

Avery's eyes lit up as he approached. "Mikael! Are you coming to dance?" She stumbled a little on her feet and he realized she'd had too much to drink. Since she was the only thing between him and the smirking lion, he glared at the other male. "Are you hiding behind a human to shield yourself?"

"You know it," Axel said as he gently nudged Avery toward Mikael.

Avery threw her arms around him much like she'd done the other night. In that moment he forgot everything else—the entire club, the noises, the sounds and scents fell away as she plastered herself to him.

Her full breasts pressed against his chest, and goddess, this was too much torture.

"I've had too much to drink," she said right against his ear, her breath warm on his neck.

"Would you like to leave?" *Please say yes.*

"Yes, but I don't think I can walk all the way home. Can I ride you?" She looked at him with such openness and he felt like a beast for the thoughts her question brought up.

It brought forth a completely different image than her meaning had intended.

"Or I can walk," she said, giggling again in that delightful way of hers.

"No. You will ride me." Goddess help him. He wanted her to ride him, wanted to see all her dark hair falling around her breasts as she took him inside her. "There's a landing area up on the roof. I can shift and change there."

Her eyes widened, the pale green lighting up. "I was mostly joking. You will really let me ride on you?"

"I told you once you only had to ask."

She made another delighted sound and hugged him again. Yes, she really must have had too much to drink. She rarely touched him this much, and definitely not after that kiss. The one that kept him up nights. It was sweet torture.

"Did you bring anything with you?"

She patted her pants pocket. "Just my phone."

He thought that was all she'd had but he wanted to double-check. Taking her hand in his, he pulled her through the throng of people, nodding once at Prima and Arthur on the way out.

They watched him speculatively but he ignored them. He was touching Avery. The world was right for these few moments.

It didn't take long to get to the roof where it was much quieter, even with the noise from the streets down below. There were far too many people here for his liking. He didn't mind it at work; he liked putting things together, simply liked being with Avery. And he liked living with his brothers but...he could do without clubs or a "nightlife" as Riel had once called it.

"What are you doing?" Avery's pink mouth was slightly open.

He noticed that she stared at him boldly, probably because of the alcohol she had imbibed. So he took his time, deciding to give her a show as he slipped his pants down his hips.

Her eyes widened and she bit her bottom lip in the most sensual way ever as her gaze trailed along with the pants. Then his shirt. Her gaze landed on his chest again and then...she went lower.

Dammit. He had to will himself not to get hard—well, harder than he already was. Her eyes were on him, he was getting a damn erection.

Suddenly she spun away from him, though her cheeks were flushed as she turned. "Sorry, I didn't mean to stare."

"You can stare all you want." She could touch him too. Kiss, touch, stroke. Do whatever she wanted.

She made a sort of squeaking sound but didn't say anything else.

In that moment he scented a hint of *lust*. It carried on the wind, growing stronger and, holy hell. This was the first time he'd ever scented something so strong from her. He'd gotten little hints every now and then but she'd always been so careful to keep her distance, to keep him in a little box where she'd categorized him as a friend only. This...was interesting. And he knew he needed to start pushing harder.

He couldn't sit on the fence anymore. He had to go for her whether he deserved her or not—and he didn't deserve her. But if he lost her without taking a chance... He didn't know that he would survive that. He'd lost so many people, so much of his family, but losing Avery? His dragon snarled savagely.

Mikael called on the change, letting the magic overtake him in a burst of sparks and pain and pleasure all rolled into one. As soon as he'd changed, a sense of peace surged through him.

Before he opened his eyes, he heard her gasp of surprise. As he peered at her, Avery was stock-still, staring at him in wonder. She'd seen him in dragon form before, but right now it was just the two of them under the city lights.

It was hard not to preen just a little bit. He stretched his wings out, showing off for her. Then he stretched his neck, rolling his head from side to side so she could see all of him. Apparently he had a vain streak. *We are glorious*, his dragon reminded him. *We are a fine specimen, of course she likes looking at us.*

"You are absolutely beautiful," she whispered. "I think that every time you're in dragon form."

He stretched out his wing so she could climb up, which she did, and only needed a little bit of help to settle on his back. He would have to be very steady in his flying tonight. He didn't think she'd had that much to drink but clearly it had been more than enough for her slight frame since she wanted to return home.

The flight back to their house would've only taken five minutes. He wanted longer with her than that so he took his time, circling around the city, savoring the pleased sounds she made as he coasted over the buildings and treetops.

"It's so beautiful up here," she called out. "If I was a dragon, I would fly all the time everywhere. I would never come back down to earth."

Sometimes he felt that way too. She was the reason he always returned to earth.

Half an hour later, he headed home and wondered when he'd started thinking of it as *home*. Because that was exactly what the house they shared was. They'd all made a home together. The yard wasn't quite big enough so he landed in the street and waited for her to dismount. Once she did he called on his magic again and shifted to his human form.

She made that squeaking sound again and turned away as he strode across the road completely naked.

She handed him his clothes, still looking to the side instead of directly at him. He bundled them under his arm and headed up the walkway with her.

"You're not putting on your clothes?" She sounded scandalized.

He lifted a shoulder, wanting her to look her fill. To see him as a desirable man, rather than just a friend. "You've already seen me naked. And I'm going to bed soon. I'll be sleeping naked as well."

"Oh..." A pause. "You sleep naked?"

"I do."

She made a sort of strangled sound as they headed inside the house. "I...if you want to hang out a bit before bed, you're going to have to put pants on at least."

He smothered a grin and slid his pants on as she locked the front door behind them. "Nudity isn't as big of a deal to my kind."

She eyed him, her gaze flitting to his chest then back up again. "So you wouldn't care if I was walking around here all naked?"

Oh, fuck. He cleared his throat. No words would come out.

When he didn't respond, she made a sort of humming sound and headed through the house, straight out the back door.

They settled on the back patio, looking out at the brightly lit yard with its lush greenery and small garden. It seemed as if the house was empty. "Where's Ivyn been?"

"Not sure. With a female, maybe." Both his brothers had been disappearing lately at all hours.

She didn't look too surprised, just pleased. "Good."

Now he was the one who was surprised. "Good?"

"Yes. He deserves happiness. All of you do."

Warmth spread through his chest at her offhand remark. She was always so kind, seeing the best in people. "I don't know that I deserve it."

She frowned at him as she stretched her legs out. "Why would you say that?"

He took the blanket from behind his chair and leaned forward to drape it over her when she shivered. "My past... I'm not a good male, Avery." *Shut up*, his dragon snarled. *You're ruining this!* Mikael wasn't even sure why he was telling her this.

"I'm gonna call bullshit on that." She yawned, pulling her blanket up higher and snuggling against the chair. "I believe in people's actions. And you are a good male, Mikael."

He didn't know how to respond, so he didn't. He leaned his head back, looking upward. The moon was half hidden by the gray clouds, but it was a bright, huge backdrop tonight. Minutes later, he turned his head to say something and realized she'd dozed off.

He watched her, drinking her in even as he stood and scooped her up. He'd done this so many times, and each time he committed it to memory. The feel of her molded up against him, her head on his shoulder. As always, the walk to her room was over too quickly.

"Don't leave me," she murmured as he took a step away from the bed.

He froze, not sure he'd heard right. "Avery?"

"I don't want to be alone tonight." Her words were spoken so low that if he'd been human, he might not have heard them. And since he wasn't a human male, he was not going to ask her if she was certain. She'd asked him. He was staying.

Mikael slipped in beside her, scooting her over slightly as he wrapped his arm around her, pulling her back against his chest.

He draped his arm over her middle and she placed her hand over his, linking their fingers together. He barely bit back a groan at the feel of her lush ass pressed up against his cock and had to will himself not to react. Sort of. It was a losing battle.

He wasn't sure what was going on with her tonight. All he knew was that he got to hold her.

Clearly her father showing up to see her, and then the Alpha, had affected her. So much so that she'd had too much to drink tonight and now she wanted him to comfort her.

As a friend would do.

"Go to sleep," he murmured. Then he called her "my sunshine" in a long-dead language he knew she wouldn't understand.

She mumbled something, briefly squeezing his fingers before her breathing evened out and she fell into a light sleep.

It quickly turned into a deep one, in which she completely drifted away.

He stayed awake far too long, memorizing every moment she was in his arms. He didn't even want to close his eyes, didn't want to go to sleep at all. No, he wanted this moment to go on forever.

CHAPTER FOURTEEN

Avery stretched, feeling the warmth of sunlight on her face. It was Saturday and she didn't have to go to work. It was also her birthday and... She opened her eyes suddenly as the events of last night flooded her. And found herself staring into stormy gray eyes.

Oh my. Not a dream.

"Morning," she murmured, fairly embarrassed how she'd acted last night. Oh God, she'd thrown her arms around Mikael and asked him to give her a ride home. And of course he had, because he was wonderful. God, he was so beautiful, all sparkling silvery gray under the moonlight. Then she'd asked him to stay in bed with her because she hadn't wanted to be alone. *Oh, wow.* So she was going to die of embarrassment on her birthday. *Awesome.*

"Morning." God, he looked so delicious this morning. Well, every morning. But he was in her bed, sans a shirt. Yep, delicious about covered it.

His bare chest was on full display as he watched her with clear gray eyes. There was a little scruff on his face that gave him an even sexier, more rugged quality. How was that even possible? She'd thought he was at one hundred percent max capacity for sexiness. Apparently he was in a different stratosphere now.

She grabbed the covers and pulled them up over her mouth. "I have morning breath."

His forehead crinkled slightly. "Now you are the one being ridiculous," he said, using a word she often did to describe him or his brothers. And her brothers.

She still didn't move the comforter. "I'm sorry about the way I acted last night. I'm pretty embarrassed." And would mentally drown in her embarrassment later. She would replay herself asking him to stay with her, throwing herself at him, over and over, until she actually expired from pure embarrassment.

"You have nothing to be sorry for. We are friends."

"True. Though friends don't normally sleep in the same bed together. I'm sorry if I made you feel uncomfortable." *Ugh.* She hadn't begged him to stay or anything, but he'd probably felt responsible or...whatever. He did this thing where he seemed to think he needed to take care of her.

He looked confused for a moment. "I am not uncomfortable. I like sleeping with you. I like holding you in my arms."

Oh. Oh... She did *not* know what to say to that. He liked holding her? She loved it too.

"I would have liked it more if we had been naked," he continued.

W*ait...what?* She stared at him, feeling a little crazy because she couldn't even blink. Did he just say... Wait, was it possible she was still dreaming? Having a stroke, maybe?

"You're not blinking," he said calmly.

"Friends don't sleep naked with each other." Her voice had gone up a few octaves. Though the thought of being fully naked with him, pressing her body against his, experiencing full skin to skin and...more. Volcanic heat erupted inside her at the mere thought.

"Maybe we can be more than friends." He said it so matter-of-fact, and wasn't freaking out the way she was. Internally at least—her head was pretty much exploding.

Maybe he just wanted to have sex? He *had* been in Hibernation for a long time and he didn't go out at night and sleep with other women. Or she didn't think he did. She...*hoped* he didn't.

"Mikael..."

"I like it when you say my name. I would like very much to kiss you now."

Oh hell. This morning had taken a wild turn. She bolted upright, shoving the covers off herself, feeling completely crazed and manic. She was still in her dress from last night.

What was going on with him? Why was he saying these ridiculous things when she hadn't even had coffee and her brain was muddled? Why was he saying any of this *at all?* Maybe she was still dreaming. Or having a nightmare.

"Avery," he murmured.

"Nope. I can't deal with this right now." She stumbled out of bed, tripping once as she made her way to the bathroom and quickly shut and locked the door. Clearly the flimsy lock wouldn't do anything if he wanted in, but she needed the distance and a small barrier between them. "I'd like to be alone now," she called out.

She groaned in embarrassment as she turned the water on. What the hell? Who just said stuff like that? He wanted to sleep naked with her, maybe do other things with her. She wanted it too, had fantasized about it, and yet it could never happen because it would destroy the dynamic of this household. She would end up wanting more—like she did right now!—and then get her heart broken. She covered her face with her hands.

Now all she could think of was Mikael naked. Naked, naked, naked... Okay she could definitely get on board with that. But sex was so complicated. Or it would be with him. It would complicate things between them. It didn't matter that she was attracted to him and *apparently* he was attracted to her. He must've been keeping his attraction on lockdown. Maybe he just wanted her because she was convenient?

No! She had to stop with the eighty billion questions racing through her head at warp speed right now. She just needed to take a shower, clear her head, and then they would have a normal conversation over breakfast.

And she would tell him he was out of his dragon mind.

Avery took a very hot, fairly short shower—long enough to wake her up and remind her of more of her embarrassment. But she couldn't hide upstairs forever. She was going to play things cool. Be like a freaking ice cube. Yep. Cool and relaxed. That was her. She would simply tell him that they would not be sleeping naked together and things would go back to normal.

Gah!

By the time she'd run a hair dryer—which was now missing one of its diffusers—over her hair so that it was only damp, and changed into jeans and a T-shirt, and brushed her teeth, she found Mikael, her brothers, and Ivyn and Cas in the kitchen. Oh, she was so happy to see them! They could be her buffer this morning because who was she kidding, she wasn't going to be able to have a calm conversation with Mikael right now. She couldn't even *look* at him right now. Not when her insides were a tight knot. And all this was happening on her birthday, no less.

Both dragon brothers kissed her on the top of her head in that sweet way of theirs.

She noticed that Mikael glared at them...which was a new development. Usually he was like her, more or less doting on his brothers as she was with hers. Though she didn't think dragons used the word "doting." Still.

"Why do you guys all look like you're ready to walk out the door?" she asked.

"We promised we'd work at the jobsite until noon. Did you forget?" Anthony asked. He hadn't even said happy birthday and she figured that her brothers had forgotten. Which kinda sucked but...it was okay. The world had imploded not too long ago. Not having a birthday acknowledged was nothing.

She winced because yes, she had forgotten. She'd been so obsessed with thoughts of Mikael. And nakedness.

"Crap, I did." And she was starving.

As if he'd read her mind, Mikael said, "I made you a breakfast sandwich. And a to-go coffee, doctored just the way you like." Oh God, he was watching her now with those stormy gray eyes, heat simmering not below the surface anymore, but right out in the open.

Her cheeks flushed and she wondered if everyone in the house could sense the shift between them and knew that he'd slept in her bed last night. Could that hole open up and swallow her now please?

"Thank you." She really didn't want to go to work, but she couldn't ask for people to come in on a Saturday if she wasn't willing to do the same herself. Besides, it would really help them stay on schedule and she didn't like the thought of that delivery of parts just sitting outside in the elements until Monday.

Anthony started texting on his phone as he and Riel headed out the door. Okay, so they had definitely forgotten her birthday.

To her surprise, Ivyn wrapped his arm around her shoulders. "Come on, let's head out."

Ivyn and Cas definitely viewed her as a sister, and this excused her from having to talk to Mikael so she was going to take it. Ignoring Mikael's gaze, she snagged the sandwich and to-go cup, murmuring a thank you.

Behind her, Mikael honest to God let out a low growl, but she was definitely ignoring it.

The bacon sandwich was absolute heaven, and for a few long moments all she did was enjoy the greasy mess, even as she cursed herself for drinking too much last night.

Today was going to be very long.

CHAPTER FIFTEEN

"Why are you so surly?" Cas asked Mikael as he hefted a bundle of pipes and headed for the building. Thanks to their supernatural strength, they should have everything hauled inside quicker than the original schedule said.

"I'm not surly."

"I think you're in what's called denial."

He snorted, his gaze flickering over to the office trailer where Avery was. She'd gone in thirteen minutes ago and hadn't come out. Not that he was counting or anything.

"Did you stay in her bedroom last night?"

He grunted in response. It had been one of the best nights of his life. Also one of the most torturous. She moved a lot when she slept, throwing her arms around him, turning over, shoving her ass against him. Heaven and torture.

"That's…interesting." Cas's gray eyes, a shade darker than Mikael's, widened ever so slightly.

"It's not anything." He didn't like talking about Avery with anyone, not even with his brother, who he loved. "So where have you been disappearing off to, anyway?" He gave his brother a pointed look.

To his surprise, his warrior brother's cheeks flushed and he looked away. He lifted a shoulder. "Just exploring the city."

"Who is she?"

Cas paused, then sighed. "A human."

"Is that a bad thing?" he asked as they stepped through the doorway into the mostly unfinished first floor of the four-story building. They'd come to a different complex today than the one they'd been working on because they'd promised to haul delivered supplies inside and out of the elements.

"She lost her family."

"So did we." It was hard, something he tried not to think about. All the loss and destruction. But it was part of life.

"No, I mean that she lost them in The Fall. Because of dragons."

Ah. Well that made things difficult. "Does she know what you are?"

Cas cleared his throat. "She hasn't outright asked. I think...she thinks I'm a bear shifter."

"A lie of omission is still a lie." Something their warrior mother had told him more than once. She also used to have this saying that would be translated to "liars should be punched in the dick" in this new language. Goddess, he missed his mother. His father too. They'd been such a guiding force in all their lives, and when they and his oldest brother had been murdered, he'd been left to lead his brothers.

"Please don't quote Mother to me." Cas dropped his bundle of pipes onto the floor, situating them with the others so they were all lined up neatly.

"Ooh, are you guys talking about Mom and Dad?" Ivyn bounded up to them in a ridiculously good mood.

"Don't start with me," Mikael growled. He still hadn't forgotten the way Ivyn had wrapped his arm around Avery and kept it there the entire walk to the jobsite this morning.

Ivyn just grinned. "Why are you in such a sour mood? You slept in the same bed as your female last night."

He glanced around, not wanting anyone to overhear them talking about Avery. She was everyone's boss and it didn't matter if they were sleeping together—which they obviously were not, unfortunately—but still, this was private. He could not imagine she would like people talking about the two of them. He didn't understand everything about this new world, but he did understand that she was a human female running a crew of mostly males, supernatural and human. He didn't want her to be the cause of gossip because of him.

"I'm simply wondering why some human males just went into her office trailer," Ivyn continued when Mikael didn't respond. "They haven't come out yet," he added before hurrying off.

"He's just messing with you," Cas said as they headed back outside to grab crates.

Mikael automatically shifted his gaze to the trailer and froze as two human males strode down the short set of stairs. One of them looked familiar but he wasn't sure why. He didn't recognize the other, however. Both tall, slender, brown skin, and one had to be older, likely in his sixties. Or seventies—he struggled to gauge human ages. Though the older of the two moved with an impressive fluidity. They were speaking to each other as they hurried out the front gate of the construction site, not giving anyone else a glance.

"I think she needs space," Cas said as he hoisted up two of the crates as if they weighed nothing.

"I'm giving her space." Mikael was now certain that he'd given her far too much space at this point. He'd scented her lust this morning, reminding him of a field in the middle of summer, the scent sweet and wild. Still she had run away.

Now that he understood her background fully, he thought he knew why. Her own father left her mother when she'd been ill instead of taking care of her, treasuring her. Shifters weren't like that but Avery very likely did not understand that. Or trust it.

He needed to step up his game, to quote what he'd heard some human say before. Though claiming Avery wasn't a game at all.

He hoisted two crates as well, not bothering to talk anymore. After hauling in the rest of the load, he couldn't stand it anymore. He needed to see Avery.

Without bothering to tell his brother what he was doing, he strode toward the trailer, only to have Avery step outside as he reached the bottom step.

She looked down at him in surprise. "Hey, ah, how's everything going?"

"We're making good time. How are you feeling?"

Her cheeks flushed a bright shade of pink. "Ah..." She cleared her throat then shook her head as if she'd changed her mind about whatever she'd been going to say. "Did you need me for anything?"

Oh, he needed her for a lot of things. He'd started to respond when he spotted a necklace hanging over her T-shirt. He frowned at it. He'd never seen it before and she had not been wearing it this morning. A teardrop-shaped crystal of sorts, purple in color, hung suspended inside a triangle. The chain was slender and was a metal he thought was called rose gold.

Had one of those two males given her a necklace? That seemed…unlikely. Or did it? Today was the day she'd been born twenty-nine years ago, according to her brothers. They'd planned a surprise for her tonight and he'd been instructed not to say anything to her. Maybe…this was a birthing day gift?

"What are you scowling at?" She hurried down the rest of the stairs.

"Nice necklace," he murmured, everything else he'd wanted to say dissipating into the wind.

Her cheeks flushed again and she tucked it into her shirt. "I've got some stuff to take care of. So unless you need me…"

He shook his head and she hurried off, an array of scents rolling off her, too many to sift through.

He needed to find out who those males were and why they had given her a gift. No male could give treasure to his female except him.

* * *

"Don't ruin the surprise," Ivyn muttered to Mikael as they stepped into the kitchen.

He glanced across the large kitchen with gray cabinets and white and gray countertops at both his brothers.

Avery's brothers were getting her cake ready. They looked confused by Ivyn's statement, and Mikael ignored all of them as he turned right back around and stalked out of the room. He didn't want to be around them, didn't want to be around anyone but her.

His dragon sliced at him, annoyed with both him and Avery. His beast didn't understand why they simply didn't get together. They had shared a bed last night. They should have been naked, as simple as that.

He was upstairs in record time and swiftly knocked on her door.

She opened it moments later, looking surprised to see him. Her hair was damp and she had on a lightweight robe—pink with yellow little flowers. It fell open slightly, the soft curves of her breasts visible. And she was wearing that damn necklace.

He growled.

"What's up?" She tightened her robe around herself, her expression almost nervous.

His gaze flicked between her breasts. That stupid necklace intertwined with one of the necklaces she'd gotten back from that vampire. Both had a similar-colored gold chain.

"Did someone give you that necklace today?" he demanded. *Smooth*, his dragon growled. *Very smooth.*

Her cheeks flushed that delectable shade and his cock stood straight at attention. Because apparently he was that simple of a creature right now.

"That's none of your business," she rasped out.

Which was answer enough. "I'll take that as a yes." He stalked into her room, moving past her lightning quick before she could protest.

She let out a huff of annoyance and even that little sound got him hard—harder. Goddess, what was wrong with him?

"Yes, Mikael, please come into my room." Sarcasm tinged her words. "What's the matter with you?"

"Nothing is wrong with me. Okay, that's a lie. I don't like that someone gave you a necklace. That a *male* gave you one."

She sniffed slightly, settling her hands on her hips. "If someone gives me a necklace, it's none of your business. *I'm* not your concern."

That was *not* the right thing to say.

His dragon flared to life and he knew his beast was in his eyes. "You are very much my concern," he growled.

Her breasts pushed out as she stood firm against him and all he wanted to do was tear her robe open and feast on every inch of her body.

"King didn't put you here so you could watch out for me. It's the other way around!" she snapped.

He knew that. King had entrusted him and his brothers not to hurt Avery or anything, but the Alpha had also wanted the sweet human to keep an eye on them since they were still adjusting to the new world.

Mikael stalked forward, every inch a predator in that moment.

She let out a gasp of surprise and took a step backward, then another. And another.

His dragon liked the hunt, kept pushing forward even as she stepped back until she was pressed against one of the walls by a window.

He caged her in with his hands on either side of her head as he looked down at her. Goddess, she was beautiful. She was breathing hard, her chest rising and falling in short little gasps as she looked up at him.

"What are you doing?" she whispered.

He wasn't sure. The only thing he knew was that he was pretty certain he'd lost his mind—but he didn't care. "If I reached between your legs, would I find you wet for me?" Hell, he hadn't meant to say that, but the words were out anyway.

Her eyes widened, and an overpowering scent of lust rolled off her so much it was like a punch to his senses. There was his answer. And it was beautiful.

Unable to hide a groan, he slid a hand down the front of her robe, waiting for her to tell him to stop, to shove him away.

She didn't.

Instead, her breath hitched in her throat and she tracked his movements, her pretty green eyes wide. When she licked her lips and nodded, the scent of her lust intensifying, he knew he was doing the right thing.

"I don't want anyone giving you jewelry," he murmured as he dipped his hand in between the folds of her robe. Gently, he cupped one of her breasts, savoring the feel of her smooth skin, the fullness. He didn't pull the robe back, couldn't even see her nipple, but he could imagine what color it was.

She swallowed hard as he rubbed his thumb over the tight bud, over and over in soft little teases. That scent grew even wilder, sweeter. Her breaths sawed in and out as he slowly, slowly, parted the rest of her robe so that it was hanging open.

Goddess, she was beautiful.

Still watching her, he ran his palm down her flat stomach, enjoying the way she sucked in a breath, the way her whole body trembled under his touch. Because it wasn't from fear, no, but pure desire. Her eyes dilated as he continued moving down, down, down, until he cupped her mound.

"Avery," he groaned. He slid his middle finger along her soft curls.

From this angle he couldn't see if her hair was dark like on her head, but as he dipped into her folds, he felt how wet she was. "You're wet for me," he murmured.

She clutched onto his shoulders, her breathing growing even more unsteady. "What are you doing?" she whispered again, her gaze on his mouth. She licked her bottom lip as she watched him hungrily.

"I think that much is obvious. I'm going to make you come." And he was making a claim, a statement. She was his. Then he angled his mouth over hers, tasting her, learning how she liked to be kissed even as he slipped a finger inside her. She was soaked, all for him.

This was definitely heaven.

She moaned into his mouth as he slipped another finger inside her. Her inner walls were tight, clenching around him as he gently moved in and out of her.

The scent of her desire was going straight to his head as he tangled his tongue with hers. He had to resist the urge to claim, to mate, to strip her completely bare and take her as rough as he wanted. No, he had to take his time, to earn her trust.

To give her all the pleasure she deserved. And she deserved everything.

He began thrusting his fingers in a slightly faster rhythm as she rolled her hips against his hand. She made little mewling sounds every time he pushed deep inside her, her inner walls tightening with each thrust.

The position wasn't the best but he knew he could get her off. And if not, he'd toss her down onto the bed and bury his head between her legs. But he did *not* want to stop kissing her, devouring her mouth. Her taste was absolutely addicting, like nothing else in the world. And he worried that if he pulled back for even a moment, she'd come to her senses and order him out. That wasn't happening until he felt her climax coating his fingers.

She still dug her fingers into his shoulders, holding on to him as if she was afraid he would leave her. No way in hell. Not in this lifetime or the next. Avery was his. He knew that. His dragon knew that. He just needed to convince her of it.

To get her addicted to him. To want him, need him like she needed her next breath. Because that was how he felt about her.

Her inner walls were clenching tighter around him the faster he thrust. So he focused the palm of his hand on her clit, moving it in tight little circles against her sensitive nerves.

She rode his hand as he moved, her moans making him light-headed. Harder and harder he thrust. Faster and faster she clenched around him.

Goddess above, she was so reactive.

He pushed his fingers farther inside her, setting her off even more.

She grabbed onto him, her back arching as her climax hit. He didn't stop moving inside her, didn't stop as she groaned into his mouth, didn't stop as she soaked his fingers with her release.

His own cock was shoving against his pants, desperate to fill her, but it was too soon. Now was just about her. Her pleasure. Her needs.

Her entire body trembled as she came down from her climax. She slumped against the wall, her eyes a little dazed as she looked up at him.

Keeping his gaze pinned to hers, he withdrew his fingers from her slickness and slipped them into his mouth.

Her own mouth fell open slightly as she stared at him in shock. He didn't think she was a virgin but she seemed very innocent and shocked by that action.

He also knew that if he stayed, he would say something stupid and screw everything up. So he brushed his lips over hers once again before he stepped back. "I'll see you downstairs for dinner." Yes, this was the right move. Bring her pleasure, then leave so she could obsess about him the way he obsessed about her.

She stared at him as he left, her eyes still wide as he shut the door.

Finally, you make your move, his dragon rumbled inside him.

Finally indeed.

Clearly he'd been handling things all wrong. He'd taken her off guard, let his jealousy control him. Something that had never been a problem before. But perhaps tonight the little overreaction had been called for. Because he still had the scent of her climax covering his fingers.

And he would definitely have to take care of himself before heading downstairs. Not like it would take long. Avery had him all worked up, and soon, very soon hopefully, he would finally claim her.

If he could just earn all of her trust.

CHAPTER SIXTEEN

Avery felt out of sorts, that being the understatement of the century. What had just happened?

Okay, she knew what had happened: Mikael had given her a better orgasm than any of her exes. To be fair, she didn't have many and her sexual experiences had been lukewarm. Still...he'd simply used his fingers.

How was that even possible?

Little trembles still rippled through her system. In fact, she could have sworn she'd even felt the earth slightly rumble, but that was just crazy.

Talk about the best birthday present ever. Not like he knew it was her birthday, but still. Now...what the heck was she supposed to do after that? He'd just left before she could offer to return the favor or potentially freak out. Maybe both.

She felt like she was in so much emotional trouble right now. Because she had no idea how to deal with what had just happened. She wanted more, *yes*. She would be insane not to. But... She didn't want a relationship of any kind. Other than friendship. Romantic entanglements were out of the question.

Ugh. She was getting way too up in her head right now so she threw on a striped blue-and-white summer dress that made her feel pretty, and a lightweight yellow cardigan over it. Yes, she was dressing up when normally she ran around in jeans and T-shirts but screw it, today was her birthday even if no one remembered.

"Avery, dinner!" her brother Anthony called down the hallway.

At that moment, she remembered that supernatural hearing was incredible so she could only hope that Mikael's brothers hadn't heard what they'd just done in her bedroom. She hadn't been loud—she didn't think anyway. Her mind was pretty much a blank from the moment he'd pinned her against that wall and taken her mouth with his. His hands had been everywhere and her entire body had felt like one giant nerve ending.

And then he'd tasted her climax!

She was going to be thinking about *that* the next time she got herself off. Okay, time to stop thinking about him, she ordered herself.

As she stepped into the kitchen, her eyes widened to find a two-tiered pale blue and purple cake on the farm-style table. And there were what looked like twenty-nine candles on the top tier.

"Happy birthday!" they all shouted, including Mikael. He had the sweetest grin on his face too.

She looked at all of them and then back at the cake and burst into tears. They *had* remembered. And they'd clearly gone to the trouble to get her a cake made.

In the big scheme of things, she hadn't even minded that they'd forgotten because the world had fallen apart, and she definitely wouldn't expect her scatterbrained brothers to remember but…*they had*. And this was all too much.

"You said this would make her happy!" Mikael growled, glaring at her brothers.

"These are happy tears," she said as she stepped farther into the kitchen, quickly dashing the wetness off her cheeks. "I can't believe you guys remembered."

"And I can't believe you thought we wouldn't," Anthony said, pulling her into a tight embrace.

"No one said anything this morning."

"We had to be really sneaky about getting the cake back here," Riel said, a grin on his handsome face.

She looked at the two-tiered confection. "How did you even get this?" She wasn't even sure if there were any bakeries open right now. For the most part they'd been getting their food from a local grocery store that had been turned into the equivalent of a food pantry. King's pack ran it and people took what they needed, but no one was allowed to hoard.

"A friend of mine made it," Ivyn said, and it looked like he was actually blushing. Wasn't that interesting.

She pulled both her brothers into a big hug, squeezing until they laughed and gently pushed back.

"Thank you guys for remembering." Then she kissed both of them on their cheeks.

After, she hugged the others, saving Mikael for last. And...she might have held him just a little bit longer than necessary. And maybe sniffed him a little. God, the man smelled like heaven. All spicy masculine goodness she wanted to bury her face in.

"You're seriously the best big sister," Anthony said as she stepped back. "We'd never forget. And I say we have cake before dinner." His grin was adorable and infectious.

She grinned back at him, the weirdness she'd felt before coming down the stairs gone for now. This was her birthday and she was going to enjoy it. "That sounds like a really good plan to me."

"How about you relax on the back porch?" Mikael said, watching her with a barely concealed intensity. "I will serve you cake."

The way he said that somehow sounded super dirty. And she wasn't sure why. But a shiver of delight rolled through her. She managed to get out an, "Okay."

He handed her a glass of...champagne? She eyed it and then him, eyebrows raised.

"I got this from a friend. I remember you liked the bubbly stuff," he murmured. "I got another bottle for you to save for something special. Happy birthday, Avery."

She felt her cheeks heat up. "Thank you."

Mikael simply nodded, watching her carefully.

"Come on, let's go kick our feet up," Anthony said, linking his arm through hers.

She laughed lightly and let her brother take her outside, her heart full even if she was still confused about what happened upstairs with Mikael.

Moments later Mikael brought her out a giant piece of cake and topped off her champagne, a wicked glint in his eyes.

Anthony shot her a pointed look but she ignored it. She was so not talking about...whatever had happened. With anyone. But especially not her brother.

This moment was absolutely wonderful and she was going to savor it forever.

***

"So you enjoyed your birthday?" Mikael's deep voice rumbled behind her as she set her empty glass in the sink.

Startled, she turned and got the full force of him. He'd shoved up the sleeves of his T-shirt, showing off ropes of muscled forearms. His eyes seemed brighter tonight even in the dimly lit kitchen. Three pendant lamps were the only lights. And now, they were alone. "I did, thank you."

"I have a present for you," he murmured.

"Pretty sure you already gave me a present," she murmured before she could stop herself. She blamed it on the champagne.

His eyes flared wider for a moment before a wicked grin fell into place. "That was just an appetizer."

She blinked. She had no idea how to respond to that.

Even though she'd started with the flirty comment, she *really* couldn't wrap her mind around anything. But they definitely needed to talk.

Without thinking, she grabbed his hand and dragged him out the back door. His brothers and hers had gone upstairs not too long ago. "What the heck is going on with you?" she demanded as they stepped out onto the back patio. "With us? You give me an incredible orgasm and then—"

She froze at the sound of someone clearing their throat.

She glanced over her shoulder to find Anthony on the back porch, his phone in hand. He looked between the two of them, eyes wide, but didn't say a word as he hurried past them. The door shut behind him with a soft snick.

Ah hell. Riel would know about this in seconds. *Gah.* She covered her face with her hands for a long moment.

"We can go upstairs and I can give you an even better orgasm," Mikael said simply. Wickedly.

She let out a frustrated growl and glared at him, which for some reason made him smile.

"It's sexy when you growl."

She reached out and covered his mouth, shaking her head. "You can't say stuff like that. I'm the birthday girl. And whatever is happening between us, it has to stop."

He gently bit one of her fingers, the action erotic and sensual. It sent a wild pulse of heat between her legs. "I will not agree to this," he murmured.

She let out a frustrated growl, yanking her hand back when the door opened. It was Ivyn. He glanced between the two of them curiously. "Sorry to interrupt but Arthur and Prima are at the door. They wanted to talk to you, Mikael. They said it's important, but I can tell them to come back?"

Even though she hadn't wanted the interruption, a small part of her was glad for it. Mikael's jaw tightened but she nudged him gently. "See what they want. We'll talk later."

Avery headed back inside with him but stayed in the kitchen with Ivyn. She heard the front door open, and instead of inviting the others in, Mikael must've gone outside because she didn't hear them talking.

"Is everything okay?" she asked, grabbing a fork and digging right into the cake. It wasn't like she needed more sugar but who cared. Her thoughts were in disarray and she needed cake. It was her birthday, after all.

Ivyn lifted a shoulder, watching her in amusement. "They might be offering him a job."

She frowned. "He has a job."

"No, I mean like doing patrols and tracking."

She set her fork down. "Why would they offer him that?"

"He's one of the best trackers I've ever known. He used to lead a special group many thousands of years ago. They were all trackers. Hunters, really," he tacked on. "I think that's the way humans might describe it. If someone needed...ah..." He cleared his throat. "He was known as an enforcer. And he's very good at what he does."

She blinked. Avery had so many questions but she wasn't going to ask Mikael's brother. No, she would ask him herself. She blindly stuck her fork into the cake again, making Ivyn grin.

"Would you like to be alone with your cake?"

"I'm about to show this cake a good time." The chocolate buttercream icing melted on her tongue.

He threw his head back and laughed. "I will tell my friend you enjoyed it."

"Good. Please thank your friend for me… And feel free to invite your *friend* over any time."

To her surprise, he quickly backtracked out of the kitchen, mumbling something she couldn't understand. Interesting indeed.

CHAPTER SEVENTEEN

At the knock on her bedroom door, Avery jumped up far too quickly from her chair by the window. She *might* have been periodically peeking outside, waiting to see when Prima and Arthur finally left.

Something fluttered in her chest as she pulled the door open and it only got worse to find Mikael standing on the other side, looking good enough to eat. "Hey," she said, feeling suddenly awkward.

"Hi." He took a step forward as if he would come inside, then placed his hands on the frame above the door instead. She wondered if he knew how delicious he looked, how the way his muscles flexed in that position made her think...lots of dirty things. How it made her wonder what it would be like for him to hold on to a headboard as she rode him. Oh, he had to know what he was doing!

"Money for your thoughts?"

She giggled slightly. "It's 'penny for your thoughts.'"

He frowned slightly. "I'm sorry for leaving to speak to them."

"It's fine." She'd needed the mental break anyway. "Is everything okay?"

He nodded once, and when it became clear he wasn't going to expand or come inside, she realized she was too curious to let this go. "Did they offer you a job or something?"

"Or something."

Was he being intentionally vague? "Look, if you're not happy doing construction, I'm sure if you talk to King, he'll find you something else."

His lips curved up slightly in definite amusement. "King has already offered multiple times to give me a position in...*security*, as he puts it."

She blinked. "Oh."

He leaned down slightly, the rich, masculine scent of him wrapping around her. His eyes had gone that smoky gray again. "I am more than happy right where I am."

Yeah, but for how long? The thought popped into her head, dousing some of the desire she'd felt before. Not all of it, of course, because she was standing here staring at him and thinking about dragging him into her room and jumping him.

"Would you like to take a walk tonight?" he asked, his gaze searching hers.

She wanted to say yes. But if they spent more time together tonight, and on her birthday when she was a tiny bit tipsy on champagne and feeling good from the cake—and the orgasm—no good would come of that.

"Well?" he rumbled.

"I'm confused right now," she whispered. She hadn't meant to confess it, but there it was.

He dropped his arms, and though he didn't reach for her, she was under the impression that he wanted to. "Why are you confused?"

She gestured with her hands because she didn't know how to say what was on her mind. He was acting as if nothing had changed after he'd given her such an intense orgasm. It was like the very fabric of her reality had been ripped in two. And that was saying something, considering that the whole world had wildly changed months ago.

She wanted him. But she was so afraid of being hurt. Of thinking she could get her happily-ever-after and then getting her heart broken. If anyone could break it, it would definitely be Mikael. "I can't talk about this right now. I'm going to try to get some sleep. Thank you for…a good birthday," she said lamely.

Mikael watched her carefully and then nodded, stepping back as she shut the door.

She covered her face in her hands. She was such a coward.

* * *

Mikael rubbed his hands over his face. That had not gone like he'd wanted. He'd wanted to give her a birthday kiss, a real one. Then to make her climax again, on his tongue this time. Then—

"You gonna stand there all night?"

He turned as Anthony strode down the hallway toward his own

bedroom. He shook his head, and cleared his throat. "Look—"

"Hey, your business with my sister is your business. She's a grown woman who knows her own mind. I feel like I should give that perfunctory 'if you hurt my sister, I'll hurt you' talk, but let's be real, I don't think I could hurt you, and second...I don't think you'll hurt her. Ever."

Mikael nodded, his throat tight as he headed to his own bedroom. No, he would never hurt Avery, but she had the capacity to destroy him. That was the way with dragon mates.

And she was his mate, he had no doubt about it. He'd known even before that first kiss, before he'd brought her to orgasm.

But when he'd been kissing her, he'd felt the very subtle shift of tectonic plates beneath the earth.

Some dragons glowed or were covered in flames when the mating manifestation kicked in. For his clan, his people, they made the earth shake.

And it was only going to get worse.

CHAPTER EIGHTEEN

Avery walked the length of the long-abandoned plot of land while her two "escorts" talked in the parking lot. She'd come here today with two shifters. Sergei, a bear, and another who might be a feline. But she couldn't tell what Olga was, and Avery wasn't going to ask because that was rude.

Mikael was off working on something for her, and part of her thought he'd jumped too quickly at the option to leave the jobsite. She couldn't tell if he was avoiding her. Yesterday—the day after her birthday—he'd been gone when she'd woken up. She'd decided to go visit friends, including Dallas, her sweet dragonling Willow, and Dallas's new mate, Rhys. After stopping there, she'd visited half a dozen places, catching up with people she hadn't seen in far too long.

It had been a much-needed break and a reminder that the world as she knew it still had a lot of good in it. It was so easy to get wrapped up in working, working, *working*. She was so busy trying to make sure people had housing that she forgot to simply stop and take a breath. Because no one was homeless right now, thanks to King. Still, she wanted to get everyone settled. Having a safe place to lay your head at night, a place to call home, meant something. Everyone deserved that. But not seeing Mikael yesterday, and him being gone now, had her off-kilter.

As she reached the end of the lot, she turned right and stopped. After making a note of the length from her walking wheel measuring tape, she clicked it again and started measuring the width as she walked. This was a good piece of property, with commercial buildings across the street—unused for now—but she wasn't sure about the soil. She knew there had been a few houses built here that had been destroyed a few hurricanes ago. Well, more than a few. Since then, the property had been sitting and collecting old air conditioners and other junk.

She paused midstride and looked around at the sound of... What *was* that? It sounded like a cat crying. Or a *baby* crying.

Mildly alarmed, she glanced over at the parking lot and didn't see Sergei or Olga.

Shaking her head, she kept walking, then heard it again. Lifting her hand to shield her eyes from the sun, even though she had on aviators, she glanced around again.

The crying was getting louder. And it was kind of creepy. She realized it was coming from the other side of the dilapidated fence.

After setting her measuring wheel against the fence, she tried some of the boards and wasn't surprised when two gave way. They weren't even nailed in. She slid them to the side and squeezed through to be faced with another overgrown lot.

This entire area needed to be rebuilt, something King was already aware of. Still, she hated seeing the disrepair and wished she had ten more crews. She hated that so many areas of the city were run-down, when once upon a time federal funding and better management could have helped out. Of course, that was a moot point now. She glanced around, looking for what she imagined were stray cats, even if their cries were sending shivers down her spine.

As she walked through the calf-high underbrush, Avery was as loud as possible in case there were snakes. She was glad she'd worn her work boots today. Still, she didn't fancy stepping on any snakes, regardless.

"Finally," a familiar voice said from her left, startling her. Lindsey stood twenty feet away, appearing as if out of nowhere—likely using her vampire speed. She glared daggers at Avery, her dark eyes slits of rage.

Avery's heart rate kicked up. "How are you out in sunlight?" she blurted. She might not know everything about supernaturals, but she knew that vampires not being able to walk around in sunlight was *not* a myth. She'd heard that there were a select few that could, but they were rare. At least that was her understanding. Not that it really mattered right now as she was staring into the very angry eyes of a pissed-off vampire who hated her.

Lindsey hissed at her and rubbed her wrist absently. "I can't believe that male wants you," she spat as she strode forward, determination in each step. "I can't believe any male wants you when he could have *me*."

Avery glanced around even though she didn't want to take her eyes off Lindsey. Taking your eyes off any predator was stupid, especially one she knew wished her harm. And Lindsey was here for a reason. "What are you even doing here?" she asked loudly as she took a step back. Where the hell were Sergei and Olga?

Lindsey made the creepiest crying sound, and it sounded just like a cat cry-screeching. Her mouth opened and the horrid sound was all twisted and broken.

Avery stared in horror. Something was seriously wrong with Lindsey. Avery wanted to run but knew it would be pointless. She couldn't outrun a vampire. She could, however, stab one right in the heart.

But first she needed a weapon.

Covertly she glanced around, unable to stop the wild beat of her heart. There were discarded pipes, old bikes and boards falling off the rotting fence. Maybe a pipe would work?

Lindsey circled her, her eyes filled with loathing as she eyed Avery up and down, watching her like a lion would a gazelle.

"If you hurt me, you know there will be repercussions." Avery was desperate at this point, sweat pooling down her spine. She spoke loudly again, knowing that Sergei and Olga had supernatural hearing. They wouldn't have left her so she had to believe they were nearby.

Lindsey laughed as she started to circle her again. "I'm not worried about that. And I won't get caught."

Avery screamed, the noise her only defense at this point. She couldn't even get to a pipe in time.

Lindsey blinked, then sprinted at her so fast that Avery froze, barely able to track the movement until—

Smash!

Lindsey flew back through the air as if...she'd run into a wall.

Looking dazed as she shoved to her feet, Lindsey shook her head and let out a low growl as she raced straight at Avery again.

Smash! The same thing happened.

Avery stared in astonishment, then realized something.

Oh God, the *necklace*. The Magic Man had given her a necklace as an early birthday present. He'd told her it would keep her from harm. He said he'd seen something, a vision... That he'd wanted to keep her out of danger. She'd thought he was just being silly but hadn't wanted to hurt his feelings.

Feeling mildly powerful, she stared in awe. "You should probably leave now," she said with a lot more confidence than she felt. Because who knew how long this necklace would hold up against...well, whatever.

Lindsey screamed this time, the sound of rage ricocheting off the dilapidated buildings as she raced straight for her, fangs out.

Two feet from Avery, she flew backward through the air again.

"You really are dumb." Avery was feeling way more confident than she should. Because if whatever was happening failed, Lindsey was going to tear her apart piece by piece and relish it.

"What the hell?" Lindsey muttered, anger and confusion competing for dominance on her face.

At a grunting sound, Avery turned to see Sergei punching straight through the falling-down fence. That was a bear shifter for you. Why bother to climb over it when you could just hulk-smash it?

Lindsey looked at the two shifters hurrying toward them, then at Avery. "This isn't over," she snarled, then turned and raced down the quiet street.

As she did, Avery thought she scented burning flesh. Maybe Lindsey could only be in the sun for so long?

"There was a fight across the street we got distracted by... What the hell happened?" Sergei demanded even as Olga raced after Lindsey.

"I don't actually know. She's a vampire. She tried to attack me but she bounced back as if... Well, as if I have a protective bubble around me."

The big shifter with dark hair and dark eyes stared at her, blinking. "Come again?"

"I think it has something to do with this." She pulled the necklace out of her shirt and showed it to him. The chain was a pretty rose gold and the little charm encased in a triangle was teardrop-shaped. "It was a gift from the Magic Man. He said it should protect me." Apparently he'd meant that in a very literal way.

"We need to go see King or one of his lieutenants right now. Because she tried to kill you in broad daylight. Or at the very least kidnap you. He's going to need to figure out what coven she's from and a bunch of other things above my pay grade."

Olga raced back up then, barely breathing harder than normal. But the tall shifter frowned, and rubbed an annoyed hand over her long, blonde braid. "I lost her. It's like she just disappeared." Then she let out a colorful curse that made Avery's eyes widen.

"Come on." Sergei motioned to Avery, not taking his eyes off the street, searching for any sign of Lindsey.

* * *

Avery stepped into the factory Sergei had brought her to and looked around, unable to contain her awe. Olga had remained behind at the empty lot to finish measuring for Avery. "What is this place?"

People in lab coats milled about, going in and out of different rooms. She could see into some of them because of the glass windows. This wasn't like any factory she'd ever seen. Behind some of the windows were labs and behind others were…what looked like different types of robotics.

"Witches and human scientists—and some witch scientists—are working on some stuff here." She wondered what "some stuff" referred to and clearly her curiosity was obvious because the bear continued. "I think it has to do with different medicines. Witches are infusing certain things into, ah, something to do with *chemistry*…and that's pretty much all my tiny bear brain knows," he said, laughing.

She laughed lightly herself—because Sergei was incredibly smart— and some of the tension inside her eased. "So, like, stuff for diabetes or depression or whatever?"

"Yes, but they're also going to be working on prosthetics and things like that. I have a cousin who lost his leg and his prosthetic was created by a witch who also has a lot of degrees, including one in robotics engineering. This was from before The Fall. His prosthetic basically bonded to his body, becoming part of it. But if it needs to be removed or replaced, it can be. It's absolutely amazing. It's…technology and magic rolled into one. I don't understand how it works, but it's incredible."

She stared at him in shock. "I don't know why I'm surprised to find out that witches and scientists were already working together. That's amazing."

"Yeah, and now they can work together out in the open. They can all share their findings with the rest of the world. This is a game changer for everyone."

This was going to have incredible repercussions for the world. She stowed those thoughts, however, as Ace, one of King's lieutenants, strode across the factory floor.

His eyes were a dark chocolate, the color complementing his bronze skin, and he was tall, but lean in the way some wolves could be. His hair was cropped close to his head and…there was a little heart shaved into his barely-there cropped hair.

Ace nodded politely at Avery then he and Sergei clapped hands, doing that handshake that all males seemed to know. "What are you doing here?" he asked, looking between them.

Avery quickly relayed what had happened, including her painful history with Lindsey. As she was talking, Mikael appeared like a ghost, slipping up beside her.

She jumped, unable to contain her surprise—and relief—and stopped midsentence. "How did you get here?"

"I flew." His expression was obnoxiously neutral.

She frowned at him and Ace cleared his throat. "I texted him. Continue, please. Do you know what this female wanted with you?" he asked Avery.

"No. I know nothing about her current life. Until recently I hadn't seen her in *six* years. I didn't even know she was a vampire until the other night."

"How did you repel her?"

She touched the pendant hanging around her neck. "The Magic Man gave me a gift. He said it would help ward off evil, basically. And he wasn't kidding."

Next to her Mikael stirred slightly. "I'll be her guard until further notice." He said it almost like a challenge, but she could see his dragon right beneath the surface, his rage and fear barely contained.

Ace gave Avery a thoughtful look, then nodded once. "Mikael will be your escort everywhere you go. It's not up for discussion," he added as if he thought she might argue. "You live in the same house so it is a simple enough arrangement. If the vampire contacts you in any way again, obviously I don't need to tell you to let me or King know. If you see her again, don't approach her. I have a team who will be hunting her down."

"If I see her, she won't be walking away." Mikael's words came out a low, deadly growl.

Ace lifted a shoulder as if to say, "That works."

There was so much she wanted to say to that but she simply nodded. Ace more or less dismissed her, telling Sergei he needed to talk to him.

If Ace wanted her to stick to Mikael, then she had no choice. Not that it was exactly horrible. Just…maybe awkward right now. It was pretty clear Mikael wasn't giving her a choice either. She had no idea who he'd been challenging before, her or Ace, about being her guard.

Once they stepped outside, Mikael turned to look at her, running his hands over her shoulders and up and down her arms in a gentle fashion. "Are you okay?" There was so much concern in his eyes, it warmed her from the inside out.

"I'm fine. Okay, I'm shaken up," she corrected, because it was the truth. "And mystified. It was literally like she hit a brick wall and bounced back when she tried to attack me."

His expression darkened with her every word and Avery figured that Lindsey was lucky she wasn't anywhere near Mikael right now.

"Hey," Ace said, jogging out of the side door. "Come see King tonight. Both of you." He gave them the address, then headed back inside.

Once they were alone again, Mikael said, "Let's go see this Magic Man now."

"Why?"

"I want to find out how sturdy his warding spell is. You might need something more. And if he had a vision, I want to know exactly what it was." Mikael clearly had heard most of what she'd told Ace if he knew about the vision.

"Okay." She didn't understand why Lindsey had come after her. The risk didn't seem worth the reward. Sure, Lindsey could kill her but…what on earth did she get out of that? She would have to know that she would be hunted down and killed.

Avery didn't understand everything about supernatural rules, but she knew that a vampire killing an unarmed civilian human—one who was doing a lot of work for the city and was friendly with the Alpha—was beyond stupid.

Lindsey was a lot of things—conniving and manipulative, yes—but she was *not* stupid. She'd married Avery's father for his money and played him for a fool, all while convincing him that she truly loved him. She'd also managed to convince Avery that they were truly friends as well, when in reality she only looked out for herself. She was a very good liar.

Avery kept her thoughts to herself as they got on one of the working streetcars. During The Fall, a couple lines had been damaged, but fixing them had been one of the first things King's pack had done.

Today it was busy, packed with people, humans and shifters alike. The only rule for the streetcar was that you could not be in shifted forms to ride them because shifters in animal form tended to take up more space. Still, she could guess at the identity of a few of the overly large or tall shifters.

Mikael wrapped his arm around her and pulled her close. There was almost no room on the streetcar, everyone squeezed together, so she nestled up against him, pressing her nose against his chest. She didn't care that she was smelling him so obviously because he smelled delicious. Who could blame her?

After being almost attacked, she was emotionally exhausted, her brain working overtime. And screw it, Mikael's arms were strong and secure.

He rubbed a hand up and down her back gently, and even though he didn't say anything his very presence and embrace was a pure comfort. And she wanted him way more than she could admit to him. She was so afraid of admitting how much she cared for him, how much she couldn't imagine her life without him.

Because what happened when he realized she was just some normal human? Not special at all? He'd end up with a fantastic, badass dragon female and she'd end up with her heart broken.

At least for now, this moment, she was able to pretend that he was hers. And she was his.

CHAPTER NINETEEN

"Can you smile a little?" Avery asked as they stepped up to the two intricately carved, oversized wooden doors of the home of the Magic Man. She'd been here before, knew that he not only lived in this place in the Quarter downtown, but also ran his shop out of here too. She pressed the buzzer.

Mikael looked startled by her request. "Smile?"

He was so tense right now, his shoulders bunched tight, and he had an expression that said *Make one wrong move and I'll burn you to a crisp.* "Ah…I don't know… Maybe just not look so scary?"

He actually grinned at that, which sent ribbons of awareness spooling through her. "You wish me to change my face?"

Despite the tight ball of tension curled in her belly, she laughed lightly. "Never mind. I don't want you to change or anything. I guess you're just intimidating and there's nothing that will change that." He looked a little startled by her words but could that *really* be a surprise to him? The male looked terrifying most of the time. Not to her or anything, but he was huge and did *not* hide the fact that he was a dragon. It could be a little off-putting to humans who were just learning about supernaturals. Dragons in particular.

The door opened before she could get tangled up in her own thoughts, and Malcolm, one of the Magic Man's nephews, opened the door. "Avery, lovely to see you." He smiled brightly at her, grasping her hands as she stepped inside. Malcolm kissed her on both cheeks, then politely greeted Mikael, who at least managed to look civil. Mostly.

"As you might guess, we're here to see Thurman, if he's free."

"He's always free for you."

Mikael made a sort of grunting sound so she nudged him slightly as they followed Malcolm into an open courtyard filled with lush greenery and colorful flowers.

"He'll be right out," Malcolm said and guided them to a seat where two glasses of cucumber water were already waiting.

Because Thurman, aka the Magic Man, had very likely known they were coming. He was eerie like that. Which was a part of the reason she wore the necklace he'd given her. He'd known she needed it.

"So what do you know of this Magic Man?" Mikael's expression was grim as he glanced around at all the pretty plants and flowers, looking for potential enemies lurking.

"We've been friendly for a few years. If anyone lived in New Orleans for any amount of time and knew about the supernatural world, they most likely have met Thurman. He runs a shop connected to this place." She pointed at one of the doors that led to a shop that operated on a parallel street. "Where he sells different types of spells. They used to be for supernaturals only. At least the spell part. He inherited his place, and his gift, from his father." She didn't think the shop was actually open, at least not in the sense it used to be when they all had currency.

She stopped talking when Thurman strode out from the side door in gray slacks, a button-down shirt and a gray vest with a purple pocket square peeking out of the pocket. It didn't matter that the world had devolved into chaos, he was always immaculately dressed.

She felt kind of like a scrub, wearing her jeans, work boots and flannel shirt, but there was no way she was ever going to pull off elegance the way Thurman did. Not even on her best day.

Smiling, she stood as he approached the table. "I'm kind of dusty so I won't hug you."

"Nonsense," he said, taking her hands in his in the same way his nephew had, before kissing her on both cheeks. "It is always a pleasure to see you. Unfortunately I think I know why you're here." His gaze flicked down to the pendant around her neck. Then he smiled politely at Mikael and held out a hand. "I'm Thurman. Pleased to meet you."

"Mikael." It came out kind of like a growl but it was better than nothing. Because Mikael was strung tight, all his muscles pulled taut as he glanced around the courtyard again—as if expecting an ambush at any moment.

"Please sit. And relax," Thurman added to Mikael. "This entire building is spelled. No one will bother us here and no one can overhear us. I'm very particular about my privacy."

Well that was interesting, but Avery shouldn't be surprised, considering his gifts. Of course he'd spelled this place.

"So you're another dragon living in the city," Thurman said as he sat down and crossed his legs.

Mikael paused before fully sitting next to Avery. He scooted his chair closer to hers. "Are you a seer or did you just guess what I am?"

"I'm a seer. So, something happened, I take it?" He looked at Avery now, jumping right into the matter at hand.

She appreciated it. "A woman from my past, who is now a vampire, tried to attack me. She bounced back as if I had a protective bubble around me."

Thurman's mouth curved up ever so slightly. "Because you do."

"How strong is the necklace? Or the spell?" Mikael cut in.

"Incredibly strong. It will take serious dark magic to penetrate it. Blood magic. Even then…" He lifted a shoulder again. "It might or might not penetrate the protective bubble around her. I used very strong magic for this. Family magic."

Mikael seemed to settle back in his seat, some of that tension fading from his shoulders like the ocean rolling back out to sea.

"So you knew something was going to happen?" Avery asked, then inwardly cursed herself. *Duh.* Of course he'd known.

"Yes and no. I saw you surrounded by darkness. And I saw blood. It was very clearly an omen for death, or at least pain, so…" He lifted one elegant shoulder. "I figured better safe than sorry."

"Why…would you do this for me?" They were friendly, if not friends exactly. But this was an invaluable gift, one he'd given for no apparent reason.

"Why wouldn't I?"

That wasn't an answer but she wasn't going to push. "I don't know how to thank you." She had no doubt she would be dead right now if not for him. "If there's anything I can do to return this kindness, please let me know."

He made a scoffing sound. "You will do no such thing. You're helping rebuild the city. *My* city. My family's city. And I'm taking a page from

King's playbook. I give this to you because it is the right thing to do."

Ah, so that was why. She blinked quickly, dashing away the tears that wanted to come. Kindness for the sake of kindness was something she could get on board with.

"Well now a dragon owes you a favor," Mikael said, putting his fist over his chest. "Thank you for protecting her."

Avery was stunned by Mikael's words. A dragon giving someone a favor was…huge.

She cleared her throat, feeling awkward and nervous as she looked back at Thurman. "Sincerely, thank you again. Is there anything else you can tell me about what you saw?"

"Unfortunately no. That's not how my gift works. Some days it feels more like a curse. I *can* tell you that you're still in danger. The darkness hovers on the horizon, just out of reach. That much I can see. Keep the necklace on you at all times. It will keep you safe." He flicked a glance at Mikael, his mouth curving up ever so slightly. "So will he."

CHAPTER TWENTY

King looked around the round table where the shifters, vampires and human he had invited all sat. Ingrid of the Cheval vampire coven, Claudine of the Bonavich coven, Santiago representing the bears, and Reaper and Prima representing dragons. Thurman was here as he was a human and a seer and everyone trusted him. King had also invited Justus, even though he was not part of any vampire coven. He'd sworn allegiance to his half-vampire half-demon mate and King respected his power level. The male had been a Roman warrior long ago.

He'd also invited three witches, but all of them had been unable to make it—for reasons he could understand. He'd kept his own pack at bay for this, not wanting to overwhelm everyone, and to make it clear that this meeting was for their leaders only. He did wish Dallas was here, representing witches, but she was questioning whether she was strong enough to represent witches. King knew without a doubt that she was, she just needed to come to that realization on her own.

"Humans are being turned into vampires, and I know it is not any of you who are behind it," he said, glancing at each vampire—Ingrid, Claudine and Justus. "I do have a name, however. Magnus." He looked at them all, waiting for a reaction.

Claudine was the only one who reacted even remotely, a flick of her eyes. It was subtle though.

"Never heard of him," Santiago said with a shrug. "He's turning humans against their will?"

"I don't think against their will. But he's breaking the mandate not to turn any humans right now." King had made that order for the time being, only a temporary ruling, and every vampire leader agreed with him. It was a miracle they all agreed on something. But while he got his territory in order, he couldn't risk having too many vampires and not enough humans to feed on. It was an unlikely problem, and vamps were usually careful about who they turned anyway, but he'd wanted the mandate official, regardless.

"I have some contacts I can reach out to," Ingrid said.

"I'll speak to my mate," Justus said. "Cynara has many contacts across species."

King figured Justus would also reach out to his former coven as well. They were located in upstate New York and had survived The Fall.

"I don't know a vampire named Magnus, but the name itself is familiar." Prima tapped her finger against the table, looking lost in thought. The ancient dragon female had been awake for a little while. Before that she'd been in a deep Hibernation. If she'd heard of the male, he must be old. Ancient like her.

"I do not know the name," Reaper said simply.

"I don't know the name either," Thurman said. "But…it makes me think of darkness. I can see it on the horizon. I had a similar vision about Avery. It's the same darkness."

King frowned slightly. The human could see things, not necessarily future events but Thurman often had feelings. And okay, was slightly psychic, was King's understanding. And he was a whiz at spells. As good as some witches. Maybe better.

He really did wish at least one witch had been here tonight, more or less because he wanted all species in the city to have a voice. He would relay everything to them later. He'd also invited Aurora for…so many reasons. But she'd been working on something else for him. For the *territory*, he mentally amended.

"I know the name," Claudine said, glancing at Thurman. Then she looked back at King.

He wasn't sure how old she was, she'd never told anyone, but if he had to guess he would say over five hundred years old. She carried herself with an elegant authority. He'd never once heard her raise her voice at her people, but he had seen them cower at just a hard look from her. He also knew that she'd once saved a bunch of children from a fire that went out of control in the warehouse district about ten years ago. She'd gained nothing from it either. So she might frustrate him on occasion, but he respected her.

"I should say I know *of* a Magnus," she continued. "He is a vampire.

This is from many, many years ago. He is…old. Much older than me. He's compelling. He fell off the face of the earth so long ago. Disappeared. I figured he had gotten bored and maybe gone into a deep sleep."

King knew that some very old vampires could go into a deep sleep much in the same way that dragons went into Hibernation. He didn't understand the details of it, however. Vampires didn't share all their secrets with outsiders—no supernatural species did. "What can you tell us about him?"

"Not much, unfortunately. I heard that he was maybe…Greek or Roman? Magnus was not his human name so I can't even guess. He was an anomaly to me. He knew magic and was a vampire, but I always felt as if he was…more. I never fought him so I do not know just how skilled he is, but he wiped out two vampire covens that tried to encroach on his territory, using a dark magic. This was a very long time ago. It was a bloodbath. Brutal and savage.

"A human village was caught in the crossfire. He could have stopped the carnage but once he and his coven won against the other vampires, he allowed his newly turned vampires to run rampant over this human village that had never harmed anyone."

Her jaw tightened once, which might as well have been actual shouting for anyone else. Claudine always kept her expression carefully neutral. She was one of the hardest beings to read—one of his lieutenants had likened her dark eyes to shark eyes.

"I've seen a lot in my life," she continued. "What he allowed his vampires to do… They defiled men, women, children alike. It was…wrong. There was no reason for it. It was evil for the sake of being evil. Whatever he wants, it is not good. If you go up against him, I am with you."

He nodded and looked around for any other additional information but no one said anything. Claudine giving her help so quickly was a sign that either Magnus was that evil, or things were changing for the better in the city. Maybe both.

Since there was nothing more to say, King moved on to another subject. They had much to discuss about the rebuilding of the city and expanding territory. But he could not allow this Magnus or his newly turned vampires to run free.

They needed to be stopped—he just had to find their nest.

* * *

King raised his hand once in greeting to Aurora as he crossed the street to see her. They'd decided to meet up near the zoo and it was quiet this time of night, with people already in their homes. As always the sight of her was a punch to his senses. Every. Single. Time.

"How was your meeting?" she asked as he stepped up next to her on the sidewalk. She was in dark pants, a dark sweater and black boots, the outfit anything but plain on her. Nothing could ever be plain on her. The female practically glowed—sometimes she actually did. Tonight her dark violet eyes were unreadable.

He fell in step with her as they walked along the sidewalk. "As well as could be expected." He didn't scent anyone other than a few humans walking nearby but wasn't going to give too many details in public like this. "I have people looking for…what we need."

"I had a little bit of luck, I think," she said quietly, tucking her dark hair behind one ear. It fell down her back in soft waves. "A few humans from the college, male and female, have gone missing. But not like a kidnapping. They've all told their friends various versions of being invited to 'become immortal' by a dark, serious man. In a few cases, they were invited by a blonde female who promised them that if they left with her, they would be turned. Only two declined and I made note of who they are. Whoever you're looking for—"

"Magnus," he said quietly. "I'm pretty sure that's his name."

She raised an eyebrow as she continued. "Well whoever he is, it sounds like he's the one turning all these humans."

"Anything else?"

"I didn't want to ask them about the dead humans since that's not public knowledge. I didn't want to start a panic or anything. Some have seen their friends since being turned and others have texted with their friends, but not seen them. So, he *is* turning them. And if I had to guess, he's not training his newly turned vamps to feed properly. If he's turning humans at such a rapid pace—when he's not supposed to be, and hasn't even told you he's in your territory—then I seriously doubt he's going to worry about following rules and not killing humans."

"I was thinking the same thing myself." There could be a serial killer from the group Magnus had turned, or a lone vampire who was randomly killing humans, but King was playing the odds on this. Usually when something was the most obvious answer, he took it at face value. "You said a blonde female has been approaching humans as well?"

"Yes. And in one case, she approached them in daylight. She didn't stay long but promised them immortality and the gift of walking in sunlight on *occasion*."

A blonde female vampire walking in daylight sounded eerily familiar. "I'm going to want to talk directly to whoever told you that. I'll need a description."

"I figured... So I drew a sketch already. I made a few sketches actually. Of her and of the male, though those weren't very good. Most people only remembered vague images of the male... It was odd. Like, they knew the basics: he has dark hair, is tall, has bronze skin. For the female, however, I have a much better description. And if they're right, she's stunning. Which will hopefully help in finding her."

"Thank you." Of course she'd already done sketches. King wasn't even surprised. Aurora always seemed to be on the same page as him.

Though the last couple of weeks things had been different between them. Not bad... Just, she'd seemed distant. And not only from him, but everyone. He didn't like that, especially not since he knew she'd been held in captivity for so long. He wondered if she was struggling but didn't want to push. He knew if he did, she would only pull back.

As they reached the intersection where a small grocery store was still operating and providing for the neighborhood, he waved at some people he knew as he and Aurora crossed the street. "Is everything okay with you?" he finally asked. No matter what, she was his friend and this wasn't pushing.

"Yes... Kind of."

He glanced at her but she wasn't looking at him. Instead she stared straight ahead as they stepped up onto the opposite sidewalk. Music and voices trailed out from an apartment two stories above them, the laughter a balm to him. Laughter was a good thing right now. "Feel like talking about it?"

She sighed and rubbed a hand against the back of her neck as if she had a headache. "I just haven't been sleeping well. I've been having dreams lately." She looked at him then away quickly and glanced around at their surroundings.

He was aware of every single thing around them—the man out on his front stoop texting two doors down, the female walking her dog on the other side of the street, the other female behind a tree smoking a cigarette, and the couple arguing with their window open four houses down. All background noise. King kept most of his focus on her, and on making certain there was no danger nearby.

"I'm just dreaming about my time in captivity. Not dreaming, having nightmares I guess." She shrugged, but the action was jerky and she let out a jagged breath. "I thought I had dealt with everything but apparently my reaction is delayed. I've…been struggling."

He didn't know much about her time in captivity, just that she'd been held by a power-hungry dragon for a year. That was a very long time to have your life stolen from you. And if the dragon who had kidnapped her wasn't already dead, King would kill him now. Slowly. Methodically. Painfully. "I'm always here to listen to you. *Always*. But if you need to talk to someone…I'm certain Greer will gladly speak to you." The dragon healer had been working with human and supernatural psychologists alike, helping people adjust to this new world.

"I've been talking to her a little bit. It helps. But the dreams are still there." She shrugged again, this time the action more fluid. "Nightmares. I just need to call them that." Another sigh, this one sad.

"I'm sorry for everything you went through," he said simply. He wished he could do more, like hold her, comfort her. But he did not have that right. And he understood more than most that sometimes time was simply the only thing that made things better.

"Thank you."

Before King and Aurora made it to the back of her house, his dragonling, who he'd started calling Hunter, flew down from one of the trees, not quite mastering stealth yet. His wings flapped too loudly but King had discovered that his dragon—and when had he started thinking of it as his own?—had a natural camouflage and often blended into his surroundings.

Hunter chirped loudly as he landed on the grass in front of them. He chirped excitedly and butted up against King until he petted the little one's head.

"He has so got you figured out," Aurora murmured.

"Oh yeah, how so?"

"He knows you have a marshmallow inside." Her smile was soft as they headed around toward the back of the house where the rest of her crew and roommates lived.

"I don't have a marshmallow inside." Not even close.

"Fine. You do for *him*."

"True enough." And he did for her too, but that didn't matter. At least not right now. He wondered if she even knew how he felt for her. Then he stowed that thought because it didn't matter. She was clearly still dealing with the aftermath of what she'd been through. And the only thing he cared about was her healing.

"Aurora!" Avery smiled as she spotted the two of them rounding the back of the house.

There was a huge spread of food on the patio table and most of Aurora's roommates were there, except Harlow and Axel.

"Avery, I'm so happy you're here." As the two women hugged, King nodded at Mikael. He'd asked Mikael and Avery to meet him here instead of at the compound as it made more sense for both of them.

"Have you had any more issues today?" he asked, though he had a feeling Mikael would have already contacted him or one of his lieutenants if he had.

One day he wanted to convince Mikael to work for him directly—he'd talked to enough dragons to know that Mikael had been a warrior and very good at what he'd done. He was supposed to be an incredible tracker, something King respected since he was one as well. He could use someone like that, especially right now.

The stronger he built up his people, his territory, the harder it would be for anyone to threaten them in the future. And he was building for the future every minute of every day. Right now the world was rebuilding, readjusting, and he would be ready once that changed—once some supernaturals decided to test limits, territories, to see if he was strong enough to hold his.

Even though he had plans for Mikael, something told King that Mikael would not be moving from his current position in construction until he and Avery officially mated. And probably not even then, not until the newness of mating wore off. And sometimes that never happened.

Hunter kept a decent distance from Mikael, sizing him up before he chirped something at the dragon shifter then flitted off toward Avery.

"Pretty sure I just got scolded by a dragonling," Mikael murmured, amusement in his voice.

King snorted. "Definitely."

"Have you named him yet?" Avery asked as she hugged Hunter around the neck, nuzzling him. "Lola says you keep calling him 'dragon.'"

"Did you change your mind about keeping him?" he asked instead of answering.

Hunter looked at him, giving him big, sad eyes, his wings drooping, and King felt like a giant dick. He'd only been joking.

"I'm kidding," he said quickly when Avery and Aurora both gave him a look of horror. His dragonling started chirping at him, his wings lifting back upward as he nuzzled Avery.

"That dragonling understands everything you're saying. I would bet any amount of treasure on it." Mikael shook his head slightly.

"I'm calling him Hunter." King sat at the table with some of the others.

"I like the sound of that." Lola grinned, her rainbow-colored hair glinting under the strings of lights above them.

"So did you find any more dragonlings?" Avery asked. "Because if you do, I want one."

"We're still looking." They'd found some scent trails, but had been unable to actually locate any more.

"Have you taken Hunter to see Dallas yet?" Avery asked as she sat back in one of the chairs next to Mikael.

"Not yet. I'm hoping to bring him to her tomorrow." He glanced at Aurora. "Will you show Avery your sketches?"

She pulled out a few from her bag and laid them on the table, spreading them out in front of Avery.

Avery froze, her eyes widening slightly as she continued petting Hunter, scratching behind his ear. And he was totally eating it up. "That's Lindsey." She tapped a finger on one of the pictures.

He'd figured, but was glad to confirm. "Do you know any of the others?"

She scanned them quickly, frowning as she looked over the pictures. "No."

Mikael, however, leaned in closer and touched a finger to two of the sketches. "Both of these two males were at the dive bar the other night. This one was wearing the same leather jacket that Aurora drew as well."

Avery looked at him, her eyes wide. "You remember that?"

Yep, King was convinced that Mikael would be an excellent tracker for him.

"Of course," Mikael said before looking back at King. "They are definitely vampires. They didn't appear to be with Lindsey, however. And when she left, they didn't follow. They also didn't intervene when I…" He glanced at Avery. "Threatened her."

"They've all been seen around Tulane asking humans if they want immortality, if they want to become vampires. I'm going to make copies of these and distribute them. If you see anyone from any of the sketches," he continued, "keep your distance." That was directed to Avery. Mikael could definitely take care of himself.

King knew Avery had a spelled pendant around her neck but he didn't want to risk her getting hurt. She was a kind human, and he liked her. So did his new dragonling.

It was also clear that Mikael liked her—in the possessive way of dragons—and King hoped the two of them would eventually figure things out and mate.

Maybe your dumb ass will figure things out as well, his wolf grumbled.

CHAPTER TWENTY-ONE

"We will discover where she is," Mikael said to Avery as he locked the front door behind them. She'd been pensive, quiet on the walk home. And he'd scented a trickle of fear when Avery had seen that picture of Lindsey.

It was now his mission to find the vampire who thought she could attack Avery. He had given the female a chance to leave town, but she'd squandered it. Now she would die.

Blinking, Avery looked over at him. Before heading to see King, they had come back here and she'd showered and changed into jeans and a T-shirt. She smelled like sunshine and peaches. And now he knew that she tasted as sweet.

"I know. Or I certainly hope so. It's just a lot to take in. I wish I understood *why* she came after me at all."

"She will not be a problem much longer." He left his boots by the front door even as she took off her sneakers.

Her pale green eyes narrowed slightly. "What does that mean exactly?"

He simply watched her.

She bit her bottom lip as she looked at him, indecision playing across her expression. "Do you mean…you're going to kill her or something?"

"Or something. But I do not wish to talk about her." That vampire had forfeited her life by threatening Avery. Her death was now imminent and he wanted to talk about other things. "No one else is home."

She seemed startled by the shift in conversation and glanced around as if looking for her brothers in the foyer. "Not even your brothers?" She pulled her cell phone out of her pocket and looked at the time. "I thought they'd all be home now."

"No. I would hear or scent them."

The look she gave him then was…interesting. Almost like a scared rabbit. But she didn't have the scent of fear rolling off her. No, something else much more complex. "I'm probably just going to head upstairs."

"Alone? Or would you like me to join you?"

She swallowed hard. "Join me in my room?"

"In your bed. Or your shower. Or up against your wall." Where didn't matter to him. Only being with her did. "Just as long as we're naked and my mouth is on you."

Now a sharp punch of lust exploded off her. He inhaled deeply, savoring every bit of her pheromones. His dragon swiped at him. *Make your move*, he demanded.

That was exactly what he was doing.

"Mikael, you can't just say stuff like that."

"Why not? I believe I have been too quiet in my desire for you." And he was remedying that from this point forward. Avery was his mate, he knew it without a shadow of a doubt. He would convince her of it also.

She stepped forward and clapped a hand over his mouth. "No, you need to be *quieter*."

He nipped at her palm and that scent of her hunger grew even stronger. "Why? I know you want me. I can smell it."

She withdrew her hand, but she didn't put any distance between them. No, her chest rose and fell, her breasts rubbing against him they were so close. "That's not fair. What..." She cleared her throat. "Ah, exactly what do you want with me? Us?"

"To bury my face between your legs. To hear you come again." He'd thought that was clear. He wanted everything from her—forever.

Her eyes went heavy-lidded and he could see the war playing out in her head. Apparently he was pushing all the right buttons. Which meant he couldn't stop now. "I also want to feel you come around my c—"

"Mikael!" she squeaked out. "You... This... Us..." She took a deep breath, but still didn't step back. That was a very, very good thing. "I just want to make something *very* clear before we do...*anything*."

"I'm listening." All his muscles were pulled taut, the center of his universe right in front of him. Everything came down to this one moment, he was certain of it in the way he was certain he was a dragon.

"I don't want a boyfriend."

He blinked. *Boyfriend?* "Good thing I am not a boy." When another punch of lust rolled off her, he took his chance and slanted his mouth over hers, desperate for more of her. All of her.

She practically jumped him, no hesitation at all as Avery plastered herself to him, wrapping her legs around his waist.

This was it. What he'd been waiting for.

He grabbed onto her ass, holding tight, and raced up the stairs. He knew exactly where he was going, could make this walk blind, and he practically did so as he devoured her, his hard length rubbing up against her covered mound.

He hated that they had on clothing—and was tempted to burn it all off now.

As they reached his bedroom door—he wanted her scent all over his sheets—he slammed it shut and locked it. Not that he thought anyone would bother them, but he did it for her sake.

She tore her mouth from his for a moment, her lips swollen, her green eyes slightly dazed as she looked at him. "I'm serious, Mikael. No *boyfriend*. This is fun. We are having *fun*. That's clear, right?"

He wasn't certain *why* she was telling him the same thing again. He did not want to be her boyfriend. He was not a *boy*. He wanted her for his mate. And he definitely wanted to have fun with her. Lots and lots of it. Forever. There was so much fun to be had during sex, and something told him that with her it would be everything: fun, intense, mind-blowing.

He nodded and slanted his mouth over hers again. She tasted sweet, with a hint of the chocolate she'd eaten at Aurora's place.

"I get to see you naked now," she growled against his mouth as she practically tore at his shirt, her hands trembling with need even as she clawed at him.

His female had claws and he liked it.

He gently set her on the bed and stripped off his shirt because he could do this part much, much quicker than she could.

And he could admit that his pride swelled when her eyes widened, her gaze hungry as it raked over him. It was as if she didn't know where to look as she drank her fill. He'd never had a female look at him like this before, with such awe.

She'd peeked at him before, had seen him naked in the moments before he shifted, but this felt different. She wasn't looking away now, not trying to avoid him, and her cheeks had flushed a faint pink. He loved the look on her, loved that he got this reaction from her.

Though he'd planned to take his time stripping her bare—and he still would do that—he decided to give her a show.

Her chest rose and fell more rapidly as he unbuttoned his jeans and sloooowly slid them down his hips and legs.

Now her breathing was jagged as she continued to stare. He had never taken the time to do this. It had been so long ago for him, but all his former lovers had been female warriors. Sex had always been after battle, when emotions and adrenaline were high. It had been a way to release, for both parties. This felt different. He wanted to savor every moment of it. Wanted to savor every moment with Avery, regardless.

Her breathing was wild and erratic as she stared between his legs, her mouth falling open slightly. He stepped out of his jeans and wrapped his fingers around his cock, stroked once.

Startled, she snapped her gaze up to meet his, her breathing still just as ragged.

"You like what you see?" he asked, because apparently he needed his ego stroked right now. As well as other things.

It wasn't enough that she clearly enjoyed it, he needed to *hear* the words on a primal level. He wasn't sure what was wrong with him, this wild hunger riding him. But he had to know that he mattered to her. Only him.

"You're huge," she blurted.

He smiled slowly, her words doing more than she likely intended. He was glad she found him pleasing. Now he needed to show her that he knew what to do with his cock. Unfortunately he didn't think she was ready for it yet. She wanted him, yes. But he needed her desperate for him, the way he was for her. Needed her to be all in.

"Lie back," he demanded.

She did as he said and he pinned her beneath him, his cock rubbing against the fabric of her jeans.

He took his time kissing her, wanting to learn everything she liked as he slid his hands up her T-shirt. It didn't take him long to divest her of it. As soon as he had her T-shirt off, he practically shredded her bra, making her laugh.

Not his smoothest moment, but as her breasts spilled free he mostly forgot any thought process, much less his own name. This was different than the heated, far too quick orgasm he'd given her the other night. She'd been half clothed in her robe then and he knew he'd barely taken the edge off for her. He'd basically been walking around with a hard-on ever since.

He got to take his time with her now, savor her. Kiss every delicious inch of her. His gaze fell on her full breasts, her tightly beaded pale brown nipples.

"Why are you looking at me like that?" There was a tremor in her voice but it didn't sound like one of fear. No, that was longing he heard.

"Because I can't decide where to start." His words came out feral, more a growl than anything, but they were the truth.

He needed to see all of her, to devour all of her. His hands trembled as he tugged her jeans off and to his surprise she didn't even have on underwear.

"I still need to do laundry," she whispered, as if embarrassed.

He stared at the juncture of her thighs, swallowed hard. A soft thatch of dark curls covered her mound. "No. You should never wear them." Ever. In fact, she should never wear anything, but he knew convincing her of that would be impossible.

He couldn't believe she'd been bare beneath her jeans all night and he hadn't realized it. Blood rushed in his ears as he leaned down between her legs. This was heaven.

He inhaled, and as he did the scent of her lust seemed to grow even stronger, wrapping around him. She squirmed against the sheets but he reached up, placed a firm hand on her stomach. She did a lot of hard work, labored with her crew, and he felt the evidence of all her effort in the flex of her taut stomach muscles.

He reached higher, cupping a soft, full breast as he dipped his head between her legs. He needed more hands. Another mouth.

She moaned as he flicked a thumb over her nipple, her whole body jolting as he simultaneously teased his tongue against her folds. She was so damn wet and it was all too much. She was turned on, because of him—

because of them. He was damn sure going to make her climax again. More than once.

The other day had been a precursor to this. He'd kept his distance the last couple days, giving her time to come to terms with this shift in their relationship. He knew human females were different than shifters. She didn't have that same mating instinct he did and he had to respect that even if it drove him crazy.

He growled against her folds and she shoved her fingers through his hair.

"Mikael," she cried out.

That's right, say my name. He might've said the words out loud or he might have thought them, he didn't know.

A growl bubbled up as he flicked his tongue up and down her wetness, inside her. He wanted to drown in her, taste her orgasm on his tongue. He wanted her trembling from the pleasure, completely wrung out when he was done with her.

From the weekend, he knew how she liked to be touched, knew what pressure it would take to get her off. He'd used that knowledge for her first orgasm from him—and he was determined that she would have more than one tonight.

It didn't take long until she was rolling her hips against his face, faster and faster. So when he finally slid two fingers inside her and strummed her clit with his tongue, she let out a surprised shout. Oh, she was so very close. His sweet Avery was strung tight and ready to come.

She dug her fingers into his scalp as her inner walls clenched around his fingers, tighter and tighter. He didn't let up, continued teasing and thrusting as she writhed against his face. He felt her release even as she cried out his name again.

Her entire body shook, her inner walls clenching around his fingers as shudders wracked her body. When she finally collapsed he looked up to find her staring at him, her expression a little more than dazed. She looked a bit like she had the other night after she'd drunk too much.

"Mikael," she whispered and trailed off because that was apparently all she could say.

Good, his entire dragon snarled. *Keep going.*

Like he needed instructions.

He crawled up her body, slanted his mouth over hers in a crushing kiss. He wanted her to taste herself, to taste her climax.

She clutched onto his shoulders before sliding her hands around until she was digging her short nails into his back. She held on tight, as if she was afraid he might pull away.

His cock lay heavy between them but they weren't there yet. Well, he was there, but he knew she wasn't ready for the next step. They still weren't done tonight, however. Not even close.

He rolled onto his back, taking her with him so that she straddled him, moving so quickly she let out a surprised yelp. As she slid over his stomach, he felt the wetness from her release on his lower abdomen and it took all his control not to slide his cock against her slick folds. He wanted inside his female desperately.

Her dark hair fell around her breasts in waves as she looked down at him, her green eyes bright with emotion. "That was incredible."

"I want you to ride my face," he growled, the words out before he could try to think of anything smoother. His control was on a razor-thin wire.

Her eyes widened and that flush was back, as if he'd shocked her. When she didn't make a move, just watched him with that adorably shocked expression, he made a motion with his fingers, ordering her to turn around.

She blinked once, as if not understanding, so he lifted her up and flipped her around. "Scoot back."

"Mikael," she whispered, apparently only able to say his name again. Goddess above, he loved it when she said his name.

"You can do whatever you want to me." He grinned as she shuddered, but she still hadn't moved back farther.

Not that he was complaining about the view. Still, he was impatient, so he grabbed her thighs and tugged her back so that her pussy was completely over his face. He knew humans had an expression for this sexual position, a number of some kind.

He did not care what it was, he just cared that she came again. That he tasted her climax again. She was his addiction, one he would gladly give in to over and over. "Have you ever done this before?" he murmured, then realized he didn't want the answer. He didn't like the thought of her with anyone else like this.

She made a sort of strangled sound before she wrapped her fingers around his hard length.

Now he was the one who forgot to breathe as he waited, impatient to feel her mouth on him.

Finally, after what felt like a century, her tongue flicked against the head of his cock, circling the crown slowly, sensually. It was even more erotic because he couldn't quite see what she was doing.

Fuuuuck. He tried to stay still, so he wouldn't shove himself into her mouth, but it was difficult.

Focus, he ordered himself even as he lost more brain cells. Zeroing in on her pleasure, he flicked along her folds, the taste of her climax still there. He didn't care what it took, she was going to come again.

She took him fully in her mouth now, up and down, then she released him with a pop of sound. He loved the angle of her mouth as she stroked him, teased him, pushed him close to losing control. And when she leaned forward, licking him down his entire length until she reached his tight sack, he nearly lost it.

Goddess, this was too much. She was too much. She was everything.

She mixed it up, taking him in her mouth fully, then simply rubbed her cheek against his length. He never knew what to expect, he just knew that the feel of her on him was going to send him over the edge far quicker than he wanted.

And from this angle he had the perfect view of just how turned on she was. He continued teasing her folds as he slid both hands up the back of her thighs and over her full ass. He loved the feel of her smooth skin underneath his palms and couldn't resist smacking her ass once. She jolted and the scent of her lust spiked, sharp and heady.

Oh, she liked that.

Wanting to push her over the edge before he came, he then slid his thumb past her slick folds, getting it soaked before he moved it back farther, teasing her tight rosette. He didn't push fully inside her, just hinted that he would. He wanted to give her a little warning beforehand.

She let out a little squeak as he pressed against her tight entrance. Her breathing erratic, coming out in hot breaths that skated over his hard cock, she went still. "What are you doing?" she whispered.

He thought it was quite clear what he was doing. "You want me to stop?"

"No."

He grinned at that one desperate word and gently, slowly, teased his thumb inside her. She shuddered around him, her muscles clenching around his digit as he pushed knuckle deep. Shifting his arm up slightly, he reached around her with his other hand and began strumming her clit even as he continued teasing her.

As he did, he realized she could definitely come again. She was trembling much the same way she had before. So he started working her again with his tongue even as she did the same to him. She sucked him into her mouth and he imagined how she would look, how her cheeks would hollow as she dragged him deep.

Oh goddess, he wasn't going to make it.

"I'm coming," she gasped, starting to stroke him with her fingers only as her entire body shook and trembled. He slapped her ass once more and her entire body jerked. "Mikael!"

Her orgasm was sharper this time, the scent of it overpowering his brain and he lost control. As she came, still gripping his cock with her fingers, he did as well.

He came with a shout, growling against her slick folds. He might've said her name or nothing at all. He had no idea as he came in long, hot strokes.

Their orgasms seemed to go on forever and when she finally collapsed on him, half rolling off his legs with a laugh, he maneuvered her until her chest was flush against his.

Her cheeks were bright red now as she met his gaze, her naked body blanketing him. Heaven.

He loved the feel of her breasts against his, savored the skin-to-skin contact. He wanted to be naked all the time with her.

"Did you like what I did?" he murmured.

Her cheeks flushing a brighter shade of pink, she nodded as she stroked her hand over his chest.

"Maybe one day you will let me put my cock—"

She groaned slightly. "Mikael, I beg you. No dirty talk right now. I don't think I can handle it."

"It was just a simple question." And okay, he wanted to see her cheeks flush that dark shade again.

She started to respond, then he heard the front door open downstairs. "Someone is here… My brothers," he finally said when he scented them.

She glanced at the locked door before looking back at him. "Do you want me to leave, or…"

"No." Never.

"Good." At that, she laid her head on his chest, splayed her arm and leg across his body and simply relaxed into him.

He didn't push her with questions about the future or anything at all. He simply held her close, savoring this quiet moment where it was just the two of them. Naked and sated.

"This is going to sound crazy, but did you feel an earthquake earlier?" she drowsily mumbled a few moments later, her breath warm on his chest.

"Just get some sleep," he murmured, stroking his hand down her back. He didn't answer her directly because she had definitely felt the earth rumble beneath them. But it hadn't been an earthquake. His mating manifestation with her had kicked into overdrive. He needed to fully explain to her what it was to mate to a dragon, but…soon.

First he had to convince her to be his mate.

CHAPTER TWENTY-TWO

Mikael stepped into the kitchen the next morning to find Ivyn leaning against the countertop, drinking coffee as a pancake sizzled on the stovetop. His brother had been cooking for all of them since they'd moved in, trying new recipes. It was very interesting and something Mikael attributed to the new human female Ivyn was pretending he was not seeing.

"You came in late last night," Mikael said, pouring coffee for himself. Avery had been right, he now liked the stuff and found it was a nice part of his morning ritual—though he would much rather eat her every morning. He'd thought about that this morning, but she'd looked so peaceful that he hadn't wanted to disturb her. She worked too hard as it was.

His brother lifted an eyebrow. "And you did not sleep alone last night."

There was a hint of something in his brother's tone, he wasn't certain what though. Both Ivyn and Cas knew how he felt about Avery. So did her brothers for that matter. It was not a secret. "And?"

"And..." Ivyn sighed and flipped the pancake. "You're my big brother. I love you and...I love her too. But I don't want you to get hurt."

He blinked in surprise. He knew Ivyn liked Avery. They all did. Hell, they all adored her because she was perfect and wonderful. "If I get hurt, then I get hurt." He spoke quietly since he could hear her descending the stairs. He patted his pants pocket, felt the little button that had fallen off one of her work shirts. He'd scooped it up this morning and liked having it with him.

Ivyn nodded once and slid the pancake off onto a plate stacked with them.

"So why were you so late last night?" he asked, mainly to needle him a bit.

Ivyn swatted at him with the spatula. "None of your business."

Avery stepped into the room, her cheeks turning pink as her eyes met his. "Morning."

"Morning." He wasn't sure how things would be between them today, if she would openly kiss him or… He didn't know how he would feel if she wanted to hide things. Technically she could not hide anything from his brothers since they had supernatural sensory abilities and would easily scent her all over him. But she might not want to acknowledge that things had changed between them. He rubbed the middle of his chest.

"Pancakes?" She stepped into the room, her eyes widening slightly. "And is that whipped cream?"

"A friend of mine said we should try it on pancakes," Ivyn said, pouring another one.

"Friend, huh?" She snorted and gave Ivyn a brief hug. His brother kissed her on top of the head in a brotherly way and only a part of Mikael wanted to smash him in the face for touching Avery. Just a small part.

"Is there something you'd like to say?" Ivyn murmured to her, a grin on his face. "Because if you want to talk about my friend, let's talk about your sleeping arrangements last night, Avery."

Avery punched him in the shoulder and went to grab her own coffee but didn't respond. Instead she shot Mikael a look, eyebrows raised.

"Avery's sleeping arrangements last night are none of your concern."

She groaned as she poured creamer into her coffee then came to stand next to him at the countertop, wrapping her arm around his waist.

Mikael stilled at her show of affection. It wasn't like she was full-on claiming him when she wrapped her arm around him. But she kind of was. At least in front of his brother, here in the privacy of their kitchen.

"So you all know…about us?" she asked.

Ivyn simply shrugged and nudged a plate with two pancakes her way. "You need to eat."

To Mikael's surprise she leaned up on tiptoe, kissed him right on the mouth, then grabbed the plate.

It didn't matter that they'd shared a lot last night, her public claiming of him did something to him. His beast settled down in a way he had never experienced.

"Look, Mikael is a grown-up," she continued, as if his world hadn't just shifted under his feet. "And so am I." She put a dollop of the whipped cream on her pancakes. Then another. "So I don't want to hear anything from any of you about what we're doing. You all just keep your thoughts to yourselves. Or I'll start harassing you to bring your girlfriend around."

Ivyn gave her a salute and poured more pancake batter into the frying pan, a half grin on his face. Then he murmured, "She's not my girlfriend."

"Yeah right. Oh my God, these are so good." Then she moaned in a way that made Mikael's dick want to stand at attention.

Unfortunately they had a long day of work ahead of them. His poor cock was going to have to wait. Especially when he glanced at his phone and saw a text from King—that he'd sent to both him and Avery. Looked like they had an errand to run today.

* * *

Avery clutched Mikael's scales tight as he dipped lower over the treetops. They were going to see Dallas for a personal visit before meeting up with a contact of King's who'd flown down from Montana. In a plane, not as a dragon, though she thought their contact might be a dragon. Flights were a whole lot rarer now and as far as she knew, there weren't any commercial ones going anywhere. Some Alphas had managed to get some people who had been displaced back home—if they still had a home to go back to. But that was a level of organization she didn't even want to think about right now.

All she knew was that she was meeting someone about kitchen supplies, but not until she'd stopped at Dallas's. She wondered if she should feel guilty for taking a break to see her friend, but she squashed those thoughts. It was okay to see her friend and it wouldn't affect her current work timeline at all. If anything, they were ahead of schedule at this point.

Still, she had this driving urge to *always* be active lately. Subconsciously worried that if she stopped, the world would stop too. It was ridiculous, of course, and she was working on it. Though last night when Mikael had been giving her the orgasm of a lifetime, she hadn't felt guilty or thought of anything at all. Her whole body was still sort of in a state of shock after that—in the best way possible.

Mikael's expansive wings made the green leaves ripple like a giant wave spreading out before them. She didn't think she would ever get used to how beautiful he was in dragon form. Well, in both forms, but as a dragon he was this magnificent piece of moving art.

The smoky gray of his wings glittered almost silver under the sunlight, sometimes almost disappearing and other times they shone a brilliant silver. She petted one of his big scales, fascinated by the texture. They were hard but smooth, and not uncomfortable to sit on. Leaning down against him, she enjoyed the wind rolling over her.

Suddenly his big body jerked and she instinctively clutched him tighter. She knew he would never hurt her but this was the equivalent of turbulence during a plane ride.

He banked right sharply and that was when she felt it... A ripple of *something*.

A heavy blanket descended on her, in the air, though she couldn't see it. It scraped over her skin like talons, making all her hair stand up even as a prickle of awareness coated her from head to toe. She looked around, the wind whipping, but couldn't *see* anything out of the ordinary.

She could feel it, however. And it was clear Mikael could too.

Suddenly he banked even more sharply, diving in a hard angle toward a spread of farmland. He skimmed over it, jerking to a halt before rolling suddenly and tumbling her off.

She landed on the grass with a thud, though it was fairly gentle considering he could've literally thrown her off. "Mikael—"

Her eyes widened as a giant seam ripped open in...the middle of the air, as if the very fabric of the world had been torn straight down the middle.

Right. In. Front. Of. Them.

He shoved her back with his wing, roared loudly and flew straight at the tear. She stared in horror and raced after him even though she had no idea what the hell she was doing. And why was he flying straight toward it? They needed to get out of there. *Now.*

He breathed fire at the giant tear and abruptly disappeared into the opening. She jerked to a halt as it vanished. Poof. As if it had never existed at all.

Her heart racing, her breathing out of control, the deafening silence shook her to her core. She spun in a slow circle, looking for any signs of life. Everything was eerily quiet, the sun shining, the grass flattened in the areas where Mikael had landed and shoved her back.

But he was gone.

"Mikael?" she cried out, her word coming out more of a sob than anything else. "Mikael!"

She sucked in breath after breath as she tried to wrap her mind around what had just happened. Only problem was, she had no idea.

Panicked, she raced across the grass as she tried to find an opening or something... Some trace of him, maybe. As she reached the area where he'd disappeared, there was nothing there. Just flattened grass.

With a trembling hand she managed to get her cell phone out of her front pocket—and was glad it wasn't broken from her fall. But she had no service, which was no surprise. Even though most of the satellites were still up and running, a lot of towers had come down during The Fall. Reception was hit or miss, especially out in the middle of nowhere.

Think, think, think. She was maybe five miles from Dallas's farm. She could run back there if she could figure out how to get to a road or cut through all these farms. She hadn't been paying attention to Mikael's path, since he'd been flying.

She needed to call his brothers. They would know what to do. And if they didn't... Then she would go to King. Because she refused to think she might have lost Mikael. No way. A world without him in it? It was unthinkable. But she knew what she'd seen. An actual rip in the fabric of reality. Or...she guessed that was what it was.

She started jogging back in the direction they'd come from, panic riding her hard as she crossed the rest of the field. A huge pond stretched out in front of her and she let out a growl of frustration. As she tried to figure out which would be the easiest—and quickest—way around it, water shot up into the air, covering her in a tidal wave as a giant dragon with glittering scales the color of diamonds shot out of it into the air.

She fell backward, covering her face and curling into the fetal position as it burst into the sky above her. Her scream caught in her throat as she tried to make herself as small as possible.

It didn't matter. The dragon had seen her. It landed in front of her, its huge jaws opening wide. Then it shook its head and wings, throwing water everywhere, soaking her even more.

No, no, no. She had nowhere to go. Not that she could actually outrun *a dragon.* She grabbed her pendant instinctively, hoping it would keep her safe. But she had no idea how it would work against a dragon bite. Or dragon fire. Or...

The dragon inhaled deeply and looked at her, its head tilted to the side slightly.

Then sparks of colors flashed into the air and suddenly a tall, broad-shouldered male stood before her with a dark beard, gray eyes and a frown.

All she could do was stare.

CHAPTER TWENTY-THREE

Mikael let out a scream of fury, his dragon unleashing the raw power of his fire on the male on the ground.

The male, face obscured as if spelled, raised his hands and shot a ball of fire at him.

Mikael barrel-rolled to the left, but the fire clipped his wings. Surprised, he felt it burning—scorching along his scales. He let out another roar of fury and returned a blast of fire. It engulfed the male.

When it cleared, the grass around the attacker was gone, replaced with black, charred earth—but the man was still standing there.

Damn it!

Mikael couldn't see Avery anywhere, desperately tried to shelve that knowledge as he focused on the immediate threat. He'd flown straight into the opening, knowing that if he didn't, the enemy would come for Avery.

Now they were in a sort of magic bubble. He'd been trapped in these before, usually by witches who thought they were strong enough to take down a dragon. They were always wrong.

Something about this power felt familiar, however. But...that was impossible. The power was ancient, from a long-dead line of beings he wasn't even certain how to define in modern terms.

He flew upward and slammed into an invisible barrier. He was definitely in a spelled dome.

Take down this threat. Get to Avery. The words were a staccato beat in his head.

A blast of fire rolled upward at him. He pulled his wings in tight and descended straight toward the male in a free fall.

The male who smelled like vampire held out his hands again, drew them back and Mikael rolled midair. As he did, the blast of fire went wild, missing him completely. He shot his own fire at the same instant, engulfing the enemy again. He wasn't sure what this being was, but if the male was anything like dragons, enough firepower would weaken their strength and eventually Mikael would be able to rip him apart with his fire. It was what he was counting on anyway.

The male stumbled once then righted himself, the remaining grass rippling out all around him under the force of Mikael's firepower. It didn't burn the rest of the landscape, however.

Risking a glance behind him, Mikael scanned his surroundings again, looking for Avery.

Nothing.

Panic like he'd never known rode him hard and he screeched, blasting fire at his target again as he swooped back down through the air. If he could get close enough, he would bite the male's head off. In his experience, nothing survived a beheading. Because nothing was truly immortal. Long-lived, yes. But everything could be killed.

Fire blasted up at him from below, clipping his tail this time. He reined in his screech of pain, not wanting his attacker to know he'd been affected as he flew upward and then dive-bombed again, blasting fire as he did.

This dome was too small, making it impossible to gain much speed or even move to attack—which was likely the damn point.

Mikael attacked again and again. He wasn't sure how long they battled, how long they blasted fire at each other. It felt as if an eternity stretched out, though in battle time was often impossible to gauge.

When the male stumbled again, Mikael felt a shift in the power of the dome. Almost like an invisible crack rippling through the air. *There!*

A seam in the enclosure ripped open. Mikael was weakening him.

He breathed more fire, this time knocking the male onto his ass.

The seam rippled again, growing brighter. He could see outside the dome now. Could see patches of blue sky.

More fire flew at him, the reddish-orange flames weaker this time, and when a wild stream hit his wing, it rolled off him. Like oil and water.

This was it. This male was finally weak. He could take him out now.

Mikael flew in a sharp, deadly line straight at his target. He opened his mouth to blast fire—and chomp off his head—when the male wrapped a cloak around himself and…disappeared.

The dome around them cracked and shattered, the sharp, sparkling shards suspended in air before they suddenly disappeared into nothingness. Just as their creator had.

Avery! He saw and scented her at the same time, far over the field below him by a glittering pond.

A male was standing next to her—a naked male.

He didn't think, simply shot straight toward them, fire building in his throat. No one threatened his female.

CHAPTER TWENTY-FOUR

Mikael pulled up short as he descended toward Avery. He recognized that scent. And the male wasn't threatening her, but standing in front of her protectively.

He called on his magic before he'd even hit the ground. Pain and pleasure punched through him as a kaleidoscope of colors burst forth, a waterfall of sparks filling the air before he was once again in his human form.

Standing ten feet away, Mikael stared, shock too dull of a word for the emotions rolling through him. "Zephyr?" The word came out a strangled whisper.

Zephyr stared at him as well but he didn't seem to have the same shock. Or maybe he did, but it was overwhelmed by pure joy at seeing him. "My brother."

"We thought you died," he rasped out, staring at his older brother. A male he'd never thought to see again. Thousands upon thousands of years hadn't erased the memory of Zephyr. Mikael had taken on the mantle and responsibility of the oldest but he'd never wanted it, never wanted to replace the male in front of him.

"As you can see, I am still alive and as handsome as ever." Only an inch taller than Mikael, he was broad in the way dragon shifters were, had the same dark hair and gray eyes of their family line. Though he had a big beard and scars covering his body that had not been there before. So many scars.

Mikael stared, the tension in his chest a tight ball, and with every breath he took, shards cut into him. This was his brother, his oldest brother who he'd thought long dead. Murdered thousands of years ago. Now he was standing in front of him as if no time at all had passed.

"Mikael?" Avery whispered and he snapped to attention.

He moved quickly, putting himself between her and Zephyr, though he knew his brother would not hurt her. Or the brother he had known long ago would not. But the mating instinct was a powerful thing. It was the only reason he hadn't hugged his brother, hadn't reached for him. He needed to be sure this male was truly his brother.

He reached behind himself, clutched onto her hip just to reassure himself that she was there. "Everything's okay," he said as he watched his brother carefully. "Are you okay? Injured?"

"Everything's okay? You disappeared into thin air, came out breathing fire, and now there is a dragon who looks a lot like you standing in front of us and you seem surprised to see him. He also called you brother. So everything is totally fine. Just peachy!" Her voice trembled and he hated the sharp scent of her fear punctuating the air.

In front of him, Zephyr snorted softly, clearly amused by Avery. "Did you kill him?" Zephyr asked.

"No. I weakened him, but he escaped." Mikael had a lot of questions, like who *him* referred to—though he had a sinking sensation he already knew. "We need to get out of here. Get back to town. You're coming with us."

His brother looked as if he wanted to argue but then nodded.

"You can follow us," Mikael said as he stepped back, keeping Avery behind him. He knew she would have questions, but he needed to get her somewhere not so exposed.

"For the record, I have a lot of questions," Avery murmured.

"We'll get all your questions answered." He paused and turned to look at her, but kept Zephyr in his periphery. "I don't scent any blood. Are you sure you're not injured?"

To his surprise, she cupped his cheek and shook her head. He leaned into her gentle touch, savoring it for a millisecond. But that was all he would allow himself. They needed to move.

"I'm fine, but are you okay?" She scanned him in a much too clinical fashion for his taste. He only wanted pleasure in her gaze when she looked at his naked body. And he really didn't like the fact that his brother was naked so close to her.

He looked back at his brother, frowned. "Shift so my female does not see you naked anymore," he growled.

His brother blinked, then strode away, muttering under his breath before he shifted into a dragon.

A beautiful form that Mikael had never thought to see again. This was truly his brother, not an illusion created by dark magic. He rubbed the center of his chest, unable to believe that his older brother was here. *Alive.*

"I didn't know you had another brother," she whispered, drawing his gaze back to her.

"I thought he was dead. We have a lot to figure out and I promise we will once we get back to the house." He cupped her cheek gently, allowing himself only one more moment of this as he placed his forehead against hers. She was okay. Avery was alive and unharmed.

The rest of the tension slid away as she leaned into him, wrapping her arms around him and burying her face against his bare chest. She trembled, as if she'd been worried about him. *A dragon.*

* * *

In the front yard of their house, Mikael pulled his brother into a tight hug. He didn't care that they didn't have clothing yet—it had been thousands of years and his big brother had found them.

Zephyr held him tight, thumping him twice on the back, hard. "I can't believe you're here," Mikael said, voice thick with emotion.

"You guys." Avery's tone was tentative. "Maybe we should get inside."

Mikael turned to find Avery waving politely at two of their human neighbors standing catty-corner across the street.

"Because if you guys plan on hanging out naked in the front yard, it's going to cause a stir."

Her dry tone dispelled the tight lump of emotion lodged in his throat and he let out a laugh as he spotted the two women watching him. Both had whitish-gray hair and were staring, open-mouthed, at him and Zephyr.

Zephyr gave them a salute and a grin before turning away.

Inside, Mikael raced upstairs to grab clothing for both himself and Zephyr, who was only slightly larger.

When he came back downstairs, Avery and his brother were still standing in the foyer, Avery looking uncomfortable, glancing away from him. Zephyr was studiously ignoring her as well. That pleased Mikael a ridiculous amount because he didn't want her looking at anyone else naked except him.

Once his brother was dressed in jeans and a sweatshirt, Mikael motioned toward the kitchen. "Come on. Are you hungry? Where have you been? How did you find us?" he asked, even though it felt weird to just blurt the questions out.

"We have so much to discuss," Zephyr said, sliding a curious gaze at Avery as they all strode into the kitchen.

"Keep your distance from her," he grumbled as he pulled open the refrigerator.

Avery blinked at Mikael. "Why are you ordering your brother to keep his distance from me?"

He lifted a shoulder.

A tiny spike of fear rolled off her. "Why? Is he dangerous?" She took a small step backward.

"Yes," Zephyr said. "But not to you."

"Oh." She frowned at Mikael. "You're being weird."

He pulled out a jug of water and lifted it. Zephyr nodded so he poured all of them glasses. Maybe he was being weird. He did not care.

"So…where have you been for however long you've been missing?" she asked before Mikael could. "And who were you talking about when you asked if Mikael had killed 'him'?"

Before Zephyr could respond the front door flew open, and moments later Cas and Ivyn barreled into the kitchen. They swarmed their oldest brother and he hugged them back tight. It was clear Zephyr was fighting emotion as he gripped the back of his brothers' necks in a tight embrace.

"My baby brothers," he rasped out.

Both males wiped away tears as they stepped back, looking at Zephyr.

"I can't believe you're really here." Cas stared in awe. "Mikael texted us and I thought maybe he was mistaken or…" He hugged his brother again tight.

"I have missed you both. All three of you," he said, looking at Mikael again with a warm smile. "So much."

"Well our family has gotten even bigger," Ivyn said, wrapping an arm around Avery's shoulders. "We have a bossy little sister who keeps us in line, and two little human brothers."

Warmth spread through Avery at Ivyn's sweet words. She'd started thinking of all of them as family too, and it made her so happy that he felt the same.

"I think little sisters are supposed to be bossy," Zephyr said. He and Mikael looked the most similar, except for the beard he was sporting. And he had a few scars on his face and neck that looked as if they'd once been deep.

Mikael nudged Ivyn out of the way and pulled Avery close. He really didn't want anyone else touching her right now, something she could appreciate. She was still feeling out of sorts after what had happened. "Maybe we could go sit on the back patio and talk? It's clear a lot is going on, and after what happened… We need to figure some things out." And they definitely needed to tell King about it.

Once everyone was settled outside, Mikael said to Zephyr, "Talk. Tell us everything."

"When he came for us…" He cleared his throat. "I think he waited until the three of you were on that mission to attack the clan. He came right after you'd left. It had been maybe two full days."

Avery wanted to know who *he* referred to but it was clear the rest of them all knew, so she decided to save her question for later.

"He slaughtered most of us—"

"Most?" Mikael demanded.

"He tossed me into a Hell realm and he might have done the same to some of our cousins. I honestly don't know. One moment I was battling and…" He shook his head. "The next I was in another realm."

"Hell realm?" Okay, she couldn't resist asking just one question.

Mikael nodded slightly. "There are different realms throughout the entire universe. Different…I don't want to call them planets, because they exist simultaneously alongside this reality. Most humans and supernaturals can live in them, though I don't see how most humans would survive. Some are hellish but many are not."

That sounded a little bit like the multiverse theory. Avery kept the thought to herself though.

"They are all rough to an extent, filled with predators." Zephyr's tone was flat. "There is no room for weakness in them."

"I felt…the deaths of our parents," Mikael said. "I felt their life force snap. I felt so many others as well. I just assumed I felt yours too." Avery must have looked confused because Mikael took her hand and explained. "When related dragons or members of a clan are born or die, we feel it. It's subtle, but it's a sort of knowing."

"I felt their lives snuff out too," Zephyr said. "It was a waterfall of loss, all at the same time. That was when I woke up in another realm. I've only been gone for forty years. Or at least that was what I had thought until I escaped a few months ago."

Mikael shook his head. "It has been much longer, my brother."

"I realized that once I escaped."

"So how did you finally escape?" Mikael asked.

A dark smile spread across his brother's face. "Technically Ozias was the one who escaped. I just followed him out."

"He was in the Hell realm with you?"

"Yes. He followed me in not long after. My perception of time is skewed so I can't even guess how long after it was, based on this reality. It had been a month maybe—so I assumed. He thought I had the key and wanted it." He cleared his throat and glanced at Avery before giving a meaningful look at his brothers.

What key are they talking about? And who is Ozias? That guy Mikael fought? She bit the questions back.

"He was very mistaken. And he couldn't figure out how to escape." Zephyr's jaw went tight. "Unfortunately neither could I."

Mikael looked at her then. "Hell realms have specific entrances and exits. Some of them are terrible, vile places. Others…well, according to human ideals they wouldn't be pleasant, but for supernaturals they are more than livable. The downside to some of them is that there is always a very specific way to leave. Sometimes you may only leave at a certain hour of the day and you might have to climb a mountain infested with scorpion-like creatures to do it. And if you miss the opening of the, ah, portal I think I would call it, then you have to wait for it to open again.

And that's if it's not being guarded. In some cases, there's no specific time they open, but once they've been opened by an individual, they won't open again for another twenty-four hours. That's just an example. There are different rules for different realms."

When supernaturals had torn apart the world, Avery had handled things much better than most of her human friends. Mainly because she'd known about vampires, witches and shifters already. But...*this* was a lot to digest. "I might have questions later." Yeah, there was no might about it.

Mikael linked his fingers with hers and held tight as he nodded.

"I've been tracking Ozias for months," Zephyr said. "I lost his scent when those crazy dragons ripped the world apart. I finally picked up his scent again weeks ago, and here I am."

She had questions about this Ozias, but it was pretty clear from their conversation that he was a bad guy and that he'd killed their parents. She'd ask Mikael more later.

"Did you ever battle him in the Hell realm?" Cas asked quietly.

Zephyr nodded. "We did a few times. We were fairly evenly matched and… My concern was escaping. It was a very vast realm and for the last decade I managed to avoid him almost entirely. Then I started to hear whispers that he was making his escape. That he'd figured out a way. No one can keep a secret like that. At least not in a place like that. So I tracked him down and watched him."

"What is this key that he wants?" Avery asked, looking at all of them. "Is it in New Orleans?" There had to be a reason this Ozias was here.

The men all looked at each other.

"It's not something we really talk about," Mikael finally said.

"Oh." For some reason she felt weirdly hurt. She'd made it pretty clear that they weren't romantically involved, not like boyfriend and girlfriend or whatever. That they were just having fun. Still...it kind of hurt that he wasn't telling her something this important, and that had affected her too.

She stood. "Well we should probably call King and tell him—"

All of the males stood abruptly, their bodies vibrating with tension.

"No." There was no give in Mikael's voice.

She blinked. "You said that there's a 'Big Bad' in King's territory. A being who can throw people into Hell realms. King needs to know. I'm not a supernatural but even I understand that is a very basic rule."

The brothers all looked at each other and sat back down, Mikael tugging her with him. "I'm not going to tell him just yet."

She bit her bottom lip, conflicted. "You're putting me in a bad position. I don't want to lie to him."

"If King asks you directly about Ozias, obviously do not lie. But we're not going to offer up the information yet."

She didn't like this at all. Especially since she had no idea what this key referred to, or who Ozias was. What if it was like the key to the underworld? Which sounded kind of ridiculous, but Hell realms sounded ridiculous to her too. "He's the Alpha," she said quietly.

Mikael's eyes went pure dragon as he looked at her and he definitely did not like her saying that.

She squeezed his hand. "I didn't mean it like that," she whispered. Not that it should matter to Mikael anyway. They were just friends…with benefits.

Her words seem to calm him as his eyes returned to human.

Feeling out of sorts, she gently tugged her hand out of his. "I'm going upstairs. I need to check in with my crew and I need to at least let King know that we were delayed. I'll just text him that we had a family emergency." She really didn't like lying. Her brothers would always tease her about it but she practically broke out in hives if she had to. She didn't want anything to shake King's trust in her.

Mikael nodded. "If you want, you can tell him we were delayed by my brother. It's the truth and he will need to introduce himself to King, regardless."

A tight ball settled in her stomach but she nodded. She wanted to call her brothers to check on them even though she knew they were perfectly fine at the jobsite. But after the day she'd had, she needed to hear their voices. She would hold off on contacting King as long as possible, but would have to text him within the next hour no matter what.

She was also way too confused. She'd only wanted fun with Mikael. But now that he was withholding information from her, blocking her out of their family secrets, she felt…loss.

Maybe simple fun wasn't going to be enough for her.

CHAPTER TWENTY-FIVE

Mikael knocked on Avery's door, unsure what his reception would be. He knew he'd upset her, and every fiber of him hated that.

The door opened and he found Avery in a set of pajamas he'd seen her wearing in the past. Blue lounge pants with little dogs on them and a light blue tank top that hugged her breasts. For the last few hours he'd heard her working quietly upstairs, making phone calls, checking in with her brothers, and handling other job-related things.

Her expression was carefully neutral. "Hey," she said quietly.

"Hey. Are you hungry? Ivyn cooked before he left." His brother had gone to go see his human female, Mikael thought, though he hadn't actually said so.

Avery shook her head. "I'm good. I have a protein bar and a couple apples stashed away."

He frowned. That wasn't good enough. "I didn't mean to upset you before." She hadn't been downstairs in hours and he could feel the chasm opening up between them. He needed to fix it.

"It's fine. You had a big shock finding out your brother is alive after all these years. I still don't like not telling King about what happened."

"We're going to tell him." Mikael just wanted more time with Zephyr.

"Really?"

"Just give me a couple days." He had to help Zephyr locate Ozias, because the male was a threat to all of them. He would always be one—but Mikael couldn't leave Avery.

As if she read his mind, she said, "Look, I understand you're going to have to hunt this guy down. He killed your family and he attacked you today. I know enough about how supernatural law works. If you need to go, then go. If you're worried that I can't function without you," she said, her mouth curving up slightly, "I'm good. Promise."

"I know you can function just fine without me. You are one of the most capable people I know. But I don't like being separated from you," he said bluntly, basically baring his soul. Because it was true. "I will *not* be separated from you." Never from his mate.

She blinked as if he had surprised her. "Oh." She wrapped her arms around herself, the little dogs on her pajamas shifting with the movement. She needed pajamas with dragons—or she should just be naked.

"I'll figure things out with my brothers and how we're going to hunt him down." He knew he should ask if she wanted company tonight, but it was clear she didn't want him with her. He tried not to let that hurt when he was desperate to touch her, hold her, kiss her.

"I have to meet with that supplier tomorrow. King was understanding about us missing the meeting. I just told him we had a family issue to deal with and he didn't ask questions." Again she gave a half-smile. "He has enough on his plate to worry about questioning and micromanaging me, I think. But this guy came all the way from Montana and he's friends with King. We need to meet up and I need to see what he's got for my projects."

"I'll go with you tomorrow."

She shook her head, and though it was subtle, she took a small step back. "You need to handle *your* family business. And worrying about me is going to distract you. Clearly this guy is bad news and doesn't need to be in our territory. I've already talked to Santiago. He and Olga are coming with me."

Mikael gritted his teeth. Yeah, he would just see about that. "You're mad at me."

"Not mad. I'm just tired."

"I can scent when you lie."

Her brow furrowed. "That's not fair."

"I have been told that life is not fair."

She full-on glared at him then. "I'm not mad…exactly. I'm just feeling… Conflicting emotions, I guess. I'm kind of hurt that you wouldn't tell me about the key, and yes, I'm probably being irrational. Sometimes humans aren't rational," she said. "I know I'm the one who said that we were just having fun, that it's not like you're my boyfriend or anything. But I thought we were friends too, and…I thought I meant more to you."

What was she talking about? How did she not understand what she meant to him? "Explain this boyfriend talk to me." There were some things he still didn't understand and he thought there might be a miscommunication happening.

"You know...like boyfriend and girlfriend. I don't know if dating exists anymore." She rubbed a hand over her face, and in that moment she did look exhausted. He didn't like contributing to part of that. "I just meant we're not committed or anything, and I'm fine with just having fun with you." Her words and scent did not match, however.

He frowned as understanding settled in. "I'm not just having fun with you!"

Her eyes widened, at his tone or words, he wasn't sure.

"This isn't fun for me. I mean..." That sounded bad. "What we've done is a *lot* of fun." So much, and they had just started exploring each other. He wanted many, many more years with her. Forever, in fact.

Her cheeks flushed red but she still didn't speak.

"But it's more than fun for me. I am *committed* to you." He wasn't sure what that not-committed nonsense was about. "I don't want another female. I only want you." The very thought of her seeing anyone else had his dragon half growling angrily.

She rubbed her hands over her face again and let out a groan. The emotions that rolled off her were sharp, tart, the scent raking against his senses. "I...I need to get some sleep. It's been a long day and honestly I'm emotionally drained."

"I take it you want to sleep alone."

She paused then nodded, and the disappointment cut through him like a blade.

"I'm heading to bed. My door will be unlocked all night if you change your mind."

She paused as if she wanted to say more, then she stepped back and shut the door.

Inwardly groaning to himself, he laid his forehead against the door. Well that had gone well.

"Still the charmer, I see." Zephyr snorted softly from down the hallway before ducking into the room they'd given him.

Oh yes. Quite the charmer. He had miscalculated with Avery. But he would be remedying that very soon.

CHAPTER TWENTY-SIX

Avery ended the phone call as she hurried down the stairs. Neither of her brothers had slept in their beds last night, which meant they hadn't come home at all. She knew them well enough that they didn't make their beds until after they'd had coffee and a shower.

Neither were answering her phone calls or texts. She desperately hoped that when she got downstairs she would find that they had simply come home late and fallen asleep on the couch or *something*. It seemed unlikely but she was holding on to that hope.

She could hear voices trailing from outside and opened the back door to find Mikael and his three brothers all drinking coffee on the patio.

"What is it?" Mikael stood immediately.

"Anthony and Riel never came home last night. And they're not answering their phones. Would that guy hurt my brothers to get to you?" she demanded before he and his brothers could do one of those silent conversation things again.

They were all quiet, until Zephyr spoke. "Maybe. But he would use them as a bargaining tool long before he would hurt them." He had a similar faint accent to Mikael's, she'd noticed.

Mikael nodded, though his expression said he didn't want to agree. She wasn't sure if that made her feel better or worse.

"You know that both of them have been seeing different people," Mikael said.

"They would never ignore my calls or texts. You know that. Ever." That wasn't the type of relationship she and her brothers had. If one of them hadn't answered she would be okay, but both of them not responding? No. Her instinct said something was wrong.

"She's right," Mikael said, looking at Cas and Ivyn.

They nodded and looked at Zephyr, and Ivyn spoke. "They would never ignore her. She's like a mom and sister to them."

Mikael pulled out his phone. "We'll start searching—"

Her own phone rang and she almost jumped. She didn't recognize the number but answered immediately in case it was Anthony or Riel. "Hello?"

"If you want to see your brothers again, put Mikael or one of his brothers on the phone," a silky male voice demanded.

That little ball of ice in her stomach spread, coating everything in its wake. With a trembling hand, she pressed speaker. "They can hear you," she rasped out.

"So you escaped too, Zephyr," the male said.

Her gut tightened. All four males straightened and gathered around the outstretched phone, staring at it as if they wanted to murder whoever was on the other end.

"Why are you calling?" Mikael asked.

"I'm pretty sure you already know the answer to that," the male said. "Mikael, I know you care for the human female. More than care for her. I have her brothers with me—"

She gasped but Mikael held a finger up to his lips. She quieted but couldn't control the rush of fear, the blood pulsing in her ears. This man, this monster who had somehow created a rip in the fabric of reality and sucked Mikael into it—someone Mikael had battled with and not killed—had her brothers.

"I want to hear their voices. I need to know they're okay." Mikael's voice was ice-cold but she saw the fury in his gaze, his dragon peering out at her as he spoke.

She took a deep breath, tried not to panic even as it swelled inside her. Her brothers were wonderful and kind and she couldn't imagine a world without them in it.

"Avery?" Anthony's voice came across the line and he sounded young and terrified.

Oh, God. "I'm right here. You're going to be okay." If she sounded confident, she hoped it would give him hope.

"We're both here. Riel... They hit him on the head but he's going to be okay. I love you, Avery." Anthony's voice slightly trembled.

"I love you too." She clenched her jaw tight, trying to force back the tears that wanted to spill over.

"You will not hurt them," Mikael snapped out, his voice whiplash sharp. "I know what you want and I will give it to you."

The male made a pleased humming sound. "You gave in to that far too easily." Then the line went dead.

"Ozias wants the key," Zephyr said, his words filled with frustration.

Whatever the key was, she doubted they'd give it up for her brothers. Mikael might care for her, but she knew how the world worked. She'd seen it firsthand. Seen the way her father left her mother when she got too sick, too inconvenient. This key clearly meant a lot to them, so much so that he wouldn't even tell her what it was.

"I will get them back, I swear," Mikael said to her.

She simply nodded, her throat too tight to speak past the tears she was trying to keep at bay. He didn't say he'd give up "the key," just that he'd get them back.

Zephyr said something to Mikael in a language she didn't understand, drawing his attention away.

"Excuse me." She hurried back inside and toward the downstairs bathroom. Inside she sat on the toilet and then leaned forward, placing her head between her legs, breathing in and out as she tried not to go into a full-blown panic attack.

Then she sat up abruptly. No way in hell was she going to panic. Her brothers were depending on her. She had resources and she was going to use them. Pulling out her phone, she started to call Aurora but then remembered that the others would likely overhear her because of their stupid supernatural hearing. So she texted furiously, her fingers flying across the screen.

Emergency at my house. My brothers have been kidnapped. I need help. Please bring King.

That was as succinct as she could be. Avery knew that King would do whatever Aurora asked, and she and Aurora were friends. Avery also knew that King would help her if she asked, but she figured she'd get faster results if the request came from Aurora. Because something told Avery that one day the female would become the Alpha female of this territory.

Give me ten minutes. The text came back immediately and some of her tension eased, but only by the smallest fraction. Because her brothers had still been kidnapped, were being held captive somewhere, and she didn't know by who. Not really, other than the name Ozias.

Think, think, think.

Okay, so Aurora would bring King. That was good. But they needed more backup. She would ask every damn person she'd ever met for help if it would get her brothers back.

Going on instinct, she sent off a text to Prima, the dragon female she vaguely knew. Mikael knew her well and he trusted her, so that meant Avery did as well. And Avery knew the female was skilled. Plus Prima had once told Avery that if she ever needed anything at all, she simply had to ask. So she was going to take Prima at face value because right now she needed all the backup and firepower she could get. And it was going to take supernatural firepower to fight supernatural firepower.

Avery received a dragon emoji moments later in response. She blinked, unsure what that meant, hoping the female would hurry over here.

Standing, she shoved her phone into her jeans pocket. She thought about texting the Magic Man, but decided to hold off. First, she would wait for Aurora and King and hope they would help. King would be able to mobilize his pack quickly—if he decided to help. And she couldn't imagine he wouldn't.

Avery had lost her mother. And as far as she was concerned, her father was dead to her. She could not lose her brothers as well.

She simply couldn't.

CHAPTER TWENTY-SEVEN

When Avery stepped into the kitchen, she found Mikael and the others waiting, all standing and talking quietly among themselves. She hadn't even heard them come inside—quiet dragons.

"We're going to get your brothers," Mikael said immediately. "We're going to reach out to all our contacts and start a manhunt. Ozias has to be in the city or nearby."

Before she could respond, her phone rang again. Unknown number.

Mikael took the phone from her and answered, but thankfully he put it on speaker. "Yes." The word was dagger sharp.

"Have you decided what you will do?" That same silky male voice.

"I already told you I'd give you what you want. I'll exchange the key for her brothers. And if you try to double-cross me—"

"I have no need to double-cross you. If you give me what I want, you'll get what you want."

"They better not be injured."

There was a long pause. "They were a little roughed up, but they have no broken bones and none of their injuries are permanent. From this point forward I will not hurt them."

Even Avery didn't believe him. This male would hurt her brothers. She bit back a sob, forcing herself to remain quiet while they talked.

"Neither you *nor* anyone else will hurt them. Say it," Mikael demanded. "Swear it."

"I swear it."

"We will meet you—" Mikael started.

Ozias made a tsking sound. "You're smarter than this. You know how this works. I make the rules. You will meet at a place of my choosing. Do you need to retrieve the key?"

"I will have it by the time you want to meet up." He flicked a glance at Avery.

"Good."

"Do you know Boswell Cemetery?"

Before Mikael could answer, Avery nodded at him.

"Yes."

"Good. Be there one hour after sunset. I would tell you no backup but I know you'll bring your brothers. So please, bring them." He hung up.

"It's a trap," Zephyr murmured.

Mikael nodded along with his other two brothers. "He'll bring backup. He wouldn't meet all of us willingly. He chose after sunset so he could bring his 'turned' with him."

"What does that mean exactly?" she asked. He'd put too much inflection on the word turned and it wasn't like she didn't know what a vampire was. So…was he something else?

"He's like a vampire but…different. He can work spells, control fire, create illusions of sorts."

"Is he like a hybrid or something? Like a witch, I guess?" She'd thought only females were witches.

The brothers all paused, then Zephyr spoke. "When I was trapped in that realm, I heard others refer to him as the Dark Mage. So, yes, like a witch I believe."

"He has vampire qualities but he's powerful, as ancient as we are," Mikael continued. "And he has now fought against me one-on-one in a tight battle, so he will come at me differently next time."

"He's grown stronger in the time we were trapped," Zephyr said.

"So have I. We need to be prepared, however."

Everyone froze at the sound of someone knocking on the door. Avery must have looked guilty or something, because Mikael's gaze narrowed slightly.

"I called in backup already," she murmured. Before she could move, he sighed and hurried past her.

She followed after him in time to find Aurora, King, and all of Aurora's roommates—or packmates?—clustered on the front porch.

To her horror, tears sprung to her eyes that they had *all* shown up. They had come because her human brothers had been kidnapped. She and her brothers weren't supernaturals or considered special or integral to the city, but they were special to *her*. They were her entire world.

Aurora shoved past Mikael and pulled Avery into a tight hug. "We'll get them back," her friend said, even as Lola and the others pulled her into a tight hug as well, surrounding her.

She was with males the majority of the day, had more or less grown up as one of the boys, but having these female friendships touched her on a deep level. She allowed herself to be vulnerable, to trust all of these women.

"Thank you," she said as she wiped her tears away and stepped back.

"I need to know everything," King said quickly, drawing their attention to him.

"Let's do this on the back patio," Mikael said. "There's more room out there."

Before anyone could respond, the front door opened again and Prima strode in, strapped down with a plethora of weapons.

Mikael turned to Avery. "You called her too?"

"She texted me. Why wouldn't she? I am excellent at killing things." Prima, tall and gorgeous, looked almost insulted that he would even ask.

It made Avery feel even better about asking for help.

As they all stepped outside, Axel, who she hadn't even seen come inside with the others, wrapped his arm around Avery's shoulders. She'd never seen his expression so serious, so deadly. He didn't look like the laid-back lion now. "We'll save your brothers. I swear it."

Throat tight, she nodded. She didn't doubt they would. But she was terrified that they might not get them back alive.

"Thank you," she rasped out. Then she found herself being tugged away from him, Mikael physically body-checking Axel as he pulled her tight to his side.

"I'm not going to apologize for contacting everyone," she said almost defiantly.

"They are your brothers," he said simply as he squeezed her once. Then he turned and looked at everyone, nodding respectfully at King.

"First of all, this is my brother Zephyr. He recently escaped from a Hell realm."

When King simply nodded, it became clear to Avery that he

understood what that was. Apparently so did the others, because no one looked confused.

"Avery's brothers have been kidnapped because an ancient male named Ozias wants something my family possesses," Mikael continued. "Putting it in his hands would be detrimental to...everyone."

"How detrimental?" King asked.

Mikael rubbed the back of his neck, looked at his brothers.

It was subtle, but Zephyr nodded ever so slightly and Avery realized that Mikael was deferring to him, even though he had not seen him in thousands of years. It was definitely an older sibling or clan leader thing.

Mikael looked back at the others. "It's a key... It has the ability to open any Hell realm. Anywhere. No dragon blood needed. No sacrifice needed. Nothing. Just the key."

The entire group went preternaturally still, some staring in shock and some in horror.

Okay, so this was definitely a big deal. Avery wasn't exactly certain how big though, because she barely understood what a Hell realm was.

King recovered first. "You can't give it to him."

"I am well aware of this," Mikael said stiffly. "Not that I was asking for permission." He continued, though King's wolf flared bright at Mikael's words. "That said, I will do whatever it takes to get Riel and Anthony back. They are family to me too."

Avery felt his words like a punch to her senses even as Mikael continued.

"He will be expecting me to bring my brothers but perhaps not so much backup as everyone here. He is strong, skilled, and he uses...dark magic, I think it would be considered. He's called a Dark Mage."

"What's his name?" Aurora asked.

"Ozias," Zephyr and Mikael said at the same time.

King nodded and Mikael continued. They all talked, with Mikael going over everything he knew, Zephyr offering input, and then the others asking questions as they came up with a plan.

Avery knew it was a good thing she had called for backup, because it sounded like it was going to be a bloodbath at the cemetery. She couldn't fight the chills snaking through her because her brothers were human and they didn't even have spelled pendants to protect them. They would be defenseless.

She'd always known she was weaker than her supernatural friends, but in that moment she felt truly mortal, truly helpless. It terrified her. She hated that saving them would be up to others—even if she trusted those others.

As everyone continued talking, Mikael squeezed her shoulders once and motioned that they should walk inside. Instead of stopping in the kitchen, they hurried up the stairs until they were in his bedroom.

"I know you have a lot of questions," he said as he sat her on the edge of the bed. "Doors, or portals, to Hell realms can be difficult to open. They require dragon blood or sacrifice or powerful spells. Some don't need to be opened at all because of what is behind them. Some are simply places to escape to, places where supernaturals choose to exist instead of here. There are many, many creatures that should never, *ever* cross into this realm."

She nodded as she digested his words. "Okay, so if this Ozias has the ability to open any of them, he could potentially create another apocalyptic situation on earth is what you're saying?"

"Exactly. But it will not be like this. It will be literal hell on earth."

She closed her eyes, rubbed her hands over them. "So what happens when you show up without this key?"

"I will convince him I have it. At least temporarily. He knows how much I care for you."

She jerked slightly. "How can he *know*?"

Mikael paused. "He just does."

Okay, that was super helpful. She wasn't going to push, however, because it didn't matter right now. "So…what is the plan exactly?"

"If my brothers and I take him on, we'll be able to get your brothers back."

"Do you think he'll actually bring my brothers to the cemetery?"

"I don't know. But it should be easy enough to break those he's turned. A little torture and someone will talk. The real plan is to capture some of his people and find out more information. He won't kill your brothers, not until he gets what he wants."

She blinked in surprise at the casual way he spoke about torture.

His gaze was hard. "This is who I am, Avery. I don't want there to ever be any doubt in your mind. I will torture and kill and do whatever it takes to get your brothers back. I will do anything for you. *Anything.*"

She reached her hands up and to her surprise he actually flinched as if he expected… Well, she wasn't sure. She cupped his cheeks. "I know exactly who you are, Mikael." She brushed her lips over his in a more or less chaste kiss, just needing to touch him. He was the male who was going to save her brothers.

He tugged her so that she was sitting in his lap, wrapped his arms around her and simply held her tight as he buried his face in her neck. She held on to him for dear life, needing this anchor, needing him.

"I'm going to give you something," he whispered against her ear, so low she could barely hear him. "It's the key."

She jerked in his lap, but he held tight.

"I will tell no one that you have it. Not even my brothers. And if asked, I will say I do not have it in my possession, which will not be a lie. I trust you more than anyone. You'll keep it safe."

She leaned back to look at him, floored by his trust in her. "I could give it to him, trade it for my brothers," she whispered.

"I don't think you will. I don't think you would put the rest of the world in that much danger. Even for them."

He was right. She would do anything for her brothers but… She couldn't sign a death sentence for countless others in exchange. They wouldn't want that and she wouldn't want that either if she was in their situation. No, they would simply have to rescue her brothers. That was all there was to it. But the truth was…if it came down to her brothers, or Mikael or Mikael's brothers, she would do anything to save those males. "You think too highly of me, I'm afraid. I will do anything to save them. You as well, if it came down to it," she added.

His dragon flashed in his eyes once, stayed there. Watching. Waiting. Then Mikael was back. "You can't come with me," he continued.

She knew that even as she hated it. "I hate being so weak."

His dragon flared in his eyes again, fiery hot. "You're not weak. You are the strongest female I know." He kissed her again, and this time there was nothing chaste about it as he teased his tongue against hers.

She jerked back when she felt the earth start to shake. "You felt that, right?" If he hadn't, she was pretty sure she was losing her mind.

In response, he sighed and brushed his lips against hers before standing, pulling her with him. Then he lifted a leather cord hanging around his neck—that she hadn't even seen until that moment—and slipped it over her head.

She looked down at it and lifted up the heavy piece on the end of it. "What is this?" Whatever was attached to the cord was covered by a piece of leather. It was stitched in place so she couldn't open it without pulling the threads free.

"The key." His voice was so quiet. "Don't take the cover off. If you do, everyone will be able to see it. It's bright. But if you need to, simply pull on this thread and it opens easily."

It was also warm, she realized as she felt the heat through the cover.

"It has a mild spell on it. No one will see the cord around your neck unless you lift it off."

She tucked it under her shirt right next to her spelled pendant, the warmth of it making her very aware of the kind of power she had hanging around her neck.

It was terrifying.

And she hated that Mikael was going to put himself in danger for her, her brothers, even though she would expect nothing less from him. She tried to put a cap on her worry for him, but it was impossible.

Stepping forward, she pulled him into a tight hug, holding him close as he held her back. She didn't want to let him go. Not now, not ever.

CHAPTER TWENTY-EIGHT

Standing in the front yard of Aurora and her crew's mansion, Mikael looked down at Avery. He didn't like leaving her.

She had her arms wrapped around herself and bit her bottom lip as she stared back up at him. "Be safe," she whispered.

"I'm a dragon," he reminded her. And nothing would stop him from coming back and claiming her. Nothing at all.

"And if fighting and battles depended solely on your ego, you would win against the entire world within two seconds flat." Her tone was dry, but her lips quirked up ever so slightly.

He grinned. "So true."

Her smile grew and he savored it, as always. Making her smile and laugh could become his only mission in life. But he didn't have time to waste so he reached for her, pulled her close. As she hugged him back, he buried his face against her hair even as he threaded his fingers through it, cupped the back of her head and inhaled deep.

"You stay safe," he demanded, as if he could will it to happen.

He hated leaving her, but he knew she was in more than capable hands. Aurora and her crew were all warriors. And he'd seen them in battle—they were fierce fighters. Not to mention she had the Magic Man's pendant protecting her. Still, he did not like the thought of being away from her at all. She was his, and as soon as this was over and he brought her brothers home safely, he was claiming her for good. If she would have him.

"I..." She cleared her throat and looked at the others who were waiting for him. "We're going to finish what we started in your bed," she whispered, but even if she thought it was low enough, he guaranteed the others heard her words.

He was glad they'd heard. His heart and body belonged to her. Everyone should know it.

"We will," he said simply. They would definitely finish what they had started. And he never planned on stopping.

He kissed her swiftly, a hard claiming of her mouth. Then he forced himself to stride away, to meet the others, to not look back. He could *not* look back at her. If he did, his resolve might falter.

As he reached the others, he was surprised to find Axel standing there, arms crossed over his massive chest, watching him. "What are you doing?" The lion might annoy him but Mikael wanted him here watching after Avery.

"I'm coming with you. I love those kids."

Anthony and Riel weren't exactly kids but… Okay, they more or less were. At least by supernatural standards. Maybe even human standards, considering how immature her brothers were. He nodded once at the lion. Then he looked at his brothers, who were clearly ready to go.

He was too. They'd opted to drive out of the city and park at a distance from the cemetery and then fly in. King had already sent a couple scouts ahead to the cemetery and they'd been keeping an eye on it all day. No unusual activity. But sunset would be in an hour and he wanted to get there before that happened.

"We need to make one stop on the way. I need to see the Magic Man before we head out of town," Mikael said.

No one questioned him, though Zephyr did raise an eyebrow, likely curious who this Magic Man was. It didn't matter.

The drive to meet him was short, with little traffic, mainly because humans were not driving nowadays. He jumped from the van, the others staying put, and as he reached the carved wooden doors, they opened.

Malcolm, one of Thurman's nephews, stepped out with a small round box. He handed it to Mikael. "My uncle said you were coming by for these. They are what you need," Malcolm said.

Mikael knew he shouldn't be surprised, but nonetheless, Thurman was very clearly a gifted seer. "Tell your uncle thank you. I know I told him before that I owe him a debt. Please convey that I am now in his debt for life. Whatever he needs, just ask."

The young man nodded once. "Good luck."

Tucking the box into his front pocket without even looking inside—because he trusted that what he needed was there—he hurried back to the van.

Prima gunned the engine and for a brief moment he wondered who the hell had thought it was a good idea to let *her* drive. Then his head slammed against the side of the rear passenger door as she took a sharp turn as if they were being chased by hounds of Hell.

"Someone else is driving on the way back," Cas muttered.

Yes, indeed. Because they would come back from this. With all of them against Ozias, they would succeed. They would save her brothers and he could return to his Avery.

CHAPTER TWENTY-NINE

"I thought you were bringing them to the meeting," Lindsey said to Magnus, keeping her tone neutral.

He shook his head, dismissing her completely as he worked on…something. He was mixing random ingredients together in a bowl, and had been quiet as he worked. He hadn't told her to leave, however, so she was watching what he did and trying to remember everything. She'd learned at a young age that knowledge was power. She'd also learned that people only respected power and money—and that so much of the money in the world was passed down within families so the rich stayed rich.

It was why she'd married into money—to a fool who'd planned to leave her everything. Until The Fall happened.

"Should I kill the brothers, then?" she asked. If he wasn't taking them, she hoped she got to kill Anthony and Riel. Maybe she shouldn't feel so gleeful, but after she'd married their father they'd cut him out of their lives. Which had made her life that much more difficult.

All of her ex-husband's attention and neediness had been directed at her. She'd married him thinking she'd get the country club life—but most of his friends had cut him out too. She'd made an error in her calculation. And the rage that lived inside her, always simmering right underneath the surface, needed an outlet. Killing Anthony and Riel would hurt Avery too.

He didn't bother to look at her. "They are my bargaining chip. Do you really think killing them would be a wise choice?" The way he asked made it sound like he thought she was brain-dead.

She swallowed hard, fighting back her anger. "No. Just trying to understand what you're doing." She hated that she couldn't manipulate Magnus. Maybe it was time to cut her losses and leave.

"You are too young and your brain is too small to understand much of anything," he said dismissively.

Anger swelled inside her like a tsunami, but she bit down hard. She *hated* how much he dismissed her, how he seemed to think she and all the others he had created were beneath him. Nothing. Yet he still needed them for whatever his plan was—and he didn't tell any of them much. So far he'd created thirty vampires who all lived at this homestead in the country with him. Thirty that she knew of anyway. And he'd had to kill a few, ones who had been stupid and killed humans, fed on them until they had no blood left to give. Fools.

She knew they were going to some cemetery with him once the sun set to face off with a bunch of dragons. He'd given her something to drink before, something that let her walk in the sunlight for a brief time, but when she'd asked him about it, he'd told her that he couldn't create the potion for all of them. He'd simply wanted her to kidnap Avery—though Lindsey had planned to make her bleed first—and bring her back. He'd been too careful to go into the city, however, worried that others would sense his power. So he'd sent Lindsey. She'd foolishly thought it was because he'd started to trust her. Now she knew better. She wanted to leave now, before the fighting started later.

He'd told Mikael to come alone but obviously the dragon shifter wasn't going to. That male would definitely bring his brothers. Maybe others too. She knew that much.

Lindsey didn't even want to go at all, couldn't see how it would be anything but a bloodbath if it came down to a bunch of dragons and young vampires. It wasn't like she was trained or very old.

Annnndd *that* was when it hit her.

Maybe that was the whole point… Maybe she and all the others were merely cannon fodder. They were the front line Magnus would send ahead to slow the fighting.

Because they were all expendable to him.

Oh God, she was so stupid. How could she not have seen this before? "Should I stay behind and watch the brothers?" she asked casually.

"I have someone coming to pick them up and transport them elsewhere. Some humans will be watching them for me." He sliced his palm and added some of his own blood to the mix of whatever that green concoction was. Then he continued stirring. Whatever was in the pot smelled like dirty socks combined with onions and gunpowder.

"Okay," she said, biting back every ounce of emotion inside her. "Should I bring any extra weapons or anything?"

He sighed and she knew she had annoyed him at this point. "Yes. Tell everyone to gear up. Bring any weapon you think will be beneficial. We leave in ten minutes."

She was going to gear up all right, but there was no way in hell she was going to fight a bunch of dragons and end up ash for him. He'd offered her immortality. She would have that.

And she was going to enjoy a lot more years to come. Unlike some of the other members of what she was now realizing was quickly turning into a cult, she didn't worship him. He'd given her a gift and she wasn't going to squander it.

She couldn't just leave though, not when it was still daylight out. She would have to bide her time, be smart about things. No, she was going to use the cover of night and the destruction of battle to make her escape. She had no idea where she was going after this, but it certainly wasn't going to be sticking around to die for another male who cared nothing about her.

CHAPTER THIRTY

Mikael circled above the cemetery, looking for Ozias and trying to catch his scent. His brother and Arthur and Prima were above him and would be acting as backup but he would be the one to meet with the traitorous male.

Ozias had no doubt tracked the key to New Orleans. It must be why the male was here. Mikael could hide its existence for the most part; it was spelled to look like an inert object, but it constantly put off a pulse of low-grade magic. At least now he knew it was in safe hands. And the truth was, if something happened to him and Avery needed to trade it for her brothers' lives... So be it.

He was not like her; he would trade it for her life in a heartbeat. And he didn't care what that said about him. He understood the concept of the greater good and for the most part he agreed with it. Except when it came to her. Avery was his greater good. Avery was everything.

The scent of Ozias, evil, ancient and putrid, drifted on the air. The male had arrived.

Keeping his camouflage in place, Mikael glided downward, scanning the cemetery.

Ten minutes ago he'd checked in with King's people and they had spotted a cluster of vampires coming from various directions, descending on the cemetery en masse.

The place was out in the country, a rural area that looked as if it hadn't been touched in months. The grass was wild and overgrown, and from the air he couldn't see many indentations in the grass, so this place wasn't well-traveled.

Which was likely why Ozias had picked it. He wouldn't have picked somewhere in the city where all supernaturals pledged allegiance to King and his group of leaders.

It was also unlikely that the male knew Mikael was, if not friends with King, at least friendly. He didn't think Ozias would be expecting

Mikael to bring more backup than his brothers.

As he descended, it was like an invisible cloak or wall dropped, revealing ten vampires lined up behind their master, who was standing tall on a gravestone.

Always the showman.

Ozias liked to create havoc wherever he went, uncaring about the lives he destroyed. No, the male simply liked power and taking more of it.

There definitely had to be more than the ten below. Not that he was worried about a bunch of baby vampires. He could handle those alone, with no backup—fire would incinerate them.

Instead of shifting, he flew down at a sharp angle, reveling in the gasps of some of the vampires behind the mage hybrid.

They really must be newly turned. Pathetic.

At least Ozias didn't flinch or act surprised.

Mikael landed on top of a row of crumbling gravestones and stretched his wings out once, showing off their great span before he pulled them in tight to his back. Then he yawned, stretching his jaws wide to show his teeth as he eyed Ozias. He wasn't going to shift until he saw Avery's brothers. He didn't scent them, however, so he knew they weren't here.

Big surprise, Ozias was a liar.

"Shift," the male demanded. He looked the same as Mikael remembered—unmemorable. Except for his eyes. It was a bizarre thing. This male was ancient, powerful, but had the type of face you would have a hard time remembering. With dark hair, and a too-slender build for his taller frame, nothing but his glowing eyes stood out. There was an eerie red quality to them.

He yawned again, knowing it would piss Ozias off. And the sight of his big teeth would likely terrify the others. Then he flapped his wings out impatiently.

"I have to see the key first," Ozias snapped.

He sighed. Apparently they were going to do this. Mikael half-shifted, something that was incredibly difficult to do and something he rarely showcased. Not many dragons could do this. He shifted partially to human but kept his wings extended.

For the first time since he had known the ancient hybrid, he saw a flicker of surprise in the male's eyes.

"I don't smell them," Mikael said simply.

"They're nearby. I couldn't bring them here. You know that."

Mikael couldn't scent if the male was lying—probably because he was what Avery called a psychopath. There were some beings that never put off that acrid scent when they lied. It had something to do with the chemistry in their brains, he'd been told. Some people were just evil, in his opinion. It happened with supernaturals and humans alike, though the psychopaths were rare enough in both species.

"How close are they?" he demanded.

"Where is the key?" Ozias countered.

"Close."

Ozias jumped down from the gravestone, the ridiculously long cloak he was wearing billowing around him as he strode forward. "You lie."

"Do I?"

"I can smell it on you."

"Then I guess we're both liars, because you didn't bring them." He breathed out fire even though he was half-shifted, giving the signal to attack. If the brothers weren't here, then he was done with this male. He needed to kill Ozias and keep at least one or two survivors. It would be much easier to torture and break one of these baby vampires into giving up the brothers' location.

As five dragons dropped their camouflage and descended from the sky, Ozias lifted his hands up wide, then brought them down with a savage scream.

The ground shifted beneath Mikael's feet as magic rippled through the air. He took to the air, his wings propelling him upward even as a vortex of swirling blue and white opened under his feet.

Oh, hell.

He strained against the wind, the sucking pull of the Hell realm door, the muscles and tendons in his wings pulling tight as he fought against the whirlwind.

Even as he struggled, he could see his brothers arrowing toward him, trying to save him. *No.* He couldn't let them get sucked in too. They needed to stay. To fight.

To protect Avery.

"No!" he screamed at them.

Surrendering, he pulled his wings in tight against his body, Avery his last thought as he fell into the vortex.

CHAPTER THIRTY-ONE

King raced across the graveyard as dragons torpedoed down from the sky, his sword singing with power. Ever since Aurora had shot it full of her lightning bolts, it was even more powerful than before.

A hideous scream went up as a couple dozen screeching vampires dropped down from the trees.

It was time to fight.

For the moment, he was going to shelve the fact that Mikael had just been sucked into a Hell realm. They would have to deal with that later and get him out. Mikael was a powerful dragon; he would survive—but King hated to think how devastated Avery would be if the dragon didn't.

He swung hard as a vampire with longer than normal fangs raced at him, hissing like a wild cat as he lunged. The thing let out a disturbing clicking sound that King would not soon forget.

As the vamp sprung at him, King sliced his head off in a simple arc. He was aware of dragon fire all around him, screams filling the air as he sliced off another head. Then another.

And another.

There was fire to his left and behind him as he and two of his wolves mowed down vampire after vampire. Most of his pack had shifted and were ripping off heads and body parts, but he was using his sword for this battle.

The leader of the group had disappeared into the melee, something that was weak and pathetic, in King's opinion. He'd sent his people off to be slaughtered so he could escape.

The fight was over in minutes, and he kicked a male vampire who couldn't have been more than thirty years old when he'd been turned. One of his wolves started to pounce on the vamp but he held up a hand and sheathed his sword. "This one lives."

The male crab-crawled away from them, bleeding from his head and wrist as he tried to escape from King and the wolves that had already surrounded him.

"It's your lucky day," he said as he stalked toward the male, his wolf in his eyes.

The stench of the vamp's fear nearly made him gag.

"You've got a couple options," he continued. "I'm going to let you live for now. But only if you tell me what I want to know. If you don't, I'm going to hand you over to those dragons behind me. And then when they're done torturing you, they'll give you back to me and you'll tell me what I wanted to know from the start. So you can save yourself a lot of time and pain by talking now. Because from your scent, I can tell you are a *very* newly turned vampire. So you won't be aware of the hierarchies of the shifter communities." He leaned close then, as if telling the male a secret.

The male stared at him, raw terror in his glowing green eyes. His fangs withdrew and now he just looked like a scared human. If he had still been human, King had no doubt he'd have already pissed himself by now.

"Dragons are very good at extracting information. And they can keep you alive for a very long time."

"I'll tell you whatever you want to know," the man whispered. "I saw Lindsey escape before we started fighting. She hung out on the outskirts when the dragon descended, and then she turned and ran." His voice was growing stronger now. "I stole a bunch of cocaine from my drug dealer before I was turned. I killed him too. But only because he was going to shoot me for not having enough money to pay off my debt. I also robbed a liquor store on Douglas Street, but that was before The Fall. I felt bad about it so I washed his windows and swept in front of his shop for a week."

Okay, so this vamp was telling King *everything*.

King thought he heard one of his people snort in amusement as the man continued telling secret after secret. King held up a hand because it was clear the young vamp was never going to shut up. "That's enough. I don't give a shit about any of that. I want to know about your maker."

"Magnus?" Fear intoned his words.

King stilled. *Magnus?* Was it possible that Magnus and Ozias were the same person? The male had mentioned a Lindsey... "Yes. Tell me everything about your maker. The male who led you all tonight."

"Boss! You're going to want to see this!" Delphine called out.

King pointed at the male on the ground and gave him a warning look. "Don't move."

Ace, still in wolf form, prowled closer, revealing his canines as he let out a low, deadly growl.

The vampire shrank into himself, curling into a ball.

Dismissing the vampire, King turned and strode toward Delphine, who was standing next to a fallen gravestone.

As King reached her, he cursed when he saw that it had been hiding a trapdoor. An escape route. The male hadn't used magic to escape after all.

"We track them," he ordered. Delphine was already jumping into the hole along with Axel, who was in lion form, before King had finished. Then he turned to the dragons. "Span out, search the area." Maybe they would get lucky and they would see Magnus—or Ozias—aerially. He didn't need to give an order to Ace, who would haul that vampire back to the compound and question him until he cried.

He'd deal with that vampire later.

No matter what happened, whether he found this vampire or not, he had to figure out where Mikael was.

He also had to tell Avery what had happened, and he wasn't looking forward to that.

* * *

Hours later, King walked into the small room where their captive was being held. Though the vampire was not in chains or restrained, there was nowhere for him to go. And he knew it. "How were you recruited?" he asked as he strode inside.

Ace hadn't had a chance to question him because something more pressing had come up.

Now King was ready to get his answers.

The man, who had been human not long ago, blinked. "Recruited?"

King kept his expression passive as he looked at him but bit back a sigh. "The male who turned you. How did he convince you?"

"A woman did, Lindsey. She's one of his. We all are. But she approached me at a bar and offered me immortality." He cleared his throat. "And sex."

"So it's as simple as that? He offered you immortality in exchange for what? To follow him? Worship him?"

The male shook his head. "No, nothing like that. It wasn't supposed to be like that. He said he was going to talk with someone and just needed backup. We were just a show of force."

Christ, this guy was stupid.

"Lindsey left though, when the fighting started. I saw her escaping and started to ask her what she was doing, but I quickly realized. She was smart enough to run. Look, I don't have any beef with you or your people. I just wanted immortality. I'm not a killer."

A dull throb started in King's temple as he leaned casually against the wall. "Good thing for you I can sense that you're not lying. So tell me more about Magnus. I want to know everything, including where you've been staying."

"A farmhouse," he said immediately. Then he started giving information, spilling every little detail he could think of.

Mid-conversation, King straightened. He knew the place this guy—whose name he still didn't know, or particularly care to know—was talking about. He turned, and before he'd made it to the door, it swung open and Ace stepped inside. He'd clearly been listening and knew the area the guy had been describing as well.

King turned back to the vampire. "You're going to stay put and write down every single thing you remember of your time with Magnus. Every. Little. Thing." Then he shut the door behind him and posted a guard there. The vamp might be too afraid to leave now, but he might be stupid enough to try later. He was young and not very skilled at fighting so he wouldn't get far if he did. But hunting down an asshole wasn't something King wanted his people to waste their time on.

As he hurried down the hallway with Ace next to him, he said, "I've got a stop to make, but I'll meet up with you guys on the way. Let the dragons know and grab four of our own. That'll be enough."

Ace simply nodded as they stepped outside onto the semi-busy street in the Quarter. King went right and Ace headed left to gather up the others.

Hunter swooped down from the top of the building across the street where he'd been patiently waiting for King. The dragonling flew right next to King as he jogged down the sidewalk, his chirping, constant companion lately. "You miss me?" he murmured.

Hunter chirped an affirmative—he'd let his annoyance be known when King had forced him to stay behind for the cemetery battle.

It didn't take long to make it to Aurora's house, where Avery was staying. Unfortunately Aurora wasn't there—she'd had to check on some supernatural friends of hers about something. Probably just as well because she was a distraction—his kryptonite.

Outside, behind the mansion, everyone had given them privacy. And though he'd sat at the table, hoping to make Avery more relaxed, she was still standing, hands shoved into her cardigan pockets. "Please tell me what's going on," she said. "I know something's happened. Everyone has been really weird. Is Mikael…hurt?" Her voice broke on the last word.

He stood, since it was clear she wasn't going to sit, and moved closer to her. The yard was lit up with a plethora of Edison-style lights and a few chickens were walking around—but keeping a wide berth from Hunter, who was a few feet from King.

"There was a battle at the cemetery. It appears as if Magnus and Ozias are one and the same. He set a trap of sorts, we believe to trigger the opening to a Hell realm." He knew she was aware what they were after the last conversation they'd had. "Mikael was sucked into the vortex before any of us could get to him."

She gasped and put a hand over her mouth but he continued.

"The good thing is, he's a dragon shifter and he'll be at the top of the food chain in *any* other realm. I know this is hard on you, but Mikael is tough and damn near impossible to kill. We're currently hunting down Ozias and will do *everything* we can to find out which realm Mikael was taken to. We're also scouring the city for your brothers."

Her breathing had increased and he could hear her out-of-control heartbeat. Normally he could tune out the sounds of heartbeats, but right now it was just the two of them plus Hunter, and Avery was close to panicking. Her eyes were dilated as she dragged in shallow breaths. "Mikael will survive a Hell realm?"

"I have no doubt he will. And I have a potential lead on where your brothers might be held—I wanted to talk to you in person but I swear we're going to do everything possible to find Mikael and your brothers. And you know his brothers won't stop until we do."

She slowly nodded, shoved out a long breath. Her breathing had somewhat evened out, but her eyes were still dilated and he could scent the fear rolling off her, the sharp metallic scent bitter on the air. "Thank you for coming to tell me in person. Do you know anything in particular about the spot Mikael was in when the portal opened? Maybe Thurman knows something we don't. Maybe he'll have some insight about the area. The Magic Man knows a lot, and if you haven't tapped him for information…I will." Her lips pulled into a thin line, as if daring him to stop her.

King paused. He didn't want Avery going off and doing anything rash, but…he also couldn't stop her from going to see the Magic Man. Besides, Thurman would talk more easily to her than one of his people, that much King knew. Thurman always played his cards close to the vest but there were a select few people he communicated fairly openly with, almost all humans or witches. So King gave Avery the details she'd need, right down to the name on the gravestone that had split open during the portal opening and Mikael disappearing.

"Thank you," she said. "I'll have my cell phone on me. If you find out anything more…" She cleared her throat. "Just don't leave me in the dark about Mikael or my brothers, please."

"Of course not." With some people he would, but not with her. She could handle honesty. "I don't think I need to tell you this, but I don't want you going anywhere tomorrow morning. No work. You stick close to Aurora or one of her people. And if you go to see Thurman, take one of them with you. In fact…" He turned to look at Hunter, who only straightened under King's scrutiny, sitting up at attention like a little sentry as he looked between the two of them.

King crouched down in front of him and found that he didn't want to say goodbye. Hunter had burrowed his way under King's skin. He was a freaking wolf shifter; they didn't have pets. But...apparently he did now.

Still, the pain leaking out of Avery's every pore was raking against his skin and all his senses. "You're going to stay here with Avery," he said, pointing at her. "You stay close to her and keep her safe, okay?"

King swore Hunter understood him because the little dragonling nodded once, then butted his head against King's before he stepped back.

Avery stepped forward. "King, you don't have to—"

"I think you need him more than me right now. And he really likes you. I can't drag him off now anyway. He's too young to take part in a hunt like this." Or King assumed he was. He had no idea. But it sounded believable, and he didn't want the little one to get hurt.

Hunter moved closer and gently patted Avery's back with his gray, sparkling wing as if he was trying to comfort her.

Avery's jaw clenched tight as if she was fighting back tears. "Thank you," she rasped out, reaching out a hand to pet Hunter.

"We're going to get your brothers and Mikael back, okay? I swear it."

Avery nodded, crouched down and hugged Hunter, who awkwardly hugged her back with his big wings.

"Go and get them," she whispered to King.

He nodded and ran off, briefly acknowledging Brielle, who was perched along the mansion's border wall, acting as Avery's security.

This was his city and these were his people. His responsibility. He was going to get all of them back home safely.

CHAPTER THIRTY-TWO

"Where are you going?" Brielle dropped down from the wall as Avery *almost* made her escape from the compound undetected with Hunter in tow.

Or maybe she was fooling herself because these shifters were stealthy. "To see the Magic Man. And I'm not asking for permission."

Brielle blinked once. "You're a feisty little thing."

Avery frowned at her and started toward the open gate. *Little thing?*

"Look, we've got a car," Brielle said. "Unless you just feel like walking."

Avery looked at Hunter and then Brielle.

"I've seen him follow King around when he's driving. He'll follow us."

Avery looked at her new shadow. "You'll follow us?" she asked, wondering how much he even understood.

Probably more than she thought. More than any of them thought. Every time she looked into his bright purple eyes, intelligence shone back at her.

Sure enough, by the time they reached Thurman's brick building downtown, Hunter swooped down in front of them as Brielle snagged street parking out front.

"No offense, but I am never riding in a vehicle with you again if you're driving," Avery said as she stepped outside and resisted the urge to get on her knees and actually kiss the pavement.

The tall redhead sniffed haughtily. "I'm an excellent driver."

"Whatever you tell yourself," she mumbled. Avery didn't like to stereotype, but something about supernaturals driving cars was terrifying. None of them drove well. Probably because they had no fear of death.

Before either of them could knock, the wooden doors opened and to her surprise Thurman himself was standing there. He pulled her into a hug and gently kissed the top of her head. She didn't realize how badly she'd needed the comfort until then. She resisted the urge to break down because she'd come here with a purpose. To save her dragon. She trusted King and Mikael's brothers to find her brothers. King said he had a lead. Meanwhile, Mikael was stuck in a Hell realm. Well, not on her watch.

He nodded politely at Brielle before opening the door fully so all of them, including Hunter, could come inside.

Hunter darted past the three of them as they entered the courtyard and started flying from bush to bush, smelling everything, his curiosity vivid.

"I won't bother with small talk," Thurman said as he motioned for them to sit at the round mosaic table.

Her surprise at his gift of "knowing" had long since dimmed, because there were three teacups already waiting and a pot of steaming tea on the center tray.

If Brielle was surprised, she didn't let on. Instead she poured tea into each dainty cup as they sat.

"Your dragon is safe for now," Thurman said without preamble, sitting across from her. "And no, I do not know which realm he is in."

The little crack in her heart split open wider at his words. She'd been banking on him knowing. She swallowed hard, forced the tears back. Tears solved nothing, her mom used to tell her, and it was true. "You don't know how I can find him?" Now it looked like she might lose her brothers *and* Mikael. She was fighting every ounce of the terror forking through her at the thought of that. Of a world without any of them. A world she didn't want to be in.

"I didn't say that. I just said that the cemetery is not a known portal. At least not to me—and I've already made a few calls. No one else knows it to be a known portal either. However," he said, glancing once at Brielle before focusing on Avery, "if you go there, you will find what you're looking for. All you have to do is use the right key and you will be reunited with Mikael."

Okay, that was about as clear as he could be. He didn't have to draw her a damn map, thank you very much. She stood abruptly, energy vibrating through her. She might not be able to help hunt down her brothers, but this she could do. She wasn't going to sit on her ass at home and wait for Mikael to come back. "You're sure?"

"Very." He looked at the tiger female again, then pinned Avery with a hard look. "You will be protected as long as you keep the pendant around your neck. Do *not* lose it," he ordered as he stood with them.

All of their dainty teacups remained untouched, steam rolling off the cups in faint white wisps.

"What key are you guys talking about? *Please* tell me you're not thinking of doing what I think you are," Brielle snarled, hands on hips.

"You can't stop me." She didn't care if she was "just" a human. She'd take on anyone or anything who stood between her and Mikael. "Try it and see what happens."

"I can haul you over my shoulder and take you out of here right now." Brielle moved toward her as if to prove just that point, but suddenly bounced back as she hit the invisible barrier created by the pendant.

Goose bumps broke out across her skin, power and urgency racing through her. "Like I said, try it." Avery motioned for Hunter to come to her and the little guy immediately flew to her side. He was definitely big enough to hold her weight, and even though she knew Brielle was going to be *really* mad, she looked at Thurman and nodded. "Thank you. I know Mikael already said it, but I am forever in your debt."

The seer, who had likely seen far too many dark things in his long life, shook his head. "I won't take any favors from you but I will from that dragon of yours. Go get him back."

Avery might only be human but she had a freaking magic key to open any portal and a spelled pendant that should keep her safe. She was probably in a lot more danger than she wanted to acknowledge, but she was getting Mikael back. And then they were going to save her brothers. Because screw this new insane world. She hadn't survived The Fall only to lose the people who meant everything to her.

Brielle stepped forward. "Let's just think about this—"

Nope.

Avery jumped on Hunter's back. He let out a squeal of delight and shot up into the air as she wrapped her arms tight around his neck. She was so glad she'd practiced flying on her friend Dallas's pet dragon, Willow. Because this felt more than familiar. It was a bit like riding a horse. *Kind of.* A wider one, and the ride was more awkward, kind of like riding a baby elephant, she imagined. But the concept was the same.

"Dammit, Avery!" Brielle cursed below them, but Avery ignored her, petting Hunter's beautiful gray wing. It sparkled under the moonlight as he flew through the opening above the courtyard and cleared the top of the building.

She was going to get her dragon back. And she didn't care what she'd said before about things being casual. She was so full of crap.

Yes, she was still terrified of any sort of true commitment because she'd seen what happened when you give your heart to someone, but... No matter what, she was finding Mikael. He would do the same for her.

And she didn't want to imagine a world without him in it. She'd been a coward so far, too scared to claim what was hers. She couldn't let Mikael go, couldn't let fear rule her anymore.

***

Avery's heart hammered a wild, staccato beat in her chest as Hunter landed in the middle of the cemetery. With all the toppled gravestones, upturned grass and dirt, and...a *downed* oak tree, it was clear there had been a battle here. Even if King hadn't told her where that portal had opened up, she could see where a huge gravestone had been split down the middle, debris sprayed in every direction around a shallow crater. Other gravestones were broken as well but this one looked like a bomb had gone off in the middle of it, carving out the ground beneath.

Mikael had been taken, trapped, because he'd been trying to save her brothers. Even though she was terrified and felt wholly out of her depth, she couldn't abandon him. She had the key that could supposedly open any door to any Hell realm. And what if he was stuck there and the only way out was with this key?

No way was she abandoning him. Maybe she should have asked for backup or asked his brothers to come with her, but she wasn't going to wait for them. She knew they wouldn't let her go and time was ticking. Besides, she had the spelled pendant and Thurman swore it would protect her. She was going on raw instinct right now and she was going to trust herself.

She stepped over a chunk of broken concrete and through piles of fallen leaves, her boots crunching softly as she stalked toward the blast site. Hunter was right with her, a silent companion. Normally he was so chirpy, but now he was simply looking around, taking the whole scene in. She could even swear his wings had changed colors a couple times so that he almost seemed to blend in with the shadows around them.

"Hey!" a familiar female voice called out.

Avery turned and frowned to see Delphine striding across the cemetery. Oh, God. Had Brielle called her?

"What are you doing here? And why is Hunter with you?" Her amber eyes flashed bright against her brown skin, her suspicion clear.

Hunter animatedly chirped in greeting, but stuck close to Avery. Facing the wolf shifter with what she hoped was a friendly smile, Avery petted Hunter's head, scratching behind his ear the way he liked. His wings flapped animatedly. In a way she was glad Delphine was here because she could leave Hunter with her. She might be on a mission but she couldn't take him and put him in danger. She was willing to risk her own neck but not this sweet dragonling.

"I was told that this is where Mikael got sucked into that Hell realm."

Delphine nodded once, her expression grim. "Yeah. Still doesn't explain why you're here."

Damn it. Okay, so Delphine wasn't buying anything right now. Avery flicked a glance at Hunter, who had inched closer to Delphine to butt his head against her once in greeting. Delphine laughed lightly and rubbed his head.

"Am I not allowed to be here?" Avery asked.

"I didn't say that."

"Okay, well I'm going to try something. I want to see if I can get the door to open again." She'd decided on full honesty right now. Delphine would scent a lie anyway. And screw it. The wolf couldn't stop her while she wore the pendant. "Can you take Hunter over there with you?" She didn't want either of them to accidentally get sucked in.

Delphine's expression hardened. "No way! In fact, I'm gonna have to ask you to leave now."

"King knows Hunter is with me," she said. That was true enough, but she hoped Delphine wouldn't pick up on what she *hadn't* said.

"Of course he does. He wouldn't leave Hunter with you otherwise." She frowned as she pulled out her cell phone. "You sit tight," she said, holding up a finger as she lifted her phone to her ear and stalked away.

Avery made a shooing motion at Hunter to follow Delphine. He tilted his head as he watched her, and if dragonlings could frown, he definitely was. But he went along with Delphine, hopping backward of all things, his wings flapping as he watched Avery intently, not taking his eyes off her for a second.

She reached under her shirt and pulled out the necklace Mikael had given her. She had no idea what to do with it or if this would even work but Thurman had made it clear that she should go after her dragon.

Well here I am, universe.

She was really putting all of her trust in him—and herself—right now. She held up a finger to her lips, hoping Hunter would understand as she tugged on that stitch Mikael had showed her and fully pulled the leather cover off the necklace.

Delphine didn't have her back to her, she was half turned as she talked on her phone, but she wasn't paying enough attention.

She was vaguely aware of Delphine getting more annoyed on the phone, and the wolf turned just as Avery held the glowing pendant out in front of her. She wasn't sure what she expected but the blast of light that exploded from the gem was not it.

"Stay back!" she shouted just as a giant, swirling hole opened up underneath her. A cacophony of noise, flashing colors as brilliant as the aurora borealis swirled all around her as she fell through space.

"Damn it, Avery—" Delphine's voice faded away.

Avery clutched the gem to her chest tightly as she fell and fell and fell—

She yelped as she landed facedown on a thick patch of grass. As she shoved to her feet, she realized a couple things at once.

One, Hunter had apparently decided to follow her, and two, she was most definitely in another realm, given the two purple suns illuminating the violet sky. Not to mention when she'd left…earth, or whatever, it had been dark. So this was wild.

All around her a beautiful forest that reminded her a bit of a Thomas

Kinkade painting surrounded her. Thick, lush trees with leaves the color of a rainbow jutted up from bright green grass. The sound of running water—like a babbling brook nearby—filled the air, and little birds were chirping.

The place was so beautiful but she remembered everything Mikael had said about these realms. It would be filled with predators.

"We are definitely not in Kansas anymore, Hunter," she murmured, reaching out to stroke his head.

He didn't look scared at all, simply curious, his big eyes taking in everything.

As she looked around, she could see heavy boot prints going in one direction. Assuming this was where Mikael had landed… She decided that was as good a direction as any. She refused to doubt herself now, refused to question her decision as she and Hunter took off after the footprints.

CHAPTER THIRTY-THREE

Mikael glided through the quiet air, scanning the dense forest below—or as much of it as he could through the triple canopy. For a moment, he thought he might be going crazy because he *smelled* Avery.

But he knew that was incorrect. Still…he glided lower, straining for another hint of the peaches-and-sunshine scent lingering on the air. He'd been here before and this was a fairly calm realm. As far as he knew, no humans or supernatural beings lived here—because the foliage itself was sentient and wild, the kind of place that could devour you in your sleep.

Luckily he knew a few safe places to hunker down before flying to the exit tomorrow. Because there was no way he would be able to make it tonight. It wasn't that far and he could easily fly at night, but he needed to recharge after going through the portal. Especially since he'd have to be in top form during the exit tomorrow.

Hurry! The urgency hit him with the intensity of another dragon slamming into him.

And that was when he scented something else. An escorpara, a predator native to the realm. He'd eaten it as a snack before. The panther-scorpion-like creature was racing through the trees below him, jumping from branch to branch. He got a glimpse of the scorpion-like tail before it quickly disappeared. The leaves rustled again, then… He heard a very soft thud.

Though he couldn't see through the thick canopy, the beast had taken to the ground.

And that was when he heard Avery's voice. "We'll just have to figure out where we're going to sleep tonight," she said.

Avery? No. She couldn't be here.

He heard a sort of chirping sound in response but…it didn't sound human. *What the hell?* He didn't question what he was hearing, if it was real or not.

He arrowed downward, drawing his wings back and out, skimming over the top of the trees. He could hear Avery far ahead, and the escorpara up in the trees again.

Fire burned the back of his throat. He wanted to simply burn away everything in sight, but he'd learned the hard way not to damage any of the foliage or plant life here. It was a quick way to make an enemy of the sentient beings that called this place their home.

When he saw the escorpara rush by underneath him, he dove down through the opening in between two purple-tipped trees. He shifted to his human form, calling on all his magic as he landed on the hard ground. In a crouch, he immediately scanned, spotted the beast. About fifty feet away, it turned and looked at Mikael, hissed—then turned away and ran off.

He could smell Avery stronger here, and didn't question that scent anymore. Did not question the need to find and protect her even if it was somehow manufactured. If Ozias had somehow created an illusion or...

Whatever. He could not ignore her scent, her voice. This could be a trap and it didn't matter.

Pulse pounding, he raced after the beast, his feet slamming into the hard earth, though he barely felt the impacts.

The animal was fast, sprinting ahead of him before it took to the trees, using various limbs to springboard itself from branch to branch, tree to tree. Hunting Avery.

They were coming up on the hill and Avery's voice was growing stronger.

He had to get the predator before it got to her. As he crested over the hill, he jumped over a thick blue root just in time to see the beast a mere twenty feet from her.

He let out a roar of fury and released a stream of fire, aiming straight at the animal, clipping its tail.

Avery screamed as he made contact.

The beast turned, baring its fangs in a raging fury as his tail grew back almost instantly. Sharp fangs similar to those of a shark descended as it raced straight at Mikael.

He breathed out another ball of fire, trying to avoid the trees and roots even as he incinerated the rampaging beast.

The beast's scream was short-lived as his fire did its job.

As his fire died down, a blur of sunshine and peaches threw herself at him, wrapping her arms and legs around him even as the dragonling Hunter swooped down, chirping excitedly to see him.

"We found you!" Avery shouted as she grabbed his face and kissed him hard. Then she peppered kisses all over his cheeks, nose and forehead.

Oh goddess, she was safe. Alive. *Here*. She shouldn't be here.

He held her close, very aware that his cock was heavy between them and that if she wasn't wearing any clothing he could easily slide inside her. Not that his thoughts should be heading in that direction right now. But he was only a male and this was his female.

"I'm pretty sure I found *you*," he murmured as she kissed his mouth again. "And that escorpara was *hunting* you." She could have died, something he wasn't going to say aloud. It wasn't something he wanted to even think about.

Still holding her tight—he was not letting her go anytime soon—he looked over her shoulder at Hunter who was basically dancing around, his wings flapping excitedly as he chirped at the two of them.

"You're going to need to work on your hunting abilities and your spatial awareness," he said pointedly to Hunter.

Hunter covered his face with his wings, as if he'd actually understood, and for a moment Mikael felt a little guilty—until Hunter drew his wings back and actually stuck his tongue out at him.

"I'm so glad you're okay," Avery said as she loosened her legs around his waist.

Though he didn't want to let her go, he did and quickly took stock of the surrounding area. It looked as if he had singed a few roots but there was no overt damage to any of the leaves or any other full foliage. Still, they needed to get out of there in case the trees decided to attack.

"We're going to talk about why the hell you're even here." The words came out harsher than he'd intended. He just... She should not be here. She should be at home, safe, protected.

"I'm here because I wasn't leaving you to rot." She set her hands on her hips. Wearing jeans, a T-shirt and a button-up flannel shirt over it, she'd at least come prepared with a small backpack, he could see.

"I'm going to kick my brothers' asses when I see them for letting you do this."

She cocked an eyebrow. "Good thing I didn't ask anyone for permission."

Ice coated his veins. "No one knows you're here?"

"By now I'm sure they do. I didn't know what would happen when I got to the cemetery. And when I unsheathed the key, things went sort of haywire." She glanced around curiously. "It's hard to tell because of the thick canopy, but is it getting darker or am I imagining that the suns are setting?"

This conversation definitely wasn't over but he nodded. "Yes. We need to find shelter before it gets fully dark. I know a place we can go. I'm going to shift and then fly up through that opening," he said indicating another breach in the canopy. "You're going to ride me and… Hunter." He looked at the dragonling. "I want you to do the same." He wasn't sure of the dragon's flying skills and right now they needed to scale up the side of a sharp mountain.

"I'll make sure he gets on with me," Avery said. "I'm so happy you're okay," she whispered, her eyes slightly dilating.

The relief that rolled off her was sharp. There was a lot he was going to say to her once they were somewhere relatively safe, but until then… He brushed his lips over hers for far too brief of a moment before stepping back and putting enough distance between them so he could shift.

She'd actually come after him. It made no sense that she would put herself in such danger for his sake, but he would have obviously done the same for her. So…he should not be surprised that she had done the same for him.

Her feelings for him were stronger than she'd admitted aloud. He'd waited millennia for her, even if he hadn't known she existed. And she was definitely worth the wait.

CHAPTER THIRTY-FOUR

Avery leaned against a snoozing Hunter, soaking up his warmth and the heat from the fire that Mikael had made. He'd brought them to a cave high up on one of the mountains and they were just inside the mouth of it.

It curved inward, almost like a giant ice cream scoop had carved it out, going back maybe fifty feet into the mountainside. The ceiling was all jagged angles but at least there'd been no animals living here. According to Mikael only a few were native to this place, with the plants being the real predators. That knowledge was... Well, it was something she was still trying to wrap her mind around.

She was very aware that there was no barrier on the protruding cliff edge and that if something happened to either Mikael or Hunter, there was no way she was getting down from here. So...that was terrifying. And she was trying very hard to pretend it wasn't true.

It was kind of amazing he even knew this cave existed. Even if it was so high up that the wind whistling outside reminded her of a hurricane, she still felt safer here than she would have on the ground. Especially after seeing that creepy thing that had been stalking her and Hunter. She had no idea if the pendant hanging around her neck would have stood up to an attack by a supernatural beast like that.

And she was glad she hadn't had to find out.

She sat up when she heard the distinctive flap of wings. A moment later, Mikael's huge form landed on the cliff edge and he shifted, magnificent and beautiful as usual. His wings glittered under the pale moonlight right before colors exploded, a wild burst of magic lighting up the darkness behind him, and then a moment later he strode through the cave opening.

The look he gave her was scorching, burning her straight to her core. Hunter barely stirred, peeking one eye open then closing it again when he realized it was just Mikael.

The sweet dragonling had definitely overindulged on the meat that Mikael had brought him earlier. Right now he was basically acting like a bear in hibernation.

"Is everything okay?" she asked.

He'd wanted to do one last reconnaissance flight before they settled in for the night. The two purple moons illuminated the land below, showing thick, lush forests sprouting in all directions, crisscrossed with a spiderweb of rivers and streams.

"Everything is quiet below. And I will be able to hear or see anything if it attempts to breach this cliff."

She nodded, some of her tension easing. "This place is pretty," she said. "I mean, down on the ground." Minus the panther-scorpion thing that had wanted to eat her. "This cave is kind of bare."

"This realm is beautiful but it's deadly. At night most of the plants...come alive, I guess you could say. Everything here is more sentient than you and I are used to."

"That's why we're all the way up here?"

"It is why almost no supernatural beings inhabit this place. Trying to settle here is not worth the hassle. So," he said abruptly. "I'm happy to see you. More than happy. But I'm angry that you went off without telling anyone. What were you thinking?"

She moved around the fire so that only a couple feet separated them, but still stayed close to the warmth. And still kept a teeny bit of distance between them. "I was thinking that my friend was in danger and he had left me with the actual key to get him." Which she'd since given back to him. He had it around his neck—apparently it was magic too and could reform when he shifted from human to dragon and vice versa. "I wasn't going to let you die here. How could I know you knew the way out? No one knew where you'd been taken and they couldn't get the door to open again. I thought...you'd be gone forever."

"You should have told my brothers. Or King. Or Aurora, or anyone in that house."

"You gave the key to me, not them," she stressed. "Besides, I talked to Thurman and he basically told me it was fine for me to come after you."

Mikael narrowed his gaze, storm clouds looking back at her. "He said those words?"

She lifted a shoulder. "More or less. I don't even know why you're upset. I'm here and I'm okay. We're together." She was still terrified about her missing brothers, but being here with Mikael eased a lot of her fear. The world seemed to make sense when she was with him.

He crossed the distance and dragged her into his lap—and he was still naked. He hadn't had any clothes on when he'd been pulled through the portal, so of course he was still naked. She hadn't even thought of bringing him anything to wear.

"If anything happened to you..." He swallowed hard, his eyes those same storm clouds.

"Yeah, well, I feel the exact same way about you," she snapped. "You're like family to me." Hell, more than that. He was things she was afraid to admit out loud. Because then it would become real and she was opening herself up to heartbreak.

"Is that all I am? You look at me like a brother?" His tone was dry.

She squirmed against him, against the intensity of his expression. "You *know* it's more than that between us."

"Do I? You told me that I'm not your boyfriend. Which is a bizarre word."

"Why are we talking about this right now?" Avery had jumped through a portal into a Hell realm to find Mikael because she would do anything to save him. But having this uncomfortable conversation? She'd rather try to scale down the side of the cliff. She loved him, but she didn't understand how anything would work. She was *human* and he was a dragon shifter.

"You have something else you need to be doing?" His gaze fell to her mouth, pure hunger there. Not even simmering at this point, but on full display.

Hunter chose that moment to stir, sitting up and scooting closer to them. He tripped over his own feet and let out a yelp of surprise as he tumbled over the log she'd been using to sit on earlier.

Though she felt like a coward, Avery took the easy way out and slid off Mikael's lap, sidling up next to Hunter on the log. She scratched behind his ear. "You are a brave little dragon," she murmured, kissing his face.

As he rubbed his head against hers, Mikael grumbled behind her.

She looked over her shoulder. "What?"

"Apparently I'm jealous of a dragonling," he muttered, but his mouth kicked up all the same.

Shaking her head, she grabbed her backpack and pulled out a sweater. "I've got some nutrition bars if you're still hungry?"

He and Hunter had devoured some sort of charred animal he'd killed—she didn't want to know what it was. Her apple and nutrition bar had been enough for her.

When he shook his head, she continued. "I'm kind of tired. We can share my backpack as a pillow if you want." She'd brought some food, water and some extra clothing, but that was about it. She really hadn't thought things through as much as she should have, and now she was kicking herself for not being more prepared.

"How about you just use me as a pillow?" His voice had dropped a couple octaves, his gaze landing on her mouth.

Oh, wow. She swallowed hard. "Okay. Are you ready to get some sleep?" Then maybe they wouldn't have to return to that conversation.

In response he stretched out on the hard stone next to the fire. She wasn't sure how it was possible that he actually looked comfortable, like a warrior god stretched out, naked and glorious, not a care in the world about his nudity or the hard ground beneath him.

Feeling flustered—and internally cursing her flushed cheeks—she stretched out next to him and laid her head on his chest. He immediately wrapped his arm around her, holding her close. Yep, there was no way to keep her hands off him. Not that draping her arm over his rock-hard middle was a chore or anything.

"My mom would have adapted well to this new world," Avery said, the sound of Hunter's breathing and the fire crackling filling the air. The winds outside had died down, making everything quieter, less creepy. "I mean, not this Hell realm, but back home."

Mikael shifted slightly under her but his grip didn't lessen. "Yeah?"

"Yeah. She was always up for adventure. I think it's why my father—" she said, managing not to want to throw up for once. "I think that's why he fell for her. She was so much fun, this bright ball of energy. They took a lot of trips over the years, all of them her idea. She would coax him to visit random destinations, to try new things. She liked meeting new people, learning about new cultures. She had an adventurer's soul. They were so different, and my father was never as involved in our lives as she was…but she still loved him. It was easy to overlook his flaws because of course no one is perfect. And if I'm being honest, the fact that my mom loved him made it a lot easier to overlook those flaws. I mean, if someone as great as her loved him, then he must be a decent person. But I guess once she stopped being fun and going on adventures, he just… God, he just proved what a needy, pathetic man he was."

"Your mother sounds like a wonderful woman who loved him despite his shortcomings and in the end he proved to be unworthy. I'm sorry, Avery." His deep voice wrapped around her, soothing her jagged edges.

A few tears spilled over but she brushed them away. "I know that. I just…I wish she'd had someone better than him at the end."

"She did. She had you and your brothers."

She swallowed hard, fighting back the burn of wetness against her eyes. She wondered where her brothers were right now. If they were okay. Whether they were cold and hungry and in pain. "Tell me about your parents," she said, wanting to talk about anything other than what she had brought up.

"My parents were both warriors, as I've told you." Though she wasn't looking at his face, she could hear the smile in his voice. "My mom was a very typical female dragon warrior. Tough, didn't take shit from anyone, loved her children more than life itself. She taught us to take care of ourselves from a young age. With supernaturals, clan or pack are always important. And our particular tight-knit clan had been tasked with looking after this key." He briefly touched it, where it hung around his neck.

"That seems like a big responsibility."

"It is."

"How did your parents first meet?"

He let out a soft snort and started stroking up and down her back gently. "My mother had been promised as a mate to my father's oldest brother. His brother was well known for his warrior prowess and my mother was as well. Both clans decided that they would make excellent allies and that the two should mate."

"I didn't think dragons were into arranged matings."

He lifted a shoulder. "Some clans are. And back then it was common enough only because dragon births had started to stagnate. Though if one of the dragons didn't want the mating, for whatever reason, then there would be no mating. It wasn't a forced thing. No one can force a dragon female to do a thing she doesn't want," he murmured, amusement in his tone.

"So, did your father steal her away, then?"

He laughed again. "More or less. From the way they told it, he was smitten the moment he arrived to escort her back to his clan's homeland. He fell hard and fast."

"Why didn't your father's older brother come himself?" That seemed like the kind of thing you'd do if you wanted to impress your future mate.

"He was busy fighting with a neighboring clan. Which my mother saw as a sign that he would not be a good mate if he couldn't even put her first enough to court her— She was a wise female. So when my father made his interest clear, and according to her, he was not subtle," he said on a laugh, "she decided that she would have fun with him before returning home. He managed to prove to her that he was a worthy mate and that her home should be with him."

"How?"

"In ways none of my brothers or I ever want to know about." His tone was dry, pulling a startled laugh from her.

"I see."

"Yes. They were very affectionate mates."

"How did their clans handle everything? Did it cause friction?" She wanted to understand more about dragons in general. They were such a secretive bunch.

His chest rumbled slightly as he laughed. "The two of them got so consumed in each other, so carried away with the mating heat, they lost all track of time. And I mean literally. They holed up on a small island off the coast of my homeland and were found months later. By that time both families had gone into a frenzy, thinking they'd been killed or attacked by neighboring clans or packs. Nope. My mother was pregnant with Zephyr already—and for a dragon to be pregnant so quickly is a big deal. Sometimes children won't come for hundreds of years or even longer, if at all. There was a big celebration that night, and the rest, as the human saying goes, is history."

She sighed against his chest, her hand resting on his abs. "That's so romantic."

"Dragon shifters mate for life," he said a few moments later.

"I've heard that." She'd seen plenty of mated shifters and they always seemed so happy. So...devoted to each other. But she'd seen humans like that too. Humans who'd ended up divorced, hating each other.

"Do you know what it means? Really means?"

"That...they're stuck with each other no matter what," she said dryly.

To her utter surprise, he swatted her butt.

She jerked up to look at him. "What was that for?"

Smoky gray eyes watched her hungrily.

Oh no. She couldn't resist that look, couldn't resist him. She ducked her head back against his chest. "Don't think about a repeat of the other day. Apparently I lost my senses for a while."

"Lost them?"

She pinched his side. "Whatever. I went crazy or something. And I don't want to talk about it. Or anything else."

"Why not?"

"Because..." Oh God, she was such a coward!

"Because?"

"Ugh. Leave me alone," she muttered. She burrowed against him, soaking up his warmth. He didn't seem to care that he was naked—and she was very much ignoring the huge cock between his legs.

"When shifters mate, it's for life," he continued, as if she hadn't spoken at all. "Our devotion to our mates is different than humans. Or...other beings I'm likely not thinking of right now. Mating is for life. We don't leave because we get tired of someone—I will *never* get tired of my mate."

Oh. *Oh, oh, ohhhh.* She felt his words deep in her core, couldn't look at him. Couldn't think as heat speared through her. Was he saying what she thought he was saying? This was what she'd secretly craved from him.

Mikael shifted his body and tipped her chin up to look at him. "I'm not your father. I am not some pathetic excuse for a male. My dragon recognized you even before I did. You are mine, Avery. Mine."

She blinked, trying to digest what he was saying as her mind refused to fully wrap around the words, the intent. He was clearly trying to kill her. "You mean... What *do* you mean?" she whispered. She needed it spelled out, apparently.

He cupped her cheek casually, his big thumb stroking over her skin. "I'm torn as to whether I should be completely honest with you, because I don't want to scare you off."

"Be honest," she whispered. She needed it. She really did.

"My dragon recognized you as my *mate* before I did."

Her chest tightened, a tidal wave of emotions welling up inside her. Mate? She'd thought that was what he meant, but hearing him say it... Saying the actual word, mate. "You say your dragon. What about...*you?*" He sometimes talked about his two halves as if they were two separate beings, and maybe they were.

"I tried to deny it at first. For an entire ten minutes after we first met. Then I growled at my brothers and told them I'd feed them their entrails if they looked at you wrong. I just gave in and accepted it."

A startled laugh escaped. "Are you serious?"

"Deadly."

She didn't know if she should be disturbed or turned on. Really, she was turned on and there was no denying it. "Mating is...a lot." And she really, really adored Mikael. Okay, she *loved* him. She'd run straight into a Hell realm for this male.

Damn it. But saying those words back to him, admitting it out loud, absolutely *terrified* her. She'd seen how heartbroken her mother had been, how those last couple months had ravaged her, both physically and emotionally, because of her father's betrayal. She didn't think Mikael would do that to her, but the memories sat heavy on her chest.

"I'm not pushing you...yet." Moving quickly, Mikael tugged her onto him so that she straddled him. "For the record, right now I want to strip you naked—but I won't take you on this hard stone floor because you deserve better."

Throat tight, heart a wild beat against her chest, she stared into his gray eyes, thinking that she didn't give a crap about the stone floor right now.

Hunter chirped suddenly, making her jump. She'd almost forgotten he was there. His eyes were open as he watched them and kept chirping. His expression said, "Please don't do that." Then he rolled over on his other side, giving them his back.

She turned back to Mikael. "We can go deeper into the cave." It wasn't much privacy, but it would give them a bit more.

Mikael watched her with those stormy eyes, his gaze telling her everything he was feeling. "Our next time together will be on a soft bed."

"I don't need soft." Maybe she was crazy, but she leaned forward, not caring that Hunter was nearby as she brushed her lips against Mikael's.

His hands tightened on her hips as he held her close, pinning her to him. She might be on top, but he was completely in control as he rolled his hips against hers.

His thick length rubbed against her jeans, right over her covered clit. Her inner walls clenched as he held her close, slid one hand up her shirt to cup her breast.

She loved the feel of his callused hand moving over her skin, exploring, touching, teasing. Sighing into him, all her muscles tightened when he tugged her bra cup down and flicked his thumb over her tightly beaded nipple.

Oh, she wanted more of this. She moaned into his mouth as she grinded against him and— The mountain rumbled beneath them.

Avery sat up with a start. "I know I'm not crazy. The earth is shaking again!"

Breathing hard, Mikael sighed, frustration flickering across his expression. "When dragons are in the throes of mating heat, they usually put off a sort of…signal. We call it our mating manifestation. It's a signal to other dragons to stay away. For some clans, they glow while mating. Some set everything around them on fire—without burning anything. It's just a visual thing. For my clan, we create earthquakes."

She blinked once. Twice. If she'd had any doubt about his sincerity, the vibrations in the mountain had just killed them all. "That's…intense. Do people know about this?"

"Not most people. Dragons do though. And some other beings—it's how Ozias knew you meant so much to me. He must have felt the vibrations of the earth and figured it out."

Oh, wow. "So every time we fool around, we'll create actual earthquakes?"

"Until I claim you for good." He rolled his hips up again and she raked her gaze over every inch of him she could see.

He really was like a warrior god, all gleaming muscles, the fire creating shadows over his already ripped body.

The earth rumbled slightly. "I don't want to stop kissing, but I don't think we should risk toppling this mountain down on our heads."

He sighed and shifted slightly, clearly uncomfortable even as he nodded. "It would be worth it, but as always you are right." He tucked her up against him once again.

An ache pulsed between her legs—how could she not be turned on when she was pressed up against the sexiest man alive? And he was naked with a rock-hard, thick erection.

But…*earthquake.*

Sighing, she tried to force her mind off Mikael's naked body. Which was hard to do when his cock was right in her line of vision. "Could I maybe stroke you off?" She wrapped her fingers around his length and squeezed once.

He groaned and little tremors shook them. Hunter chirped without turning around. Loudly.

Okay, then. She sighed and splayed her hand over Mikael's stomach instead.

"Later," he said, his words a dark promise.

He'd better believe it. She…trusted him. She'd never thought she'd trust anyone the way her mother had, but Mikael was a male she could count on.

And even though she was sexually frustrated, she knew they needed to get sleep. They needed to get out of here once the suns rose. They needed to get back home. Together.

CHAPTER THIRTY-FIVE

Zephyr was frustrated that King had called them back from searching for Ozias. But he was the Alpha, and Zephyr would respect his calls for now. His brothers seemed to like the Alpha well enough and he would be staying where his brothers did.

As they arrived at the big compound, a guard standing on the wall motioned that they should enter. He scented wolves and other creatures milling about the yard. This was a much different world than the one he had left before he'd been sucked into the Hell realm. And much different than the Hell realm. A place he did not miss.

Before they had reached the end of the driveway, King opened the front door and jogged toward them at a steady pace. The male moved with the grace and confidence of an Alpha. *Even if he is young*, Zephyr's dragon sniffed.

"Avery followed after your brother," the Alpha said without greeting.

Next to him both Cas and Ivyn cursed.

Zephyr blinked, not sure he understood. "Followed?"

"She opened the portal somehow. I'm guessing with the key. Both her and my..." He cleared his throat. "My pet dragonling Hunter fell through it with her." And the Alpha looked worried.

Ivyn let out another savage curse.

"Fuck. Fuck, *fuck*," Cas added.

Hell realms were no place for humans and not for dragonlings either. And Avery was...soft and gentle. This was not good.

"I've spoken to Thurman and he seems to think she will be okay."

Zephyr had no idea who Thurman was, but his brothers relaxed slightly at King's words.

"I called you here for two reasons. To tell you that, and to ask you to carry out a retrieval mission. We've discovered that Ozias, aka Magnus— the vampire who has been changing humans into vampires with abandon in my city and subsequently letting those turned run rampant with no control—are one and the same. And one of his acolytes escaped earlier." He looked at Ivyn and Cas. "Lindsey, the female Avery knows. Do you know of her?" There was a slight question in his voice.

Both his brothers nodded.

"Aurora mentioned that Mikael retrieved some jewelry from this vampire for Avery. It should still have the vampire's scent on it. If she's in the city, I want her brought to me. Can the three of you retrieve her?"

Zephyr nodded along with his brothers. "We will. If you receive any news on Mikael—"

"I'll contact you immediately."

As they left, he looked at his brothers as they hurried down the sidewalk. "Mikael really cares for her, doesn't he?"

"She's his mate," Cas said without hesitation. "He's just been *very* slow to court her. Until now."

"She's been so oblivious to him anyway," Ivyn said, a hint of amusement in his voice even though his expression was tense. "I thought she would break his heart, but those two are perfect for each other."

"I never thought he would mate with a human." Or someone who seemed so kind and soft.

Both his brothers looked at him, their expressions going...almost neutral.

"What? I like her. I was not saying anything negative about Avery."

They didn't respond, simply looked away as they hurried down the street. It wouldn't take long to get back to their home.

"If I have said anything to offend either of you, I apologize," he said stiffly as they reached the house. He had not seen his brothers in so long, and he did not want to lose them because he'd chosen his words incorrectly.

"You didn't. It's just... We like humans," Cas said bluntly. "A lot."

"I like humans too," he said simply. He had met some in the Hell realm he'd been stuck in. And they were definitely not all bad. And after being separated from his family so long, feeling like a savage, he never wanted to inadvertently offend his brothers. They were the only family he had left.

"Good, then." Ivyn threw the front door open. "Sit tight. I'll grab the jewelry."

* * *

Zephyr and his brothers had their prey cornered—even if she had no idea she was about to be captured.

The female vamp had left a wide trail straight to a condominium complex in what his brothers informed him was called the Central Business District. Or had been before The Fall.

They hadn't even had to break into the place, they'd simply used the elevator. And now they were standing outside a door where he could scent the faint hint of death and blood.

Instead of kicking the door in—which would have been gratifying—he simply broke the handle off and shoved it open.

They moved silently into the open foyer, with the scent of blood growing stronger. As they reached the middle of the hallway, a naked blonde female vampire stepped out of an open doorway. She tensed, her fangs dropping as she got ready to run. He could see it in the tense lines of her leg muscles.

"We are all dragons and ancient," he said quietly, inserting power into his words. "We will catch you. And we won't be gentle if you run."

She met his gaze dead-on until finally she had to drop it. She was no Alpha. Not even *alpha* in nature.

Letting out a hiss of frustration, she reached through the doorway she'd come out of and pulled a robe out a second later. She tightened the thick blue robe around her middle. "Who are you and what do you want?" she demanded.

Zephyr lifted a hand and his two brothers passed by him to search the apartment.

Instead of answering, he pointed at her. "Sit. Living room, now." He'd never been in here, obviously, but his knowledge of this modern world was that most homes had similar rooms.

She stalked away from him, her movements light and quick.

As he followed her, he tried to ignore her scent. It was devoid of...life. And not all vamps were like that. This one, however, scented of almost nothing. It was disturbing to his dragon. He'd felt that when tracking her, that something about her natural smell was…wrong.

"Got a body in here," Ivyn called out.

Both Cas and Ivyn stepped into the living room seconds later, their expressions grim. Even though it was still dark out, the drapes were pulled over the windows.

"Who did you kill?" he asked.

"My ex-husband. I was thirsty," she said dismissively. "He was old anyway. And he hated this new world. I did him a favor."

"It's Avery's father." Ivyn spoke to Zephyr, his dragon in his gaze, ready to attack.

It was very clear that Ivyn and Cas adored Avery, but from what they'd told him, he did not think she would mind too much if her father died. Though humans could be strange about some things, so she would likely have feelings about his death.

"Yes," Lindsey said, absently toying with a lock of her hair.

He could see why her maker had turned her, at least from a physical standpoint. She was beautiful, but it was clear that it was only on the surface.

"Tell us about your maker," Zephyr said bluntly.

"Or what?"

He allowed his dragon to bleed into his eyes. "You really want to find out?" he growled. "We can keep you alive for decades, centuries. You will exist in a state of pain so that it is all you know." Zephyr would not do that to another being, but he had learned that the threat of torture was often powerful enough to make someone spill their secrets. Especially someone who was weak mentally.

"What do you want to know?" she asked as a tiny thread of fear spiked in the air, sharp and pungent.

"Where did he go?"

"How should I know?"

"That is not an answer," he bit out.

"Fine. I have no idea."

"Where are Avery's brothers?" Cas cut in, stepping forward slightly.

The vampire eyed him up and down, licked her lips once. "What do

I get if I tell you?"

"You get to live."

"You dragons are so boring," she pouted. "I want a deal if I tell you where they are."

"What kind of deal?"

"I want...immunity from everything I've done up until this point. I want to leave the city. Which was my plan to begin with. I just needed sustenance—"

"You didn't need to drain him," Cas cut in, but there was no heat in his voice.

"Yes, but I wanted to. I had to screw him for years. I wasted a lot of time on his needy ass. He deserved to die." There was disdain in her voice as she dropped the strand of hair she'd been playing with. "Like I was saying. I want immunity. Other than him," she jerked a thumb over her shoulder, "I haven't killed anyone. I'm not stupid. I won't kill my food sources. I want you to vow that you won't kill me. Any of you. I know vows are important to supernaturals."

"I can't grant immunity as I'm not the Alpha of this region," Zephyr said because otherwise she would know he was lying. "But each of us vow on the Cathasaigh clan name that we will not kill you. Unless in self-defense."

"And unless you try to kill anyone close to us—including Avery and her brothers," Ivyn added.

The vamp nodded once. "And you'll let me go if I tell you where the boys are."

Zephyr watched her carefully for a long moment. "If the information you give *leads* to the rescue of Avery's brothers, we will let you go," he finally said.

She stood then. "Fine. We have a deal."

"Talk. Where are they?"

She paused, sizing him up, her eyes calculating. Whatever she saw, she didn't like. "Magnus had them drugged up in a place nearby. A house where a couple humans he feeds from live. They're in an attic, tied up and docile. They're totally fine. And he doesn't even know I know. I followed the vampire who delivered them." She sounded smug about that.

"Address. Now."

She sighed and stood.

All three of them fanned out, ready to attack.

She paused. "Jumpy, aren't we," she murmured, but he scented the fear, the stench of it beneath her bravado. She picked up her cell phone from a nearby table and typed in commands. Then she held it out so they could see the screen. "That's the house. I took a picture of it before I left." Then she gave them the actual address.

Cas already had his phone out and was texting quickly. He snatched her phone from her. "What's your code?"

Her lips pulled into a thin line, but she finally gave it to him.

Cas then texted someone, Zephyr assumed King. Instead of giving it back to her, he shoved her phone in his back pocket then grabbed her upper arm. "Let's go."

"Hey! You said you'd let me go."

"We said we'd let you go if your information led to us finding them. We're not letting you out of our sight until then." Cas spoke to her as if she had rocks in her head.

Which only seemed to enrage her, given the way her fangs descended. "At least let me put on clothing!"

"Your robe is fine." Cas continued herding her toward the door.

She grumbled but didn't complain as they hurried her outside. The sun would be rising soon enough and he imagined she wanted to be indoors for that.

He had no idea what King would do with her, but Zephyr would keep his word. Funny thing about vows, however. He only had to keep his word. Whatever happened to her after he and his brothers eventually let her go was on her.

CHAPTER THIRTY-SIX

Avery crouched down against Mikael's scaled back, Hunter right next to her, his wing wrapped protectively over her even though she knew he was scared too.

So she wrapped her arm around his neck, hugging him back as Mikael silently glided over the exit to the Hell realm.

If she'd been here by herself, she never would have found the exit. And even if she had by some miracle actually found it, she wouldn't have made it through alive. Or she couldn't see *how* that was possible.

At the top of a mountain, trees waved softly around a giant crater which Mikael had told her was the opening aka exit they had to go through.

But first, they had to *not* die.

The crater was guarded by trees that didn't actually look like any tree she'd ever seen in her short existence. The tall, thin trunks had a similar length as pine trees, but moved with the flexibility that looked like…cilia. The trunks sparkled white in the light, giving them an almost teeth-like appearance.

So creepy-ass trees were guarding the crater, ready to devour anything that dared to enter it. Because, oh yeah, Mikael had said that if one of them snagged you, it would eat you through osmosis. Not exactly, but that was her takeaway.

She dared to peek over his back again, watching the trees wave back and forth so peacefully, gently. As if they weren't plotting to kill them.

But Mikael had said he was counting down, watching the movements of the elongated trees. He swore they would try to attack, which seemed insane to her. Attack trees?

But she was in a Hell realm with two suns, riding on a dragon shifter's back with a dragonling as her companion so…she believed him. White sparkly trees were going to attack them as they tried to escape.

Just peachy.

Next to her, Hunter trembled, his big body humming with anxiety.

It was easy to forget that he was still a baby since she could actually ride on him. But he was just a child, basically, a sweet little dragonling. And he was afraid.

She made soft little crooning sounds and murmured that everything would be okay as she rubbed his head, which seemed to settle him down. He tried to burrow his head against her but failed because he was the size of a small pony.

"This will be okay," she murmured, patting his head. "Mikael has done this before. He'll get us through this. Those big stupid trees don't know what they're up against. He'll just burn them to a crisp."

She had no idea if Hunter actually understood the words, but maybe he understood the sentiment because he settled and wrapped his wing around her, pulling her closer. She was really going to miss him once she got him back to King—and they *would* get this little guy home.

Mikael's body tensed suddenly and she knew they were getting ready to dive through.

She took a deep breath, pushed it out. Then she repeated it over and over as she tried to force herself to remain calm. Panicking wouldn't do anyone any good and she needed Hunter to remain calm too.

This was why she liked yoga. It helped her de-stress and forced her not to think about everything else in her life, all her surroundings—

They dropped suddenly, with Mikael going into what felt like a free fall. She grabbed onto his scales even as Hunter held her down against him. She knew that neither Mikael nor Hunter would let her fall off but her stomach dropped to her feet as he arrowed straight toward the giant crater. The trees whipped at them like blades, the slashing sounds through the air as terrifying as the sudden groaning of the crater below them.

She stared in horror as Mikael flew right at the hard rock surface. He'd told her that this was an exit, that it would open and free them, but all she could see was rock coming up at them faster and faster as he flew downward, his wings pulled in tight.

Oh, God!

She yelped as one of the trees swung at them. Mikael twisted in midair, avoiding a direct hit. She gripped his scales even tighter, breaking a fingernail off as she held on.

Another tree swung at them, clipped his tail, but he continued flying downward.

This was it! They were going to crash-land and it didn't matter if she had a spelled pendant, they were totally going to—

A starbright kaleidoscope of colors exploded in front of them, the crater opening to reveal an entire other universe.

Stars and planets scattered as far as the eye could see as they fell, fell, fell through the opening. Hunter squealed next to her as she stared in wonder at the blast of color surrounding them.

When she'd fallen through the first portal she'd been caught off guard, terrified. This… There were no words. An eerie silence descended around them as she tried to memorize every second of what was the equivalent of the aurora borealis on steroids.

CHAPTER THIRTY-SEVEN

Normally King wouldn't take part in an operation this simple but it involved Avery and her brothers. This was personal. He looked up, motioned to Aurora, who was hovering next to the window in the third floor.

She nodded once, her pale blue phoenix wings moving so quickly he could barely see them, but the fire they created flickered wildly. Then she whispered so low that only supernaturals could hear. "Anthony and Riel are in there."

Adrenaline surged through him. This was it.

Turned out that vampire had been telling the truth. He only scented humans inside, and perhaps it was overkill but he'd brought half a dozen pack members. He would be going in with Ace and Maria, while Aurora would be busting in through the upper window.

He held up his fist, counted down and slammed his boot through the side kitchen door. Sure it was overkill but he was going to teach these humans a very valuable lesson.

As he moved inside, he heard glass breaking above, and shouts of alarm in the house. He moved quickly, not bothering to draw his sword on a bunch of humans. As he stepped into the kitchen, two chairs clattered to the ground almost simultaneously.

A human female had plastered herself against the refrigerator, her fingers splayed against the stainless steel, her eyes wide. The male hovered near the sink, a beer can in hand. And they both stank like drugs.

Hell.

King hated dealing with addicts. They would lie, do anything to get their next fix.

"You're officially in my pack's custody for the kidnapping of two human men." Even though he could smell beer and heroin, he wanted it clear why they were being taken from their home. Not that he was certain these two humans would remember. They needed a detox.

By the sink, the man with slicked-back hair that hadn't been washed in at least a week held up his hands. Track marks were visible down his skinny wrists. "Hey man, we didn't do anything wrong."

King simply lifted an eyebrow as Ace stepped in behind him. "Aurora has them. She's transporting them to Greer. They're alive. Barely."

A burst of rage surged through him. Feeling testy, King withdrew his sword, because fuck it, he wanted these two scared. "What did you give them? Did you pump them full of heroin?" he growled, his wolf prowling right below the surface.

"No, no!" the female by the fridge said, her hands now raised in the air and trembling. "The guy who dropped them off told us what to do. He gave us basic instructions… He wrote them down," she added. She didn't smell as bad as the male who was now staring listlessly at King and Ace. "I've been giving them what he prescribed every six hours just like he said. And I've been making sure they ate food. I've been keeping them alive, I swear!" She cleared her throat. "It was the only way he'd get our drugs. We had to keep them alive," she whispered, shame in her voice and expression as she looked down at her feet.

He wasn't sure if he believed her, and that was the problem with addicts as well. It was hard to scent out the truth over the drugs and what they'd convinced themselves to be true. You could rarely take anything at face value. "I want the drugs you've been giving them, and you two are coming with me."

"Where are you taking us?" Fear rolled off the female, but the male was still watching them with a sad vacantness.

"You're going to detox and then you are going to work off what you've done." Some people could be saved, others couldn't. But unless these two were hardened criminals, he was going to make sure they got off drugs and then get them into therapy. And they were going to pay for their crimes as well. But he wasn't going to toss them in some cell and forget about them. He believed in rehabilitation.

The human male stepped forward then, as if to argue, but the woman snapped at him, telling him to shut up. Her voice quivered with fear. "This is King, you dumbass. He's Alpha of our city. We're going with him and we'll do what he says."

At least one of them had a brain. He looked back at Ace and Maria, who'd been silent. "You guys got this?"

They both nodded.

"Good. Take care of them. I'm going to go check on the boys and I'll meet you both at the holding center." He needed to see for himself that Avery's brothers were okay. He certainly prayed that they were.

He didn't want to have to deliver the news to her that they'd lost Anthony and Riel. If they ever got her back. But that was something he refused to consider right now. He had to believe that they would, and that she and Hunter were with Mikael.

Sweet Hunter, he thought. He didn't regret leaving Hunter with her but… *No.* He couldn't let his mind go there either. He'd lost too damn much. He would get all of them back and stave off any more loss to his city.

***

"They're going to be okay. I've gotten the drugs out of their system," Greer said to King, standing just outside the room she'd put both brothers in. Her copper-colored hair was pulled up into a ponytail and though he knew she'd been working long hours, he didn't see any fatigue in her green eyes. The dragon healer never seemed to need sleep.

"Will they have any permanent damage, or is it too soon to know?"

She leaned against the wall. "I can say with a pretty fair amount of certainty that there will be no permanent damage. They were kept on a low dosage so they would stay compliant and tired. But they haven't been tortured or otherwise mistreated—other than a couple punches Riel took. And they were a little dehydrated but that's easily fixed."

Likely why Magnus, or whatever his real name was, had put their care in the hands of drug addicts. He'd just needed the humans compliant. "Keep me informed."

The tall, striking female nodded once. "Of course. Did you want to talk to them?"

Yes, but he didn't want to answer questions about their sister and they would want to know why Avery wasn't here.

As if she read his mind Greer said, "They're resting, so I'll tell them—"

He shook his head. "No, it's my job. I need to talk to them." Being Alpha meant sometimes having uncomfortable conversations.

She nodded and stepped out of his way, letting him open the door.

Sheer gauzy curtains were open over each window, with moonlight spilling in, though they had two lamps on their bedside tables, giving them plenty of light. It would be sunrise in just an hour or so, and he hoped they got a full day of sleep.

Decorated with art he recognized from local artists, the room was large, with two full beds. Quilts likely donated from his pack or local humans covered each bed, and though there were human-made medical machines in here, it felt more like a bedroom. A place to feel safe. Not a hospital room.

"Hey guys, how are you feeling?" King grabbed a chair and sat in between their beds.

"Been better," Anthony rasped out, a small smile on his face.

Christ, they looked so damn young just lying there with the fluffy quilts pulled up to their chests. Their normally vibrant bronze skin had paled but he saw sparks of light in their eyes.

"Where's Avery?" Riel asked.

Hell, he'd known this was coming. "She's with Mikael right now. They're working on helping us find out who did this to you. She's on her way back," he said, because it wouldn't be a lie. Not that they would be able to smell a lie from him anyway, but all the same he didn't like lying, regardless.

"I knew there was a reason she wasn't here," Anthony said, laying his head back against the pillows as he closed his eyes.

"I guarantee your sister wants you to sleep right now, so please try to rest. If there's anything you need, let Greer know and she'll tell me."

"I'd like a phone," Riel said. "There's someone I want to call before I pass out."

Anthony nodded, opening his eyes again. "Me too."

"No problem. I'll speak with Greer and make sure you can contact anyone you want." King turned at a slight shuffling sound from the door to find Ivyn and Cas hurrying inside, worry etched into their faces.

When he'd placed the three brothers with Avery, he'd known that she would look out for Mikael and his brothers, but he had not foreseen how close all of them would become. And it was clear that these two ancient dragons looked at Riel and Anthony like younger brothers.

He pushed his chair back and moved out of the way. "They're okay and I've already let them know that Avery is with Mikael and on her way back here." He gave them a meaningful look—no need to tell them she'd rushed into a Hell realm and that both she and Mikael were stuck in one. King also noticed that Ivyn carried two pendants similar to the one Avery wore. "What are those?"

"From the Magic Man. Mikael got them before..." Ivyn cleared his throat. "He got them from Thurman and asked me to hold on to them for safe keeping for Anthony and Riel. For when they were rescued. He had faith they'd be found."

King nodded once and the two dragons hurried forward toward the resting brothers. He then murmured a goodbye, not that anyone was paying attention, and hurried out.

Zephyr leaned against the wall outside, his hands shoved into his jeans pockets.

"I'm sure you can go in," he said.

The dragon with similar gray eyes as his brothers lifted a shoulder. "I'm going to give them this time together—they've been worried. I am surprised that the vampire was telling the truth."

King nodded, eyeing the ancient dragon. He needed to learn more about this male—though according to Prima and Arthur, he was a decent male.

"What will you do with her?" Zephyr asked.

"I promised her immunity, promised to allow her to leave the territory."

Zephyr's jaw tightened. "I don't like it."

"I don't like it either. But I'll have one of my wolves escort her to the border of the territory." Though he did not owe this stranger any explanation he decided to give one anyway. "She will barely make it to the next territory by sunrise. And that territory is run by a wolf I am friends with. I've already spoken to him—she will have one day to sleep in his territory before she will be forced to move on to the next one. That territory is run by a vampire who is very good friends with Olga. She's already contacted them and asked them to reject her request for sanctuary. I don't think Lindsey Baird will make it out of *that* territory alive." King would keep his word, but at the same time ensure that the vampire was executed for her crimes. It was a win-win as far as he was concerned.

Surprise flared in the dragon's eyes, but the tension in his shoulder eased. "Good."

"Are you planning on staying in my territory?"

Zephyr straightened slightly. "As long as my brothers are here, yes. I know this is your territory so if there's anything particular you need from me, just let me know. If you want me to leave, Prima has already told me her nephew has a place for me in his clan."

King wanted to learn more about this Zephyr, his skills as a warrior, his ability to help rebuild New Orleans. He was good at reading people and something told him this male would be an asset. He kept his expression neutral as he said, "I will be in touch."

CHAPTER THIRTY-EIGHT

Just as quickly as they flew through time and space, the real world rubber-banded back to them as they flew out into… "Oh, hell!" Avery grunted in surprise as Mikael landed roughly on a patch of earth and grass. His wings stretched out as he steadied them.

She held tight to Mikael's back as did Hunter…then looked around in confusion. It was dark now, not just after sunrise. Mikael had told her that this might happen, that time could shift or pass differently, but it was still jarring.

Mikael had said that one of the gifts of his key was that they could dictate where they spit out of any portal. It was why the thing was so rare, apparently.

But when she spotted a familiar water tower in the distance, she knew they were outside New Orleans. Not in the territory proper—not home, where they'd planned to land. And she knew exactly where they were, in a small farming community, so maybe they'd screwed up in the exit somehow.

Mikael growled beneath them and suddenly twisted, sending both her and Hunter sliding down his back. She let out a yelp as her butt hit the cold grass.

Hunter didn't land, but instead took flight, flapping his wings and very clearly annoyed as he hovered and chirped in that sweet way of his right next to Avery. He looked as if he was telling her that Mikael had been very rude. But she quickly realized *why* Mikael had done what he'd done.

Oh, no. Noooooo.

She could feel that familiar darkness from before, the one scraping along her arms, down her legs, coating her entire body with a nasty, invisible film of evil.

Hunter abruptly stiffened, gliding down next to her and getting very, *very* quiet. She looked around, the moonlight fading, but still bright enough to illuminate the field in front of them. A couple houses stood in the distance, but everything was quiet.

Eerie.

From a cluster of trees, a shadow moved. Then another and another. Her heart jumped into her throat.

A taller figure leading the group came out in front, a cloak billowing around him. His eyes glowed in the darkness, bright red as he strode straight toward them.

Mikael roared, looking back at her as if telling her to run.

She didn't want to be a distraction and she wasn't stupid enough to go up against a Dark Mage—or whatever the hell he was!—so she got on Hunter's back and he immediately took to the air.

As they lifted up, Ozias threw out an arm. A bolt of fire streaked through the air, orangey-red flames flying straight for them.

Hunter swerved wildly and tossed her off his back. She landed on the hard earth. Pain fractured through her hip even as Mikael let out a roar of fury, fire erupting from his giant mouth.

That was when she saw the other vampires break away from their leader.

They ran at her so she went on instinct and turned and *ran*. Or limped was more like it. She was clearly no match for Ozias, and Mikael would need all of his strength and attention to kill him. Meanwhile she just needed to stay alive long enough for Mikael to kick ass.

Her legs and throbbing hip burned as she ran from the vampires, limping as she tried to hurry.

Slam! She felt a reverberation as someone hit the invisible bubble around her.

She turned, and fell on her ass more out of surprise than anything else.

Four vampires stared down at their companion. The one who'd ricocheted off her protection bubble was still on the ground, eyes wide. But he got up again and now the five of them rushed at her. She winced, curling up as they all slammed into that invisible bubble, bouncing back almost in unison.

Before she could get up, or react really, Hunter swooped down from the sky, a tiny warrior spitting fire at the hissing, fanged vampires.

One caught fire immediately, its head bursting into flames. The other screamed and ran—which only seemed to excite Hunter more.

He looked at her, chirped loudly, then raced after the vamps into the woods, bursts of purple and orange fire lighting up the darkness.

* * *

Mikael released another stream of fire, determined to destroy Ozias once and for all. This bastard had taken his family from him, his parents, locked his brother in a Hell realm for thousands of years. And he had tried to kill Avery.

He would pay with his life.

Pain shot through the underside of his wing, something slicing through the soft tissue.

He reared back, magic bursting through him as his body involuntarily underwent the transformation. He turned from dragon to human, skin replacing scales in moments.

Breathing hard, he crouched down, his hands digging into the dirt beneath him.

"I'm going to kill you today." Ozias stalked toward him. "Just like I killed your parents. Then I'm going to kill your pretty little human. Or maybe I'll turn her into a vampire and keep her as a pet. She has very soft-looking skin and a pretty mouth." The male's voice dripped with lust as he stalked forward, acting like a conquering king.

But he was nothing. He was simply another problem to be eliminated.

"Are you wondering what's wrong with your body right now? Why you're internally screaming in pain?" Ozias smiled, pure evil looking back at Mikael. "It's an ancient concoction I've only made stronger in the last few years."

A heavy weight settled on him, telling him to lie down, to give up.

Mikael forced his legs to obey him, forced himself to stand up as he called on the deepest vestiges of his dragon, every single bit of magic he possessed, even as the poison coursed through his body, surging through his veins, his *blood*, trying to destroy him.

He refused to give in, refused to let this monster take Avery from him. From the world. He let out a scream of rage as his wings extended from his back, the burst of magic eating away at some of the poison.

He couldn't shift fully, couldn't get a word out to even respond to Ozias.

But he could fight with everything he had. He was vaguely aware of Avery and Hunter in the distance, but kept all his focus on the threat, the one true problem.

A dark grin spread across Mikael's face as Ozias stared in fear at his wings.

He couldn't lift very high off the ground, but would not give himself away. Would not wince at his internal pain. Instead he lifted up and flew straight toward Ozias. His fist caught the male right in his face, bone crunching as he flew backward.

Mikael barely felt the impact on his fist, just joy at knocking the male down.

Ozias jumped up, tossed a glowing green fireball at him. Mikael dodged, but poison was making him sluggish, slowing him down too much. The fire clipped his left wing—the agony of a thousand angry hornets stinging his scales made him stumble.

But he attacked again, this time with fire and his fists.

He knew he was attacking on a physical, primal level, but he let all his rage and anger out as he punched the male again.

And again and again.

Ozias's fingertips glowed with magic but each time he would have released a fireball, Mikael ducked or punched him. He kept their fighting ring close, refusing to let the Dark Mage unleash himself fully.

Ozias slammed his fist into Mikael's gut, then a blade flashed under the moonlight, slicing into his shoulder.

He slammed his foot into Ozias's stomach, sending him sprawling onto the ground. He needed to get the male down and remove his head from his body.

Ozias jumped up, his eyes bright red as he threw another wild ball of green fire at him.

Mikael ducked and swiveled, avoiding a direct hit.

The Dark Mage threw another ball of fire.

He swiveled again but it grazed his left leg. Fire shot up his calf and the back of his thigh, the angry buzzing hornets back.

He rushed the male, breathing fire out of his mouth as he did. Brute force was the only thing that would win now. No finesse, no beauty to this battle. Just raw, primal death.

His fire was weakening even as he sprayed it, covering Ozias—Suddenly a sharp blue fire like he'd never experienced burst from his mouth and fingertips. He had no idea what was happening, but didn't care. He saw the fear in Ozias's face. The red in his eyes dimmed as he took a step back, then another, trying to run.

Even as the poison ate away at Mikael, made him sluggish, ready to collapse to his knees, he stumbled forward, the fire erupting from him wild and raw and beautiful.

A stream slammed into Ozias's arm and the male screamed as he fell backward, his arm disintegrating as blood poured from the open wound.

Ozias kept screaming and tried to reach into his cloak with his only hand. He withdrew something, then lifted a vial high into the air.

Mikael vaguely heard a scream in the distance. Avery or Hunter, he didn't know.

He couldn't afford to look away and Ozias didn't either, never took his gaze off Mikael.

"Say hello to your parents," Ozias shouted as he started to throw the container of green liquid at him.

Suddenly the male's eyes widened, and—a sharp blade erupted from the middle of his chest.

As he fell forward, Mikael saw Avery standing behind Ozias, trembling as she stared at the falling male. Ozias tried to turn toward her even as he fell.

Protectiveness Mikael had only ever known with her erupted in him once again, pushing back the fatigue and the poison as he let loose another stream of raging blue fire. It wouldn't stop as it devoured Ozias, engulfing him at first, his screams filling the air but quickly silenced as he turned to ash.

His ashes scattered on the wind as Mikael fell to his knees. Avery was alive. Safe now.

When he opened his eyes again, Avery was in front of him cupping his cheeks, her green eyes wide, the scent of her fear sharp. "Stay awake," she ordered. "You better stay awake! Oh God, Mikael, please don't die. No, no, no! You can't leave."

"Avery," he managed to rasp out. Just *Avery*. He loved her. He needed to tell her. Had to tell her. He had been showing her every day since he met her how he felt, but he needed to give her the words. Needed to say them before he died.

She looked up at something in the distance and screamed, "Hunter!"

Darkness edged his vision, pulling Mikael under even as he tried to hold on to her hand, tried to hold on to Avery. He didn't want to die. Didn't want to leave her.

But the pain and darkness were too much.

* * *

"Oh no," Avery muttered as she tried to lift Mikael. But he was dead weight.

Fear, sharp and stinging, punctured through her as Hunter landed next to them. There were no more vampires following him so she guessed the dragonling had destroyed every single one of them. "I need you to get Mikael home. Home!" she shouted, unable to control the volume of her voice. Because nothing mattered if he died.

Hunter nudged Mikael, making sad whining sounds as he tried to get him to wake up.

She crouched down with him and lifted Mikael up by the shoulders. "That's right, he's hurt. You need to help. Get him home. To King," she added. "Take him to King."

Hunter crouched as low as he could and was very still as Avery managed to drag Mikael onto Hunter's back. She tried to get on with him, but it was quickly clear that combined, they were too heavy for Hunter to go very fast. So she slid off and took Hunter's big face in her hands. "You keep him safe," she said. "*Please* save him."

Hunter chirped at her and actually nodded.

"Get him home. You go home to King!"

Then she pointed south, in the direction he needed to go. It wasn't perfect but she knew he could fly pretty far, at least according to King. And she really hoped that someone from King's pack would see them and know what to do if Hunter couldn't make it back to the city.

"Please get him help," she rasped out, her throat tight with emotion. He'd fought to the death for her, had put himself in danger and might die because of it. She loved him so much, wished she'd told him. Wished she hadn't been such a damn coward. And now…she might never get the chance.

Hunter chirped as he took off, not looking back as he flew a little awkwardly through the sky, but the beat of his wings was determined.

In that moment she was going to hope against hope that he made it home, that he got Mikael to safety and to a healer. She had no idea what that monster had done to him but it had been enough to bring the dragon down. One of the strongest males she knew.

In the silence, she looked around at the charred grass and small crater where Ozias had once stood. The long knife she'd picked up from a dead vampire and stabbed Ozias with was gone, incinerated, but a small vial with the green liquid still lay there, somehow not destroyed even after Mikael had completely obliterated the vampire-mage.

She picked it up and put it in her pocket before she turned in the direction of one of the homes far off in the distance and started limping away as fast as she could.

Hopefully she would be able to get help for herself and make it back to New Orleans sooner than later. She would find her way back to Mikael no matter what. Even if she had to walk the whole way.

CHAPTER THIRTY-NINE

King burst out of the mansion's front doors when he heard his name being shouted. As he raced into the front yard, he saw Hunter on the grass and that weird tension that had been sitting in his chest since his dragonling had disappeared eased just a bit.

Hunter didn't approach him, however, just kept jumping and loudly chirping. It took a millisecond for King to see the body draped over the dragonling.

"Hell," he growled as he reached Hunter and a bloody, naked Mikael. He could see the rise and fall of Mikael's chest but his skin had gone a pale, pale gray.

He put his hand on Mikael's forehead. Cold. *Dammit.* Dragons and other supernaturals ran a lot hotter than humans, but especially dragons.

King turned, barked out an order to his nearest packmate. "Call Dallas. Tell her mate to fly her directly to Greer's healing center. Now." Then he stripped off his clothes, tossed them down. "Hunter, follow me," he said, even as he shifted to wolf and raced off along the driveway. He could get to Greer's a lot faster in his wolf form than by driving.

He glanced up once to see Hunter following close behind.

His heart raced as he hurried down street after street, heading toward the Irish Channel District. And he tried very hard not to focus on wondering where the hell Avery was.

Because there was no way in hell Mikael would have left her if he'd had a choice. No way Avery would have left him either.

* * *

Mikael heard voices, familiar ones.

His brothers.

And...someone else. A female, though he couldn't place who she was. Her voice was commanding but soft. But she wasn't Avery.

Avery! He needed to get to her.

Ice coated his veins as he tried to open his eyes.

"What the hell is happening?" Zephyr's worried voice.

"He's fighting the poison." The commanding, female voice. "And if you don't back up I'm going to have to ask you to leave."

A warmth spread through him and it felt…so good. So soothing. He was growing tired, but he couldn't sleep. Couldn't rest for even a moment.

Had to move. Had to shift. He tried to move his limbs. Or he thought he did. He could hear a growling sound, realized it was coming from him.

"Avery," he murmured before darkness swept him under again.

* * *

Mikael wasn't sure how much time had passed, but he was aware that it had.

He hadn't been in Hibernation. No… Where was he? Why did he feel cold? He could smell his brothers. Even *Zephyr*.

Wait, Zephyr was dead.

Had Mikael died? No…Zephyr was alive. That was right. He'd come back and— Avery!

He jerked upward, his eyes flying open.

All three of his brothers stood by a big bay window, quietly talking, but they stopped and stared before striding to the bed.

Zephyr spoke first, reaching for him. "My brother. You're alive."

"Avery," he managed to get out through his parched throat.

Cas hurried out the door. "I need Greer! And water!"

Mikael shifted slightly, forcing his legs to obey as he got off the bed. The room was all soft blues and greens, a healing center of some sort, he thought as he managed to stand upright.

"Damn it, Mikael, get in bed." Ivyn tried to move toward him but Mikael growled, baring his canines. "King has his packmates out searching for Avery. And Prima and Arthur are out there too. We were waiting until you woke up to search."

"We need the healer faster," Zephyr snapped, his body vibrating with tension.

Mikael ignored them and stumbled toward the door. Or tried to. He made it to the wall by the door and held on to it.

A wave of nausea swept through him.

"You need to get back in bed." Zephyr stood in front of him, his mouth pulled into a thin line. "So many people are out looking for your female now." He reached out a hand, but Mikael swatted him away.

"Touch me again and lose your hand," he growled. He just needed to get outside, needed to shift. He needed to get to Avery.

As he made it to the door, Reaper strode in with a glass of water. He didn't question what Reaper was doing here, simply took the water and gulped it down in seconds.

"Like your brothers said, we've got people—wolves, dragons and witches—out searching for your Avery," Reaper said quietly. "So now you need to get your ass back in bed."

"If it was Greer out there, what would you do?" He was breathing hard, drawing in breath after breath as he clutched onto the wall. *Fuck.* Every part of him hurt.

Reaper paused for all of a second before he slid a hand under Mikael's arm and propped him up. "Come on."

He was aware of his brothers cursing behind them but he did not care. "Where's Hunter?"

"Downstairs. He's agitated. He brought you in and you both passed out pretty quickly. How much do you remember?"

"I don't remember him bringing me in. But we killed Ozias. Avery and I."

Reaper jerked in surprise and he heard his brothers exclaim behind him.

"Yeah, he's gone." And never coming back. But where was Avery? Another burst of panic blasted through him. He had to get to her.

Zephyr moved in on his other side as they reached a set of stairs and wrapped his arm around Mikael as well, helping him.

He just needed to shift to his dragon form. Once he did that, he'd be able to move better. The magic of the change always helped heal him.

"I think your little friend is waiting to fly with you. He was injured as well, though we can't figure out how. One of his wings was slashed up.

It looks like from claw marks. Greer has healed him completely now as well," Reaper told him as he pushed open the front door to the healing center. "You were both out for about twenty hours."

Twenty hours? Where was Avery? Why had no one found her yet? *Goddess no.* That was too long.

As he stepped outside with the two men propping him up, Hunter flew across the yard, chirping wildly at him. He turned and looked at the sky, then looked back at Mikael expectantly.

He couldn't tell what time it was. Maybe two in the morning, given the position of the moon. And if he'd been out twenty hours… He needed to get to Avery.

"I can stand," he said to Reaper and Zephyr, who slowly eased back. Then he reached out and patted Hunter's head. "Good boy. We're going now. We're going to get her." There was no way Hunter would have left Avery behind unless he hadn't had a choice.

Satisfied and definitely understanding him, the little dragon backed up as Mikael strode away from the others toward the middle of the yard. Though strode away was probably a bit of a stretch. He more or less stumbled until he fell on his hands and knees but he did not care. He let his dragon take over, the magic rolling through him with a wild swiftness. Pain and pleasure intermixed as a kaleidoscope of colors sparked everywhere, scales replacing skin, his beast side taking over fully.

As he blinked down at Hunter, the little dragonling zoomed up into the air and pointed north. Mikael inhaled deeply, trying to sense her on the wind. He didn't bother to see if his brothers followed, he simply took to the air, following the dragonling.

Moments later he heard the steady flap of multiple wings behind him, and when he glanced over his shoulder saw that his brothers and Reaper were following. Good. If he needed backup, he would take it. Anything to get his Avery back. But he remembered her stabbing Ozias and there hadn't been any other vampires he could remember either. Maybe Hunter had killed them.

He just knew that she'd been alive, shouting at him to not die, when he'd passed out.

She cared for him more than she wanted to admit. He knew she did.

Now he simply had to find her.

CHAPTER FORTY

Avery inhaled the cool country air, still feeling groggy and disoriented as she pulled out of the driveway in her borrowed car.

She'd found an empty house with a fairly thick layer of dust covering everything, which told her the house had been abandoned. Probably a result of The Fall. Which was why she didn't feel too guilty about breaking that window today. Er, yesterday.

She'd passed out on one of the couches from sheer mental exhaustion and slept almost an entire day. It was still dark out, but close to sunrise and now…now she needed to get home.

Needed to find Mikael and Hunter. She had to tell Mikael she loved him and that she'd been a fool to fight it. He had to be safe by now. Hunter would have made it back and Mikael would likely be with a healer. He'd be fine. He had to be. She fought a sob that wanted to rise in her throat. Oh God, what if… *No. No, no, no.* If she gave in to that, into the what-if game, she would lose focus. Right now she simply had to get home, to Mikael.

Glancing in the rearview mirror at the farmhouse, she hoped the people who owned it were okay, but… She couldn't think about that now. Instead, she was simply grateful that there had been a sedan in the garage with a half-full tank of gas. It had taken two tries but the engine had started.

The GPS wasn't working and she figured that had to do with some towers being down. She knew some were still up because a lot of cell towers were still working, but not all of them had survived.

She knew where she was though. It would just take some figuring out how to get to a main road. She just wished there had been a phone or something because she had no clue where hers was—maybe it had been destroyed in one of the portal jumps.

There were no lights out here, just a fading moon and stars and of course her headlights. She kept the brights on, since there was no one else out here that she could see, and holy shit, blinding another driver was the least of her worries right now.

Half an hour later when she pulled onto a two-lane country highway that she knew would take her back to a main road, she blinked in surprise to see a lone figure walking along the road.

From the slight build it was clear she was a woman. Worried for her safety, Avery started to slow down, rolled down the window as she did. "Hey," she called out, surprised the woman had turned at all when she'd been driving up on her.

When Lindsey *freaking* Baird turned to look at her, her eyes going wide at the sight of Avery, her fangs descending, Avery shook her head. "Nope." She rolled the window back up and pressed on the gas. She didn't care why Lindsey was out here, she wasn't helping her.

No way in hell.

As she sped up, a thump rattled her trunk.

Avery let out a scream as she saw Lindsey in the rearview mirror, poised like a cat on the trunk. Her eyes were wild, her fangs out as she punched her fist into the trunk again.

"Holy hell." Avery pressed on the gas and started swerving the car back and forth, trying to dislodge the vampire, but the female was supernaturally strong.

Suddenly, Lindsey disappeared from sight, and for a moment Avery experienced a tiny thread of relief.

Until a hand punched through the roof as if it was made of papier-mâché. The vampire grabbed the wheel and yanked hard from above as Avery tried to hold on for dear life.

It was useless. Lindsey was too strong. She wasn't touching her, so she couldn't hurt her that way, but she could sure as hell kill Avery with a head-on collision.

She hit the brakes, trying to slow down as Lindsey swerved the sedan into a one-eighty, her wicked laugh ringing through the air as she tried to kill Avery.

Avery finally slammed on the brakes as Lindsey wrenched the car straight toward a cluster of trees. She clutched at Lindsey's arm, tried to tug the woman's arm free, but she couldn't budge the vampire.

Heart thumping out of control, Avery threw open the door and curled into herself as she dove out onto a patch of grass.

She winced at the second impact to her hip but managed to jump to her feet. Probably because adrenaline had taken over.

The sound of crunching metal filled the air as the car slammed into an oak tree. As smoke started billowing out from under the hood, that adrenaline surged. She started to run, but jerked to a halt when Lindsey slid quickly in front of her.

Stupid vampiric speed!

Lindsey's eyes glowed wildly, her fangs and—oh shit, were those claws?—extended. "I don't care how long it takes, I'll kill you. I don't care what's protecting you, I'll keep you captive and just starve you to death," she snarled as she started circling around her. Her blonde hair was wild and unkempt around her face and flecks of dirt and blood streaked her neck.

Then Lindsey picked up a rock and hurled it straight at Avery.

Avery ducked on instinct but was too slow. It hit her in the shoulder, making Lindsey blink.

Oooooh, shit. Avery started running, even as she knew that it was likely pointless, her flight instinct kicked in. She couldn't take on a vampire in a fight and she knew it. Neither could she escape from one on foot, but she was damn well going to try.

Her feet slammed against the grass as she raced across the field. With each step, Ozias's vial in her pocket rattled.

She shoved her hand in her pocket as she reached the desolate road.

A wisp of noise flew past her and suddenly Lindsey was standing in front of her. Grinning like a wild hyena. "I'm going to have so much fun killing you," Lindsey snarled. "I had to fuck that bag of bones for years and pretend to like you."

Yeah, like that was Avery's fault.

"I'm going to make you pay for every single—"

Avery didn't want to hear this cartoon villain rant and rave at her. She tossed the green liquid straight at Lindsey's face, having no idea if it would actually do anything but she had to take the chance.

She had to survive this.

Lindsey stared in shock at her, her eyes going wide as her skin started... Oh God, peeling off her face!

A scream died in her throat as she started disintegrating, just... Turning to ash right in front of Avery. She was like a pillar of salt, crumbling, crumbling, crumbling, the wind carrying pieces of her away.

"Oh my God," Avery breathed. "Oh. My. God."

She sucked in a shaky breath. Then another. But she couldn't give in to the panic as gray ash fluttered on the wind away from her. She was going to have nightmares about all of this, she had no doubt.

She just wanted to get home. To find her brothers. To make sure they were safe. And she had to get to Mikael.

Because he had to be okay. They all did. She'd survived too much to deal with any other outcome.

As she started walking along the highway, she froze when she heard... Was that wings? There were so many of them.

Feeling crazy, wondering if it was even him, she started screaming his name anyway. "Mikael!"

As the sun peeked above the sky in the east, a brilliant, smoky gray dragon, wings sparkling like jewels, ascended over the tops of trees, arrowing straight for her. A sob caught in her throat as she veered left, running off the road and across the field toward him. He was moving so fast that he made her feel as if her legs were trapped in molasses.

He dipped toward her, the span of his wings incredible. That was when she saw little Hunter flying above him and angling downward as well. They were both okay!

The moment Mikael landed, colors exploded everywhere and moments later the man she loved stood before her. The warrior god turned from dragon to man, all hard muscles and wild gray eyes as he ran for her.

"Mikael!" she cried out again as she raced at him.

He met her halfway, pulling her into his arms and crushing his mouth to hers even as she sobbed out his name.

Far too many emotions bubbled up inside her and she pulled back and buried her face against his neck. "I thought I'd lost you," she cried. She couldn't stop the stupid tears.

"Never," he growled, his grip crushing. "I love you, Avery."

"I love you too! And I wanted to tell you first."

"You can tell me as many times as you like," he said, cupping her face with his big, callused hands, swiping all the wetness away.

"I killed her," she said suddenly, the words tumbling from her. Everything felt so surreal, as if she was coming down from a high.

He frowned. "Who?"

"Lindsey. She attacked me on the road. I don't even know how she got out here." Avery was vaguely aware of a cluster of dragons landing all around them but she didn't care. She only cared about Mikael.

His expression hardened, even as his eyes shone with pride. "She deserved to die. And your brothers are alive and safe."

As she digested his words, another cry tore from her throat, one of relief and happiness. All her fear and worry exploded out of her in more and more tears until she couldn't stop herself at all. He hugged her tight, rubbing a soothing hand up and down her back as he murmured calming words to her. She had no idea what he actually said, just that he was okay and so were her brothers.

Next to them, Hunter was making sweet little crooning sounds as he patted her gently on the back with one of his wings. Which just made her cry even harder. At some point she realized she was crying for everything and everyone she'd ever lost.

Eventually, completely wrung out, she lifted her head, so damn grateful that this big dragon had chosen her for his own. She'd held back because of fear and insecurities, but she wouldn't allow that to dictate her future—*their* future. "I really want to go home," she whispered.

His gray eyes were bright under the rising sun. "Me too."

CHAPTER FORTY-ONE

Avery wasn't sure how long she'd slept, but when she managed to sit up in Mikael's bed, she saw that it was dark outside. She took a moment, sitting there, just being quiet and savoring the peace. Though she wished Mikael was next to her, she knew he hadn't likely gone far. He'd probably gone downstairs to grab food and she wasn't far behind him.

She stood to go find him, and as she did she saw a flash of material peeking out from the nightstand drawer. She opened it and started to tuck the material back inside and...blinked.

Pulling open Mikael's drawer fully now, she stared and started sifting through all of her things. Her mouth tugged up into a smile as she saw multiple hair clips, some plain brown, others sparkly. There were some of her missing buttons too. And one of her hair dryer diffusers! "What the heck?" she murmured. She picked up a lightweight silky purple-and-cream-colored scarf she'd gotten at a craft fair years ago. She hadn't even realized this was missing. Was Mikael...hoarding her things?

He really was wonderfully weird.

Laughing to herself, she shut the drawer and finally stumbled downstairs, ready to see her dragon. By the time they'd gotten back to New Orleans proper, it had been close to eight in the morning—then she'd gone to see her brothers and hugged and kissed them to the point of overkill. After that she'd had to talk to King, and finally she and Mikael had come home and crashed together.

And she still felt like she could sleep for another... Who knows, maybe another day or two. She felt physically and emotionally exhausted, but she didn't want to go back to sleep alone. No, she was only going back to Mikael's bed if he came with her.

She found him outside on the back patio with his brothers, her brothers, and Rhys and Dallas—as well as Willow, who was currently doing figure eights in the air around a frustrated Hunter, who was chirping at her as if telling her to slow down.

Mikael of course spotted her first and crossed the few feet to her, pulling her into his arms and holding her tight.

She closed her eyes for a long moment and buried her face against his chest. She was so happy he was alive, that they were both alive. And he was warm, wonderful and all hers. Soon she was going to fully claim him forever. Soooo soon. "So, I think we need to talk about the fact that you've been stealing my things," she murmured against his chest.

He froze then looked down at her, a bit of guilt flickering into his gray eyes.

She giggled slightly. "I'm not mad. Is this like a dragon thing?"

"Yes. We like treasure."

"And my buttons and hair clips are treasure?"

"They smell like you." His words were so simple and made her heart expand three sizes. Oh, this male was too much.

"Oh, Mikael."

"Avery!" She pulled back at Dallas's voice, hating the interruption even though she loved her friend. "We joined the search for you!" her friend said, pulling her into a hug.

"Thank you so much," Avery said as she stepped back, immediately missing Mikael's warmth. Right now she was already close to feeling overwhelmed. But she was so glad her friend was here.

Dallas watched her carefully, looking her up and down worriedly. "How are you doing? Truly? Do you want me to whip up a special tea brew?"

"I'm dealing with everything." Her father's ex-wife had tried to kill her, she'd also learned that said ex-wife had killed her father, her brothers had been kidnapped and saved, she'd gone to a Hell realm and survived, and she was wildly in love with a dragon shifter. Avery had no idea how to emotionally handle all of that right now. She kind of just wanted to go back to bed.

But she did *not* want to go alone. Whatever was on her face must've been pretty clear because Dallas gave her a quick kiss on the cheek and then turned to her mate. "Let's get Hunter back to King. And I think it's time we get Willow home anyway." Then she turned to Avery. "Honey, get some sleep and call me when you're awake. I'll come back into town so we can talk. Or you can come visit us on the farm for a break—with your dragon, obviously," she added, giving Mikael a look when he started to growl.

"You are truly the best."

Zephyr, the male she didn't know well but really appreciated in that moment, said, "And the rest of us are going to head over to that lion's place. We'll hang out there for a while," he added, looking between Avery and Mikael pointedly.

Anthony started to say something, but Riel elbowed him, and not subtly.

She laughed to herself and leaned into Mikael. Having some alone time in the house right now sounded amazing.

So did a hot shower. And…other things.

"I need a shower," she murmured to Mikael, watching as his eyes went all smoky gray. "I hope it won't be alone."

"Dude, we can still hear you," Anthony mumbled as he walked by, but not before kissing her on the cheek.

"Then you better hurry and get out of here," Mikael said dryly.

"I'll be upstairs," she said quietly as Zephyr pulled him aside for something.

Feeling slightly more awake, she hurried back up the stairs. She had a lot of questions she wanted answers to, but the Dark Mage, or hybrid or whatever he was, who had been turning vampires and letting them run loose on the city, was dead. And so was Lindsey. Something she wouldn't lose any sleep over. That lunatic had tried to kill her. If there were still vampires running wild, she figured King's pack could take care of it. She also needed to check into her jobsites, but right now she was going to let other people worry about the details.

She wanted to get naked with Mikael more than anything. They deserved it—they deserved a happily-ever-after.

She didn't wait for Mikael, instead stripped off her clothes and tossed them into his hamper before starting the shower. As soon as the steam rose she stepped inside, sighing at the force of the jets cascading over her body. This was heaven.

As she was wringing her hair out and getting ready to lather it up with shampoo, the gray-and-white-striped shower curtain jingled slightly as Mikael stepped inside—thankfully fully naked. *Yes, please.*

His biceps flexed as he pulled the shower curtain closed and she stared at each wonderful ripple of his muscles as he moved. The male was walking art.

Her gaze raked over his body once, twice, as she tried to drink him in. He was already rock-hard, his cock curving up thick against his abdomen. She tried to look everywhere at once, couldn't get enough of her male.

He immediately reached for her, his big hands settling on her hips as she stepped into his body. "I only left you alone because you were sleeping so hard," he murmured. "I'd planned to be back upstairs before you got up."

She slid her hands around his waist, pulling him to her so that her breasts rubbed up against his chest. Oh, she liked that. "I know. I didn't think for one second that you'd left me. I'm glad everyone's gone though."

"Are you hungry?" He was holding her close and gloriously naked, but hadn't made a move to touch her other than the gentle hold on her hips. "You have to be starving."

Oh no, no polite and nice dragon. She wanted something else from him right now.

He abruptly stopped when she reached between them and wrapped her fingers around his thick length. "I'm hungry, but not for food." She wanted to be filled by him, claimed by him. She wanted forever with him and she now understood what being mated to a dragon meant. He'd explained everything to her once they'd gotten back to the house. They'd be linked to each other, and if one of them died, so did the other. She was his weak link—not according to him though. Even though she didn't like the idea of being a weak link, she loved him too much to walk away. They were meant to be together. And her life span would be expanded so she'd live as long as he would, so at least she wasn't depriving him of that.

He let out a low growl as he pinned her to the slick tile wall. "What exactly are you hungry for?"

"Everything." She paused. "What you said about me being your mate—"

"I meant every word. You are mine. Don't want to scare you, but I'm not letting you go. If you let me claim you, you're stuck with me forever. Not that I'm going to give you a choice, regardless," he added, as if he needed to clarify. There was the sexy, possessive dragon she knew and loved.

Maybe that kind of possessiveness should scare her, but he was so damn protective and he had shown her who he was in a thousand different ways. *Not* being claimed by him scared her more than anything. Not having him in her life terrified her. He was this subtle force of nature who'd quietly ripped down her walls one by one until she had nothing to hold between them. And she didn't want to. Being vulnerable with someone else was scary, but it was worth it.

"What does claiming involve, exactly?" Because he'd been vague on that one point. Though he'd already showed her that he liked to get creative in the bedroom, so maybe it was something kinky. *Oh, yes please.*

As if he read her thoughts, or more likely he'd just scented the sharp spike of lust that rolled off her, he said, "I would give up my entire trove of treasure to know what you're thinking right now."

She arched into him, her nipples beading tight. "You have treasure?" Other than her buttons and hair ties.

"Don't change the subject."

"Claiming?" she continued, pushing him.

"I'll bite you during sex," he said bluntly, his words wrapping around her and sending a rush of heat surging through her, right to her core. For some reason biting sounded insanely hot. "You like the thought of that." His gaze dipped to her mouth, his eyes practically glowing with heat.

That was when she felt the soft rumble of the earth—and didn't care if they brought the whole damn house down on them as long as they got mated.

In response she stroked him once, twice, until he took her hand and pinned her wrist against the wall above her head. Then he did the same with her other one as he crushed his mouth to hers.

She moaned into him as she teased her tongue against his. She arched her back, but he kept her in place, basically immobile. For some reason she liked the sensation of being helpless even while knowing she held a whole lot of power where he was concerned.

Jets of water cascaded around them, creating a cocoon of extra privacy. Or what felt like it. The house was empty and right now she felt like they were the only two people in the world. As if they were back in that nearly empty Hell realm and she could be as loud as she wanted.

But she needed more.

He must have read her mind because he suddenly dropped one of her wrists, only to grasp both of them with one hand as he reached between her legs, cupping her mound.

Ooooh, yeah. She rolled her hips against his hold, her entire body on fire for him.

"You're so damn wet," he growled against her mouth. Then he slipped two fingers inside her and she nearly combusted.

Her inner walls clenched around his fingers in response. He didn't even warm her up with one finger, he just slid two right in there.

His fingers definitely weren't enough. She rolled her hips against him as he started thrusting slowly, tortuously, clearly trying to send her into madness.

She bit his bottom lip, struggled against his grasp. His hold eased but only for a moment.

Letting her wrists go, he kept her pinned in place in other ways. He cupped one of her breasts and slowly circled his thumb around her nipple. Then he dipped his head to her other breast, teasing both of her nipples simultaneously.

A bite there, a suck here, a pinch there. The torture, the pleasure, his mouth, his fingers. He was driving her crazy as he teased her body.

She was going to explode from pleasure and they had just started. Needing to touch more of him, she reached between their bodies and wrapped her fingers around his thick length, stroked once. She loved being able to touch him all she wanted, had thought about this so many times. The reality was better than her fantasies.

His big body trembled, but he didn't stop thrusting his fingers inside her. Didn't stop at all. That rumble was all around them now, but it didn't feel scary. It was…comforting almost. A huge public acknowledgment that she was his mate.

She dug her fingernails into his back. "I want to feel all of you inside me." Her inner walls were clenching and begging for it. She needed a release so badly her body was trembling.

He lifted his head, his chest rising and falling wildly as he looked down at her. Then he took his cock in hand and stroked it once, twice, three times. She couldn't tear her gaze away as she looked at all of him, this warrior god who wanted to claim her.

A low growl emanated from him as she stared unabashedly at him, drank her fill and still wasn't full.

She clutched his shoulders as he grabbed her hips. Then oh so slowly, and with a precision and patience that impressed her, pushed inside her, every thick, delicious inch.

She sucked in a breath as he pushed all the way to the hilt, her mind going into sensory overload as she settled onto him.

When she looked at his face, saw the intense lust and love as he watched her, she knew she was going to come soon. She was right on the edge, barely holding on, and as he hit her G-spot she arched against him. Right now she was beyond words—almost beyond thought. She rolled against him, needing him to meet her stroke for stroke now, needing more rough than soft in that moment.

Growling low again, he reached between their bodies and started strumming her clit with enough pressure that yep, she was about to climax. But she needed more stimulation.

He started teasing her as she pushed up with her thigh muscles, then slid down on his thick length again.

He took over immediately because that was exactly who he was, and began thrusting, hard. Just like she wanted—craved.

He moved inside her like a male possessed, taking and giving, claiming her.

It didn't take long for her climax to hit, sharp and wild as he thrust inside her with abandon, not treating her like some soft human who couldn't handle it. The friction against her G-spot combined with clitoral stimulation pushed her over the edge far too fast. She hadn't been prepared for it.

Pleasure exploded out to all her nerve endings, and as she started coming, her entire body shaking, he buried his head against her neck.

His growl reverberated through her right as she felt the prick of his canines. Piercing her skin, he bit down hard.

The burst of pain was over so quickly, before it gave way to even more pleasure, as if the pinpoints against her neck were connected to her clit.

Another wave of pleasure pushed out to all her nerve endings as another, sharper orgasm slammed into her. Wave after wave cascaded through her as she held on to him for dear life.

He let go in that moment too, and she was vaguely aware of the sound of crumbling tile as he slammed a fist against the wall next to her head as he roared out his climax.

His thrusts were wild and uncivilized as he came inside her in long, hot strokes.

Time seemed to lose all meaning as they both came together, panting and still desperate for more.

When she finally came back to herself, she looked up into his smoky gray eyes, and saw her future in front of her.

This male was everything to her. Her whole world. She was just glad that she'd been brave enough to take the chance. Hell, she was glad he hadn't given up on her because of her baggage.

"I love you," he said quietly before brushing his lips over hers, gently, the opposite of the way he'd claimed her just now.

Then he started to get hard inside her again.

She pulled back to stare at him, her eyes widening.

"Dragon shifters are different than human males." He looked positively smug about that. "And I am definitely not done."

She grinned at him and grabbed his face, pulling it to hers. "Neither am I."

CHAPTER FORTY-TWO

Three weeks later

Avery curled up on Mikael's lap, perfectly comfortable exactly where she was as she looked at the party going on in Aurora's backyard. "You think they'd even notice if we left?" she murmured against his ear before biting the lobe gently.

Axel, sneaky lion, jumped down from the big oak tree. "Yes, we would know, so you're not going anywhere." He snagged a quick kiss on the top of her head but didn't escape a swat from Mikael's hand.

Her big dragon didn't even crack a smile or betray any expression, simply reached out and smacked Axel on the side of the head. It was kind of impressive.

"I love you," she murmured, kissing him on the mouth this time as she fought a laugh. His possessiveness was never going away.

"Come on you guys, you can't sit here the whole time." Dallas's voice interrupted them.

Groaning, Avery pulled back and looked up at her friend. "Yes we can."

"No way." She grabbed Avery's hands and tugged her off Mikael's lap. "We're about to have a dance party."

Avery snickered slightly as she saw that they were indeed clearing out some space on the patio for... A dance party, apparently.

And Dallas was leading the way, her dear friend very clearly tipsy already.

"Come on," Riel said, coming up to sling an arm around her shoulders even as he placed a glass of champagne in her hand. "Mom's earrings look good on you," he added, smiling in a way she hadn't seen in ages.

She touched the dangling diamonds. Wearing something that had belonged to her mom made Avery feel connected to her. "Thank you. So where did we get all the alcohol?" Certain things were very hard to come by these days and if they weren't a necessity, they didn't get them. Some people were making moonshine, but no thanks. She'd rather be sober for the rest of her life than drink that crap.

"Dallas made it all. She said she did some kind of cloning spell to create all of it. This is top-shelf stuff." Her brother's voice was appreciative. Both her brothers were completely fine since the kidnapping, had rebounded so fast she was kind of surprised. And now they both had pendants like hers that would protect them from any potential danger. It helped her to sleep easier at night.

She'd been worried her pendant was useless after Lindsey had been able to hit her with that rock, but after talking to the Magic Man, he'd assured her it was something that had happened because she'd gone through two portals back to back. It had screwed with his magic, but he'd fixed it—and she didn't plan on jumping through portals any time soon. Neither she nor Mikael had the key anymore either. Zephyr had taken it and…she wasn't sure what he'd done with it. Hidden it somewhere. She didn't want to know where it was either.

She took a sip of the champagne and sighed appreciatively. Avery was going to file Dallas's skills under things that kind of blew her mind. She looked over her shoulder, ready to tell Mikael that he better get his ass over here, and realized he was right behind her. Because of course he was. He never let her out of his sight.

She blinked up at him, smiling. He was always her quiet, unassuming shadow and she couldn't get enough of him.

"I need to find a male who looks at me like that," Lola said, shaking her head as she looked at the two of them. "If I didn't like you both so much, I might throw up a little bit."

"You changed your hair. I like it," Avery said as she slid her arm around Mikael's waist and leaned into him. Her brother Riel had already joined Dallas and Rhys—who was actually dancing with his mate—on the dance floor.

A burst of music went up, someone clearly having found another stereo system because Harlow had broken the last one with a basketball and a Roman torch. Apparently tiger shifters couldn't be trusted with fire either. Or basketballs.

Lola ran her hands over the sparkly purple tresses. "I'll go back to the rainbow eventually, but I really like this."

"It suits you," Mikael said, almost double the number of words he'd said all night.

Avery looked up at him and he shrugged, a grin playing across his hard mouth. One she wanted to devour right about now.

Her dragon of very few words was in a good mood tonight even though he hadn't been talking much. She knew because they were in tune with each other in more ways than one. Now that they were mated, it was almost like they were linked somehow and she could sense his moods. The last three weeks, he'd been stuck to her like glue.

Though to be fair, the first week they'd barely even left the bedroom. She'd let the very capable people she worked with take over her jobsites even though she felt a little bit guilty. But King had assured her that mating only happened once in a lifetime and that she needed to enjoy herself. He'd actually insisted that she and Mikael take the week off and not show their faces anywhere.

So she had taken that week, much to the horror of her brothers and Mikael's brothers, because they'd basically disappeared for a week straight and had been spending all their time over at Aurora and her crew's place.

Aurora had decided to throw a party for Avery, Riel and Anthony because they'd "lived through a bunch of crap" and, according to Aurora, her crew didn't need an excuse to celebrate during these times anyway. She'd already promised Avery that in another week or so they'd have a celebration for Avery and Mikael's mating.

Avery looked up at her mate, her heart full. "You feel like putting on your boogie shoes?"

Mikael blinked at her. "Is that a reference to dancing?"

She grabbed his hands and dragged him toward the marked-off part of the patio, shaking her hips as she did. "Why, yes it is."

He grinned down at her, a look of such raw adoration on his face that she felt it like a punch to her heart. She couldn't believe she'd found such incredible happiness. A male she could always depend on—a best friend. He'd become her family in such a short time and she knew that he would never betray her, never let her down. That simply wasn't in his DNA.

"I will do anything to make you smile, my mate," he said quietly, intently, as he joined her on the dance floor.

She wasn't sure why she was surprised, but as he started moving in tune with the music, she realized that the male had serious rhythm. But *of course* he did—she'd seen it in the bedroom firsthand.

Over and over, in fact.

When an old-school KC and the Sunshine Band song came on, a cheer went up from the crowd and she laughed at the wonderfulness of it all.

The world was still rebuilding, and some days were harder than others, so right now she was going to grasp onto her happiness for all that it was worth.

She and Mikael had worked hard to get here. So she was going to dance with her mate and, as soon as they could, sneak away and she was going to enjoy the rest of the night wrapped up in his arms.

ACKNOWLEDGMENTS

As always, I owe a huge thanks to Kaylea Cross, the best critique partner and best friend a writer could ask for! I'm also grateful to my editor, Julia Ganis—maybe one day I'll write a series about just the dragonlings! Thank you to Jaycee for another amazing cover, to Sarah for proofreading, and of course I owe a lot of gratitude to my fabulous readers! Thank you all for your support. As always, I'm grateful to have such a great team to help me get my books in shape for publishing. This includes my two favorite writer pups, Piper and Jack, the duo who sleeps in my office day in and day out while I work.

BOOKLIST

Ancients Rising Series
Ancient Protector
Ancient Enemy
Ancient Enforcer

Darkness Series
Darkness Awakened
Taste of Darkness
Beyond the Darkness
Hunted by Darkness
Into the Darkness
Saved by Darkness
Guardian of Darkness
Sentinel of Darkness
A Very Dragon Christmas
Darkness Rising

Deadly Ops Series
Targeted
Bound to Danger
Chasing Danger
Shattered Duty
Edge of Danger
A Covert Affair

Endgame Trilogy
Bishop's Knight
Bishop's Queen
Bishop's Endgame

MacArthur Family Series
Falling for Irish
Unintended Target
Saving Sienna

Moon Shifter Series
Alpha Instinct
Lover's Instinct
Primal Possession
Mating Instinct
His Untamed Desire
Avenger's Heat
Hunter Reborn
Protective Instinct
Dark Protector
A Mate for Christmas

O'Connor Family Series
Merry Christmas, Baby
Tease Me, Baby
It's Me Again, Baby
Mistletoe Me, Baby

Red Stone Security Series®
No One to Trust
Danger Next Door
Fatal Deception
Miami, Mistletoe & Murder
His to Protect
Breaking Her Rules
Protecting His Witness
Sinful Seduction
Under His Protection
Deadly Fallout
Sworn to Protect
Secret Obsession
Love Thy Enemy
Dangerous Protector
Lethal Game
Secret Enemy
Saving Danger

Redemption Harbor Series®
Resurrection
Savage Rising
Dangerous Witness
Innocent Target
Hunting Danger
Covert Games
Chasing Vengeance

Sin City Series (the Serafina)
First Surrender
Sensual Surrender
Sweetest Surrender
Dangerous Surrender
Deadly Surrender

Verona Bay Series
Dark Memento
Deadly Past

Linked Books
Retribution
Tempting Danger

Non-series romantic suspense
Running From the Past
Dangerous Secrets
Killer Secrets
Deadly Obsession
Danger in Paradise
His Secret Past

Paranormal Romance
Destined Mate
Protector's Mate
A Jaguar's Kiss
Tempting the Jaguar
Enemy Mine
Heart of the Jaguar

ABOUT THE AUTHOR

Katie Reus is the *New York Times* and *USA Today* bestselling author of the Red Stone Security series, the Redemption Harbor series and the Ancients Rising series. She fell in love with romance at a young age thanks to books she pilfered from her mom's stash. Years later she loves reading romance almost as much as she loves writing it.

However, she didn't always know she wanted to be a writer. After changing majors many times, she finally graduated summa cum laude with a degree in psychology. Not long after that she discovered a new love. Writing. She now spends her days writing paranormal romance and sexy romantic suspense. For more information on Katie please visit her website: https://katiereus.com

Made in the USA
Las Vegas, NV
01 July 2021